THE CLOVIS DIG

A Novel by

TERI FINK

THE CLOVIS DIG

FIRST EDITION SOFTCOVER
ISBN: 1622530861
ISBN-13: 978-1-62253-086-1

Editor: Robb Grindstaff
Cover Artist: Dale Robert Pease
Interior Designer: Lane Diamond

www.EvolvedPub.com
Evolved Publishing LLC
Butler, Wisconsin, USA

Printed in Book Antiqua font.

BOOKS BY TERI FINK

Invisible by Day
The Clovis Dig

DEDICATION

To my sister, Tracy Fitzwater, an avid reader from an early age. "Maybe I was born reading," she says. Tracy dedicated her life to books and reading in her long career as librarian, teacher, and book reviewer. My love of books was inspired by her.

Chapter 1

"I think we all have some parcel of the past which is falling into disrepair or being sold off piece by piece. It's just that for most of us, it isn't an orchard; it's the way we've thought about something, or someone."

Amor Towles, "Rules of Civility"

***

East Wenatchee, Washington, July 1987

Claire stared, numb, at the chaos before her—two sheriff's cars, two city cop cars, a fire truck, and an ambulance crowded her driveway.

The trouble had begun twenty minutes earlier with a scream.

The sound had turned her gut to ice. She had raced through the apple trees toward the sound, ducking branches, as the scream lured her out of the orchard. The sound was coming from the dig site, and for that, she felt a modicum of relief—it meant no worker had been run over by a tractor, mauled by the mower or shattered bones in a fall from a ladder. The sound led her to the chain-link fence that surrounded the pits, and she hooked her fingers through the gaps.

She panted. "Is someone hurt?"

The gate to the fence creaked open and slammed shut. Spencer skirted the corner and put an arm around Claire, pulled her into him and gently guided her away.

"We need to call the police," Spencer said in the same tone and volume that someone might say, *we need to make a cup of tea*. He navigated her toward the house. "We're going to call 911, but there's no rush. Dead is dead." His voice was flat. "Everything will be okay. Trust me, Claire."

Trust him? Someone was dead and she didn't know who or how or why. She only knew it happened on her property, nearly in her own front yard.

When they got to the house, Spencer called 911. Soon, sirens wailed up Grant Road. Lots of sirens. Men and women jumped out of cars and trucks, and Spencer led them calmly to the body.

Claire stood on the veranda, stunned. An hour passed before a man with a long, craggy face walked up to her with Spencer and a gangly deputy on his heels.

"I'm Detective Wayne Taggert," the man said. "May we talk in the house?"

A homicide? Queasy, she turned to go inside.

Spencer asked, "Claire, are you all right?"

The deputy stopped him. "You need to stay here, sir."

"I'm okay," she managed, embarrassed to discover her throat had tightened.

"Don't say anything to him." Spencer ignored the deputy. "We need to call your attorney."

"My attorney?" she repeated dully.

"You *do* have an attorney, don't you?"

"No."

"Then don't say anything. I'll find one for you."

He turned to the detective. "Hear that, Detective? She's not going to talk to you until an attorney is present."

"I'll wait. Meantime, you tell your people no one goes anywhere until we say."

"I will, but first I'm going in to use her phone." Spencer walked past the detective into the house.

Claire gazed out toward the yard. Her thoughts drifted back to the day she had made the phone call that started all this. Carlos had tried to talk her out of it. He'd said what's buried should be left buried.

Why in God's name hadn't she listened?

Chapter 2

Four Months Earlier, March 1987

Claire Courtney tramped through the orchard, a willowy figure in a long-sleeved, blue cotton shirt tucked into Levi's. Her wheat blonde hair, streaked by the sun, roped down her back in a loose braid.

Carlos Barbosa, the foreman, stood between rows of trees, turning something over in his hand.

"What's going on?" Claire had been working since dawn and hadn't slept much the night before. She glanced at the gas-powered trencher they had rented to dig the new irrigation line. "We're getting charged by the day on this trencher, Carlos. Shouldn't someone be using it?"

"Juan was digging the trench, and this came up." Carlos held up a cream-colored, chiseled, pointed rock, about ten inches long.

Claire took it, brushed off some dirt, held it up to the light, and turned it back and forth. "Wow. It looks like a gigantic arrowhead," she said, tiredness evaporating. "I found stuff like this as a kid down by the river, but nothing this big or this color."

"There's more." Carlos pointed to the ground where two more like it lay.

She knelt down, brushing dirt away. "What do you think they are?"

"I think they are trouble."

She almost laughed. Carlos wasn't usually given over to dramatics. "Really? Trouble?"

"I have a bad feeling about these rocks. Let's stick them back in the ground where they belong and bury them. Whatever they are, they don't want to be found. They belong to the earth. Let her have them."

"They're probably nothing. Maybe Dad used to bury garbage here. Do you remember this part of the orchard before the trees were planted?"

"Your dad never put garbage on the land. We burned what we could and hauled the rest to the dump."

"I'll take these to the house." She gathered the rocks and stood. "Keep the trencher another day. Have Juan keep digging. If any more of these pop up, leave them in place until I decide what to do."

"I should have buried the damn things," he muttered, and Carlos Barbosa was not a swearing man.

***

Claire lay the pointed rocks on her desk and dropped into a worn, wooden chair. She ran her hand over the smooth wood of the desk. Her dad had worked here every night, smoking, going over paperwork, and reading. The years he had run the orchard had been prosperous, before all the suffocating government rules and regulations. Before people sued over spray drift. Things were different now. Now the desk belonged to her. Now the orchard wasn't so prosperous.

She ignored the rocks for the moment and picked up the ledger of orchard accounts. She turned page after page until she came upon the newest entries, ran her finger over each line for the fifth time this month, hoping against hope she had made some stupendous error, and the ink would turn from red to black. She owed the bank a frightening amount of money, and she needed more to make it to harvest. If the crop didn't do well this year, the orchard wouldn't belong to her anymore. Her family home would host yet another farm auction where tractors, trucks, furniture—generations of accumulation—were auctioned off while the family sits, hollow-eyed, watching the very fiber of their lives unravel thread by thread.

She closed the ledger and pulled open a desk drawer, fished out a glass and a bottle of R&R. Canadian whisky. She poured a stiff one, downing it in one swallow, then splashed a refill and groped in the drawer for a cigarette. Camel straights. Her dad's brand. She scraped a match into flame and touched it to the stumpy, filterless cigarette. The acrid smell of tobacco filled the room. She inhaled, and the harsh, stale tobacco seared her lungs.

"Jesus," she sputtered, coughing. She rarely lit a cigarette, only when life squeezed in on her and she longed for her father's presence, as if smoking one of his cigarettes might bring him back, or at least impart some paternal wisdom.

She stood and reached through white linen curtains on the window next to the desk and pushed it open. The smoke drifted out. The window framed a view of the Cascade Mountains, snow-capped and rugged, towering over the Wenatchee Valley. The valley lay before her like a rough-hewn bowl, cut down the middle by the Columbia River. The Courtney Orchard spidered along terrain that rose to the east toward arid basalt cliffs.

She sat back and gazed up at the old family photos that hung on the wall. In the first, she had been five, a tow-headed girl in pigtails fastened with bows in a lacy dress, white ankle socks, and black patent leather shoes. Her dad's hand rested on her shoulder with his other arm wrapped around her mom, who held the baby and smiled broadly. The smile transformed her mother's face as she held her baby boy, little Joshua, an expression Claire rarely saw in later years. Claire, too, had doted on Josh.

In another photo Claire, a teenager now, stood tall and proud between her dad and Carlos. Carlos had driven up from Mexico with five other young men in an old pickup. Earl Courtney, Claire's father, had hired them on a warm July afternoon to pick cherries, then later, apples. Claire had been a freckled-faced, pig-tailed ten-year-old, and she had taken an instant liking to Carlos, shadowing his every move. His English had been pretty cryptic in those days, and Claire had been fascinated with his strange accent and words—there weren't many Mexicans in the valley back then. Most of the migrant workers came from the south—Arkansas and Oklahoma. After the first apple season, when his companions piled into the truck one crisp, cold October morning to head back to Mexico, Carlos had remained with the Courtneys, hired on permanent. Over the years Claire and Carlos taught each other their native languages.

In another photo, fifteen-year-old Claire stared at the camera with crystal blue eyes. Pigtails had given way to braids, and the dress had become denim overalls with a red plaid flannel shirt. She remembered exactly how she had felt at the snap of the photo—like one of the guys, an orchardist like her dad and Carlos. She already knew the business of growing apples and cherries, of thinning, fertilizing, spraying, propping, and picking. She had thought she knew it all.

In the next photo she stood, a young woman now, between her brother Josh and Keith—her fiancé, once upon a time. She stared at Keith's image, his carefree grin, his beautifully tousled hair. Her eyes trailed down the photo to Keith's cowboy boots. Not too many guys around town wore them, so she had called him her cowboy. He looked damn fine in those boots. Her heart still ached at the sight of him, all these years later.

She looked away, puffed on the Camel, careful not to inhale this time, and picked up one of the rocks from the desk, and turned it over in her hand. It looked like an arrowhead on steroids.

Back in the seventies, the county had built a bridge across the Columbia at the north end of town. No sooner had they started excavation when they discovered a trove of Native American relics, mostly pottery and tools, including arrowheads. Archaeologists had arrived from Washington State University, and the construction of the bridge had been put on hold while they investigated. The local newspaper ran a series of articles on the historical life of the Wenatchi Tribe who had lived along the river before white men arrived. After a few months, artifacts were displayed in the local museum, the WSU people left, and the bridge was built.

Claire sipped the whisky and tried to remember if there had been any talk about the worth of the stuff they dug up. Maybe arrowheads were worth something to somebody. Lord knows she could use the money. Or maybe she should listen to Carlos. Ignore the damn things and get on with the business of growing fruit.

As the spirits warmed her blood, she decided to call Washington State University, her alma mater. She'd start with WSU's Tree Fruit Research office in Wenatchee, talk to people she knew, see if the pointed rocks were something important or nothing at all.

***

Carlos picked up the last dish, drying it by hand in a kitchen devoid of dishwasher and microwave oven. A birch kitchen table with two chairs stood in the corner - wood sanded smooth by Carlos himself. He had laid the rustic terra cotta tile of the kitchen floor. It reminded him of the noble buildings of his boyhood town in Mexico, like his church, Our Lady of Angels, with its sturdy floors of tile and stucco walls. No linoleum for Carlos. He loved most things about America, but linoleum floors and kitchen gadgets did not number among them.

After twenty years, the small rooms felt as much a part of him as his black hair, now peppered generously with gray, although his thick mustache remained stubbornly black.

He pulled a broom from between the old Frigidaire and the wall, briskly swept a few remaining crumbs out the kitchen door and replaced the broom. He opened a drawer and pulled out a pipe and a pouch of tobacco, pressed tobacco into the pipe and stepped onto the back porch, his nightly ritual. He scratched a wooden match along the railing and puffed the tobacco to life.

Cherry trees surrounded the house. The orchard could be noisy during the day with tractors and sprinklers and workers, but at night the trees buffered him from the world, especially after the leaves came on; their denseness absorbed sound like a blanket, cocooning him from the world.

He stepped down into the yard and strolled into the orchard. Usually he enjoyed this evening routine, but tonight he felt troubled. He ambled toward Claire's house, moving steadily until he could see it through the trees. The light in the study glowed, like every night. Claire would be going over the books or reading one of her agriculture magazines. Working, always working, the weight of the world on her shoulders. A pity she had never married. A woman blossomed as a wife and mother. But then, Carlos had never married either. Not yet.

He stared at the house for a long time, smoking and thinking about the strange rocks they had found. The study went black, and minutes later a light flicked on upstairs. Carlos tapped his pipe against the trunk of a tree, the ash flaking to the green grass below. He stared at the window for a moment longer, then turned back and made his way home.

Chapter 3

Joe Running dropped his lecture notes into a leather briefcase – a briefcase so new, not a scratch marred its surface – as he emerged from the lyceum and squinted at the bright afternoon. High cheekbones and a straight nose chiseled his face into angular lines, tempered by full lips that would have been too much on another man's face. He set out across campus with long strides. At six feet two, his black, straight hair rose and fell rhythmically with his gait; his eyes were nearly as dark as his hair. The long braid he had worn since his teens had recently been abandoned on a barber shop floor, and he missed the heavy weight of it upon his back. He regretted the decision, not only because his long hair had been a part of his identity, but because he realized, too late, he had cut his hair because of his new job at Washington State University. *Professors didn't have braids*, he had reasoned at the time. Horse shit. He had never looked like anyone else at school before, so why now? He determined to grow it out straightaway.

He liked Washington State University—WSU—or Wazzu, as the locals called it, with its campus of meandering sidewalks, aged brick buildings and oak trees that had witnessed the turn of the century, all folded into the rolling wheat fields they called the Palouse. He especially liked the solitude of southeastern Washington, where the coyotes and jackrabbits outnumbered the people. His type of place.

The only Native American on the faculty, he melded nicely into the eclectic collection of professors from around the world. Students of a calculus professor—an Indian from New Delhi—complained to one another that his thick, singsong accent implied meditation rather than calculation. WSU seemed to pride itself on luring an international faculty to its rural setting.

"Finally, a Native American on staff," one colleague had welcomed Joe. "We get the occasional question from prospective students as to the danger of," he had cleared his throat, "well, wild Indians, because we're so far out west." Joe had laughed, thinking it a joke, but the slow smile on the colleague's face had told him otherwise. Joe liked the idea actually, people still believing in the wild west. In honor of the idea, he began wearing the cowboy boots he always wore during the summer when he worked on his cousin's ranch in Idaho.

He savored the university life. He attended the requisite staff meetings and once joined a few faculty members on a Friday afternoon for a beer at Rico's Public House, which turned awkward when he ordered a cup of coffee instead of the Grants Scottish ale the others favored. But mostly he kept to himself, pretty much like he always had, with the exception of baseball. When it came to baseball, he was a team player all the way.

At College Hall, the old, brick building that housed the anthropology faculty offices and the Museum of Anthropology, he took the concrete steps two at a time. His office was on the third floor, and its size matched his status as a first-year, non-tenure-track associate professor—bigger than a closet, but barely. Setting the briefcase on the desk, he picked up the day's mail and shuffled through. A green telephone message slipped from the pile—a message from WSU Tree Fruit Research in Wenatchee. Why would Tree Fruit be calling him? The message had originally gone to Bradley Randall, chairman of the Anthropology department, and Randall had forwarded the message to Joe, scribbling in the margins. *Read your email Joe,* it said. *Message from Tree Fruit waiting for two days now.*

Email. A new and bothersome technology. He flipped on an IBM PC which begrudgingly came to life. The college had recently made the leap from terminals linked to a mainframe—which they still used for data and research—to the personal computers, or PCs, as they called them. Joe discovered twenty unread messages—staff memos, notices for meetings he had already attended, and the message from Bradley.

An orchardist in East Wenatchee had contacted the Tree Fruit Research station after finding some large arrowhead-like rocks buried in the ground of an apple orchard. They wanted to know if someone from WSU might want to come take a look. Bradley asked if Joe could squeeze in a visit. A name, Courtney Orchards, address, and directions followed. Joe printed the message, the dot matrix chattering like a toy machine gun. He had driven through Wenatchee but had never stopped to look around. He plucked the message from the printer. With no plans for spring break, a drive to Wenatchee might be interesting.

He finished his paperwork and headed home for lunch. His apartment was within walking distance, even in the winter, but far enough away from the hubbub of student life. The single-level apartment complex took up a city block, crisscrossed with sidewalks, with old maples and oaks towering overhead. He loved the gigantic, old trees, so big most places would have taken them down by now.

Back at his apartment he grabbed a quick bite then headed to his bedroom. On his dresser were his favorite baseball mitt, two autographed balls from his junior and senior years at the University of Michigan, and a couple of trophies. He changed into sweats and a t-shirt and took off for a run, wondering, as he loped up the hills of Pullman, what this Wenatchee orchard might have in store for him.

***

There were shorter routes to East Wenatchee from Pullman, but Joe had a stop to make on the way, so he headed to Spokane, and took Highway 2 to Reardan, his old stomping grounds. He pulled his 1977 GMC pickup—white beneath a fine coating of dust—into the parking lot of the Red Rooster restaurant and flipped off the ignition. The truck coughed once, then shuddered to a standstill. Joe sat a minute, searching for a car that wasn't there.

He took a deep breath, let it out slow, climbed out of the truck and headed inside, pausing before he pushed open the glass door to examine the fading and peeling painting of a rooster on the front window. At the bottom right there was a signature —*Janet*. Joe felt a tug of emotion.

Inside, the first two booths on either side of the aisle were packed full of stuff. Manila folders, shoe boxes bursting with receipts, even a cash register sat not on the table itself, but on the overstuffed, cracked vinyl seat. Joe passed the disarray and walked to the first clean booth he came to and slid in, facing the street. Behind him, snippets of conversations, all male voices, talked about crops and traffic and how much they liked the Hollywood actor turned president.

A full four minutes passed before a cup of coffee appeared on the table before him. "She ain't here."

Joe looked up. "Roger. How are you?"

"Same." Thin-faced with floppy gray hair, Roger had been the handsome, blond quarterback of Reardan High School a couple of generations before.

"How's Mike?"

"Mike's still trying to make a living ranching, which ain't a living at all. I'll tell him you said hi. Now Christian, my grandson, he's another story. Between Mike and I and a bunch of scholarships, Christian's at the UW Medical School. How 'bout them apples?"

"That's good news."

"Shit, yeah, that's good news. I hear you're doing pretty good yourself."

"Can't complain."

"You been going to school for a long time, and let me tell you, my grandson's going to make more money in his first year as a medical doctor than you're going to make in a decade. An archaeologist is a doctor who don't make shit for money."

"You're right about that." Joe laughed.

"I highly recommend the eggs and ham with hash browns this morning. Eggs are fresh, ham is nice and salty and full of flavor."

Joe picked up his coffee cup and drank. "Sounds fine."

Roger pushed through a swinging door next to the counter into the kitchen, in full view of the booths. A slice of ham hit the griddle with a sizzle, followed by a dollop of grease and a mound of shredded potatoes. He flipped food and shuffled to the refrigerator in the back of the kitchen. Soon came the crack and sputter of three eggs frying. Joe watched as the old cook piled everything onto a hot plate and retraced his steps back to the booth. Another customer, a farmer no doubt, passed Roger and let himself in behind the counter, where he refilled his coffee cup before retreating to the back of the café.

After a bit, Roger filled a cup of coffee of his own, pulled off his apron, revealing a U.W. Husky t-shirt, and slid into the booth opposite Joe.

"How's the grub?"

"Delicious, as usual," Joe said between mouthfuls. "Thanks."

"Well, it ain't on the house. I need the money to get Christian through med school." Roger took a drink of coffee, squinted at Joe. "Your mom, she did real good for almost six months. Then February or so, went back to the same old same old. She'd be late on a Wednesday morning, but right as rain on Thursday. Then she quit showing up on Wednesdays and Thursdays. Never called in, just showed up on Friday like nothing happened. Finally, she quit showing up at all."

"You should have called."

"I called your brother. He said he'd take care of it. Gonna go see her?"

"Yeah." Joe sipped his coffee. "Looks like you could use a new rooster painting on your front window."

"Is that a roundabout way of asking how Janet's doing?"

Embarrassed, Joe answered, "I guess."

"She's not doing much painting anymore. Three kids, oldest one's seven, and I think they go every other year younger after that." Roger drank his coffee. "Whatever happened to the two of you, anyway? Didn't she go off to Michigan with you?"

"She did," Joe replied. "She decided she missed her family and friends more than she would miss me. Simple as that. Ancient history."

"She probably wanted to start having them babies, and I would guess you weren't much interested at the time. More interested in baseball than babies." Roger stood, his slight stoop making him an inch or two shorter than he'd been in high school, and unconsciously rubbed his right knee where arthritis had set in after one too many sacks when the front line couldn't save the quarterback from getting flattened. "Good to see you, Joe. Glad to see you made it off the rez. That you're making it on your own, whether you get paid shit or not."

It was nice that some people never changed. "Thanks, Roger."

By the time he sopped up the last of the egg and polished off the ham and hash browns, most of the breakfast crowd had gone. He left a larger than usual tip, to help in a small way with the grandson's medical school. Outside, the morning air was fresh. He took a deep breath, glanced at Janet's painting one last time, then headed north towards Wellpinit on the Spokane Reservation. His hometown.

***

Joe drove through the familiar landscape, scattered pines and irrigated fields, until he took a left at Little Falls Road. He followed the pavement as it crossed the river in front of a dam where once a set of rapids had churned the waters of the Spokane River white, where a waterfall had spilled the river down a chunk of elevation after the rapids. No longer. The landscape turned to dry sagebrush as he drove, and a few miles before the town of Wellpinit, he took a left again onto Wynecoop-Cayuse Road, which meandered down toward the river, and pulled into a dirt driveway.

He turned off the ignition and sat in silence. Nothing had changed since he moved out in 1970 to go to college. Patchy grass, overgrown in some spots, bare dirt in others, fronted the place. Two cars sat haphazardly on either side of a mobile home that was showing its wear badly. Rusty, corrugated metal siding, shutters begging for paint, faded yellow curtains fluttering in the windows. The 1966 Ford Galaxy he used to drive to high school, once maroon, now faded to a sickly pink, slept like a fat old cat deep in tall grass and weeds. The '72 Chevy Impala, the car his mom drove to work at the Red Rooster, likewise had grass growing around the tires, about a month's worth.

As dismal as the place appeared from the road, the other side was a different story. It overlooked the river, where steep, sandy banks dotted with pine trees made for a fine view. Growing up, he had gazed at that sight endless nights from his bedroom, trying to ignore the loud ways of his mom and her friends as the night wore on and the bottles emptied.

He steeled himself to see his mom, hoping for the best. He knocked once and cracked open the door. The smell of stale cigarette smoke wafted through the opening.

"Mom, it's Joe. You home?"

His mom sat at the Formica kitchen table, cradled a cup in one hand, and held a cigarette in the other, its long ash threatening to drop on the table before she could tap it into the overflowing ash tray. As a kid, he had eaten bowl after bowl of cereal at that table, always from white cartons with black lettering —*corn flakes or puffed rice.* Government-issued food had no need for colorful characters on the box.

"Joe." She snuffed out the cigarette and stood, then indulged in a coughing fit. She wore a thin, terry cloth robe and fuzzy slippers. Her straight hair, which had been jet black a few years back, had faded to gray. "Coffee's on, help yourself," she croaked when the coughing subsided.

Joe walked over to her, wrapped his arms around her and kissed the top of her head. It felt like hugging a broom, all stiff wood and bristle. She patted his back with one blue-veined hand. "Go on now, get some coffee." She stepped out of his embrace.

What had he expected? He poured a cup and they both sat on opposite sides of the table.

"What brings you home?"

"I'm on my way to Wenatchee, so I thought I'd drop by. Had breakfast at the Red Rooster."

Her face fell at the name. "What lies did Roger tell about me?"

"He said you quit showing up for work. Again."

She shrugged, reached for another cigarette and lit it with a plastic lighter of pale red. "I'm ready to retire."

"You have a retirement income?"

She waved her cigarette at him as if it were a magic wand that would turn him to dust. "I'm fine. I get a little something from the Tribe, like we all do, and a check for the years I cleaned up at the tribal school." She brightened, "I started getting disability checks on account of my COPD."

"It might have been nice to let Roger know you were quitting."

She laughed, a raspy sound like crumpling parchment paper. "He's a big baby if he couldn't figure it out. Too busy bragging about his grandson. But I had you to brag about."

A rare compliment. That was a fast ball he hadn't seen coming.

Outside came the deep rumble of an old diesel pickup. A minute later, his brother George filled the doorway. "Joe. To what do we owe the pleasure?"

Nearly as tall as Joe but heavy in the gut, George's black hair poked out from beneath a tattered baseball cap. He cradled paper grocery sacks in each arm.

"George. Good to see you." Joe stood.

George set the bags on the counter and the brothers shook hands. George fished in one of the sacks and pulled out a gallon of Wild Turkey Rye and held it up. "Ma?"

"I could use an eye opener," his mother grinned, then glanced at Joe. Her grin faded. "It's not even noon yet. What were you thinking?"

George stashed the whiskey and the rest of the groceries, then regarded Joe. "What's up?"

"Nothing much. Passing by and stopped in to say hello. I'm on my way to Wenatchee to check into something dug up in an orchard."

"The world-famous grave digger," George snickered.

"How's work?"

"Good. Working security for a concert tonight."

"Anybody I'd know?"

"It ain't Wayne Newton."

They sat around the table and chatted about nothing much until the last of the coffee was gone. Joe drained his cup and stood. "I better hit the road. You two take care."

"Don't worry about me," his mother smiled. "I'm fine." She held her coffee cup up in a salute.

Outside, a rush of cool air washed over him, filling his lungs until he could breathe again.

***

Joe doubled back to Highway 2, followed the asphalt as it eased through acres of sagebrush country where hawks perched on the cross-arms of utility poles. *Leave the past behind,* he told himself, but the whole morning had been a baptism of memories, and they crowded in on him like a smothering membrane, blurring the sagebrush landscape.

Growing up, his mother had been there physically, but not there—not in the sense of what a mother should be. He wasn't alone. A loving two-parent household wasn't exactly status quo on the reservation. As a teenager, he decided to go to Reardan High School instead of the reservation school, and his mother definitely did not have his back. Oh, she went along with it when she was sober, but when the booze flowed, she let him know what she really thought—that he was a pain in the ass who thought he was better than everybody else. She hoped he didn't expect her to drive him to school every day. It was thirty miles away, for God's sake, she had ranted. *And what about your friends*?

What about his friends, indeed. They pretty much sided with his mother. They couldn't figure out why he'd want to go to school off the reservation. *Baseball,* he had told them. But they didn't buy it. They called him a pussy, said he wanted to be white. They said by leaving the reservation, he was walking out on them, so they abandoned him.

He hadn't realized it at the time, but he had needed a friend. He met Janet the first day of school at Reardan High, in first-period English class when everyone was staring at him as if an alien from Jupiter had suddenly landed in their midst. The only one he didn't mind staring at him was blonde, blue-eyed Janet, because she had given him a shy grin. When the lunch bell rang, he took his battered paper sack containing a peanut butter sandwich and potato chips outside. The September sunshine made him long to go back to the familiarity of the rez. A few kids were scattered around, but he found an empty picnic table and turned his back to the school. A few minutes later, Janet plunked herself down across from him. *Hi, I'm Janet. You're new. It's nice to see a new face. I've been going to school with the rest of these goofballs since kindergarten. Who are you?*

And so it began. First, they were friends, then by their junior year, a couple, which didn't exactly thrill her parents. She became his lifeline. His confidant. Unfailingly trustworthy in a way nobody had been so far in his life. And, he had baseball. The first year, the coaches and kids had welcomed him in a thin, artificial way with fake smiles and suspicious eyes. The more they played, the better things got, because Joe could play, by God, and he loved baseball, along with Janet. Baseball was the other steady constant in his life. By his senior year, the coaches and team accepted him as one of their own. He and Janet even double dated with some of the guys from the team and their girlfriends.

He had gotten a baseball scholarship to the University of Michigan, and by the time they graduated and headed off to university together, Joe had figured they'd be one of those couples who met young and stayed together forever. They would eventually marry, have kids and grow old together. In the meantime, they had years of school ahead of them, and he had baseball to play.

Janet hadn't lasted a year in Ann Arbor, Michigan. Halfway through spring term she told him she was going home and wouldn't be coming back. Her words hit him like a kick in the gut. She cried, and told him she was sorry, but she didn't like college and she missed her friends, and now that he was busy 24/7 with baseball and classes, there was no time for her. The biggest thing was that Ann Arbor was over 2,000 miles away from home. The trees were weird, the weather was frigid, and as much as she loved him, she just couldn't cope any more. He took her to the bus station two days later, staring vacant-eyed at the back of the bus as it pulled away.

After the initial blow and trauma, he had no choice to but harden his concentration into his studies and baseball. He couldn't afford to mope. A psychiatrist would probably tell him he was suppressing his emotions, and that Janet leaving him was one more blow, along with having an alcoholic mother and an absent father, that would leave him with abandonment issues. But what was done was done. He had work to do, and so he showed up to class every day, suited up for practice every afternoon, did his homework, and played his heart out on the diamond.

Life went on.

***

Hours later, the highway dropped into the steep, winding road of Pine Canyon, then along the Columbia River to outskirts of East Wenatchee, Joe shook himself back into the present. He found Grant Road, which climbed gently east until town faded away and orchards took over.

He was gazing up at basalt cliffs that loomed behind the orchards when something ran in front of the car. He braked hard. A coyote stopped at the edge of the road and glanced back at Joe with savvy eyes.

If a coyote crosses your path, the Navajos say, *turn back and do not continue your journey.*

The coyote trotted away, and Joe tried to shake off a sudden chill. A mile up the road, he spotted the mailbox for the Courtney orchard.

He pulled into a long, dirt driveway, killed the engine and looked around. Purple crocus mingled with blood-red tulips grew against a white, two-story farmhouse. Dormer windows looked out from the second story like veiled eyes. A roof of cedar shakes, darkened with weather and time, sloped down to cover a veranda running the entire length of the house. The driveway continued to a large, old garage before turning into a two-track road along the edge of a sizable orchard.

Overhead, islands of brilliant-white clouds drifted against a turquoise sky.

Joe got out, all long legs and cowboy boots, stuffed latex gloves in his back pocket, and took the steps to the house two at a time. He knocked, his gaze returning to the orchard as he waited, then knocked again. No answer. A motor hummed in the distance. He followed the sound into the orchard, passing a cluster of small, white cabins before he finally spotted a guy in rain gear—a yellow hat and slickers—driving a tractor pulling a sprayer.

The spray whipped tree branches and thickened the air with an acrid chemical bite. Joe kept his distance. He watched and waited until the roar of the sprayer stopped. The tractor pulled in front of a large, open-sided wood building, up to a black hose hung from a tall metal pipe. The engine sputtered to a stop. The driver jumped off and pulled off the yellow hat. A thick blonde braid uncoiled and fell halfway down his back, or rather *her* back. Definitely *not* a guy.

Joe's hand rose automatically to the back of his neck, where his braid had always rested. He stuck his hand in his pocket and walked toward the woman.

"Excuse me," he said. "I'm looking for Mr. Courtney."

The woman glanced his way. A natural beauty, he thought. No makeup, and she sure didn't need any.

"There is no Mr. Courtney. I'm Claire Courtney. Who are you?"

"I'm Joe Running from Washington State University – the archaeologist. You called about some arrowheads?"

Her gaze slipped down to his cowboy boots and lingered there. Her eyes returned to his, and she studied him a minute, then she turned away, stepped on a tractor tire in one, fluid motion, grabbed the hose and turned on the water.

"Let me clean up here," she yelled over the sound of water thrumming inside the sprayer.

After she finished, she slipped out of the yellow slickers and wiped her hands on a rag and tossed it aside.

Joe stepped closer and held out a hand. "Nice to meet you."

She hesitated, shook his hand briefly, then took off walking. "They're up at the house."

Her house, inside, had a vintage look with hardwood floors and well-worn braided rugs. He followed her down a hallway and into a study, where textbooks, magazines, and manuals spilled from bookshelves onto two chairs, an oversized wooden desk, and the floor. *New Directions in Tree Fruit Pest Management, Tree Fruit Nutrition, Pollination & Fruit Set, Intensive Orchard Management,* and *Good Fruit Grower.*

There on the desk, arranged on a folded newspaper, lay three of the largest arrowhead-like artifacts Joe had ever seen, cream-colored with rusty highlights, eight to nine inches long. The tips were pointed, the sides were flaked smooth.

He pulled the latex gloves from his back pocket.

"Uh oh," Claire said. "If you're putting on those gloves to protect the, uh, rocks, we already handled them pretty good."

He picked up one of the points and held it to the light, turning it over. *Holy shit,* he thought. Out loud, he said. "Looks like agate. Maybe even a man-made tool. Both sides look chipped to form a knife-like point." He ran his finger from the tip to the base. "This could be a channel to attach to a handle. I've seen similar knives and tools, but never anything this large."

"Are they important?"

"Maybe," Joe said.

Claire shifted her weight from one foot to the other. Crossed her arms. "So, what happens now?"

"I'd like to take these back to the university lab. If they appear to be authentic, I'll come back with a radar crew to survey the ground. Will you show me where you found these?"

"Yeah. Let me get you something to put those in." She left, returning with a paper sack.

Joe carefully placed the artifacts inside, eager to get these, whatever they were, back to the lab. They were either an amazing find, or fake. He glanced at the photos above the desk as he peeled off his gloves and felt an unexpected pang of envy. Somewhere in the world, apparently here, families really did come equipped with two reliable parents and a stable home.

Joe pointed at the picture of young Claire in the dress. "Is this you?"

She glanced at the photo. Flushed. "Yeah."

"And this must be you with your father?" He indicated another other photo.

"And Carlos."

"You grew up in this house?"

She regarded him for a moment. "Yeah. I inherited this place from my parents and have been running the orchard myself since my dad passed away. Listen, if you want to see where we found the rocks, let's go."

They didn't have to go far. About a half mile west of the house, a gash in the ground revealed dark soil.

"We're putting in new irrigation lines to complete a system we started last year, and dug them up with a trencher," Claire said. "If we don't get the pipes laid soon, we'll be moving sprinklers above ground all year again, which is a pain in the..." She glanced at Joe. "Backside."

Joe knelt and fingered the soil.

"You'll figure out if these are real?" Claire asked. "Maybe important?"

Joe stood. "Yes. If they look promising, I'd like to do a preliminary study."

"I decide, right?" Claire pressed. "This is my land and these rocks, or whatever they are, belong to me. Right?"

"They're your property, yes. The game changer would be if we find human remains, burials, or associated burial objects—sacred objects."

She crossed her arms. "How?"

"It's still your private property, but the Tribes will get involved. They'll probably be involved anyway. I'll notify them before we dig. But if this is a Native American burial site, the Tribes won't want anyone digging around their ancestors' cemetery."

Claire stared at him, chewing on her lower lip. "Why should I take a chance? I'm running an orchard and I can't have people getting in my way."

This woman had a hard edge to her. "You've grown up here. All your life memories are tied to this place, right?"

"Yeah," Claire's eyes narrowed.

"These artifacts might be evidence of people who lived here long before you and your family. Who were they? How long ago? How did they live? Are these spearheads? Why are they so large? Why did the people leave them here, and where did they go? These are the questions. The answers may lie beneath the ground."

"Could they be valuable?"

"You never know."

"If something is valuable, would it still belong to me? Could I sell it?" Claire looked up at him.

So that's where she was going with this. Money. Disappointing. He chose his words carefully. "It depends—possibly. This is buried treasure of a different nature. Artifacts like these, if authentic, are a crucial part of human history."

Claire studied him for a full minute. "Okay. I'll figure out what I want to do."

They turned back to the house. As they walked, Joe noticed a man standing in the shadow of the apple trees, watching them. It looked like the Hispanic man in the picture in the study. Joe raised his hand and waved, but the man turned and disappeared into the orchard.

Joe headed toward his truck, and Claire climbed the steps to the front porch.

"I'll be in touch." Joe said, but Claire disappeared inside with an absent wave.

Joe stared at the door and the orchard where Carlos had stood. Not exactly a warm reception. He headed back to Pullman.

Chapter 4

"Look at the size of them!" Bradley Randall peered through reading glasses at one of the oversized arrowheads. They were in Bradley's office, with a large window overlooking the campus. "Too big," Bradley pronounced.

Bradley flipped the artifact back and forth in his gloved hand.

"I've done some research," Joe said. "If they're authentic, the size and structure correlate with the Clovis culture."

"Now we're talking too big *and* too old," Bradley countered. "Ten thousand years old. Seems unlikely since they were found pretty shallow in a working orchard that's been operating for decades."

"Yeah, pretty unlikely, but possible." Joe walked to the office window and gazed out at the oak trees sprouting glossy, new leaves. "If these turn out to be worth pursuing, I'd like to lead the dig myself."

"Why not? After classes wrap up, you're free to go."

That had been too easy. Obviously, Bradley didn't think the find was authentic. "Great. Thanks. I'll prepare the state application and the letters of notification to local Tribes—one to the Colvilles, one to the Yakamas."

Bradley removed his glasses, rubbing the bridge of his nose with his thumb and forefinger. "I should never have become a department head. Nobody ever wanted anything from me when I was teaching, except my students."

"Thanks, Bradley." Joe moved toward the door. "You won't be sorry."

***

Joe met the geologists at the Courtney orchard a few days later. They hauled what looked like a lawn mower out of the back of a trailer. It was, in fact, state-of-the-art ground-penetrating radar equipment. After a brief introduction to Claire, the geologists took hundreds of measurements in a crisscross grid, and at the end of a very long day, headed back to Pullman to create a three-dimensional interpretation of soil, sediment, and whatever else might buried down there.

The report came back in a week. A concentration of objects populated an area more than six meters square, with smaller objects scattered outward. Many of the objects looked similar in shape—too similar to be random rocks. Joe called Claire with the good news.

She listened in silence.

"If possible, I'd like to start as soon as classes are out in early May."

Still silence.

"Are you there, Ms. Courtney?"

"Call me Claire," she said. "I'm thinking. This would be just a small investigation, right?"

"A preliminary dig, yes. To decide if this is a site worth further excavation."

Joe waited. He imagined Claire standing in her study, chewing her lip, trying to decide. After a long silence she said. "Okay. May."

"That's great. By the way, I noticed some buildings, they looked like cabins, not too far away from the dig site."

"Pickers' cabins," Claire said.

"Are they suitable for renting?"

"They have to be suitable, or the state would have my..." she paused. "The state has strict regulations on housing for migrants. My cabins meet those regulations."

"I'd like to rent a few of them for myself and a couple of grad students while we're there."

"I'm definitely interested in rent."

"Perfect. I'll be in touch with more details and paperwork soon," Joe said.

After they hung up, he couldn't get her out of his mind. Strange woman, Claire Courtney. Aloof with a tinge of anger, if he read her right. His thoughts turned to Idaho. Working on the dig meant he wouldn't be able to make the trip this year. He'd spent every summer since he was eight on his cousin's ranch near Pocatello. Those months had been the saving grace of his youth, a chance to escape the smoke-filled trailer and the nights when his mother and her friends kept him awake with their loud talk and cigarette after cigarette.

He loved working on the ranch in Idaho—the clean air, outside all day, bucking hay, riding horses, rounding up cattle and swimming in the creek. He grew to love his much older cousin, aptly nicknamed 'Tuff,' and Tuff's mom Esther, like parents.

He had known those summers would come to an end when he got a real job, but he planned to visit each year for a week or two, and be grateful for whatever Idaho time he could squeeze in.

***

The semester ended at WSU the fifth of May. Joe scheduled the dig to start the following Monday.

He pulled his truck into the Courtney Orchard driveway, followed by a well-used Volvo station wagon that kicked dust into the air as Claire watched from the front porch, frowning.

Yup, aloof with a touch of anger, Joe thought, climbing out of the truck. "Good morning, Claire," Joe said.

"That your crew?" Claire nodded toward the station wagon, where a young man and woman stood awkwardly outside the car.

"Yes," he said waving the two over. "This is Scott Carlson and Gabriella Cortez, graduate students in anthropology as WSU. This is Claire Courtney, owner of the property."

Scott wore tortoise-shell framed glasses beneath a headful of curly, brown hair.

Gabriella was petite, with dark eyes and brown hair cropped short. "Call me Gabby," she said.

"You'll want to see the cabins," Claire walked down the steps and past them.

The pickers' cabins were about a half a mile west from of dig site. Six identical, wooden cabins sat in two rows of three, compact and freshly painted white.

"They're nothing fancy." Claire opened the door to the first cabin, stepping aside so the three could peek in. "One room, two beds, a kitchenette with sink, small refrigerator and stove top. No ovens."

She pointed to a building made of concrete blocks in the center between the two rows of cabins. "Showers and bathrooms—his and hers. State law requires adequate sanitation and cooking facilities. That little piece of legislation tacked a second mortgage onto my house."

"This will be perfect." Joe turned to Gabby and Scott. "Let's grab our gear and choose a cabin."

Joe wanted to make sure everything went smoothly. Clearly, university administration didn't think they had the eighth wonder of the world at stake here, or he would never been assigned to lead the project. Eight years of college and a year of teaching behind him, his time had come.

The three of them made a few trips back to his truck for equipment and supplies, then they roped off an area four and a half square meters and set up two sifting stations.

Joe hesitated before they began, savoring the moment. A ceremony seemed appropriate. He cleared his throat. Gabby and Scott watched him expectantly.

"We need to be meticulous, as you both know, because every square inch of soil could hold something important."

Gabby and Scott glanced at one another. "Don't worry about us, Professor," Scott said.

"Why don't you call me Joe." So much for ceremony. He picked up a sod lifter, a long-handled garden tool much like an edger. "Let's get started."

Joe began at the trench where the artifacts had been unearthed, and carefully cut and removed sod. He handed each patch of sod to Scott, who placed it dirt-side down on the flat screen of a sifter, shaking it until the last remnant of dirt sifted through, then he studied the underside of the sod for any sign of artifacts.

Gabby leaned over her own sod lifter and excavated on the opposite side of the trench from Joe and Scott. Although she knew the theory of excavation, she watched Joe's every move, and copied him. When he sliced into the earth, she sliced. When he lifted out sod, so did she.

They worked for an hour, digging a small area down nearly a foot. Then Gabby's shovel clinked. "I hit something," she said. "Probably just a rock."

Joe walked over and squatted down, troweled dirt away from around the object while Gabby grabbed a small brush and began to sweep the away the soil. Millimeter by millimeter the tip of a large, flaked point emerged from the dirt.

"It looks like the other three," Joe said. "Let me grab my camera."

***

Joe took off and returned with a camera strapped around his neck, and knelt at the edge of the trench. He focused the lens and began snapping photos.

"Nice Nikon," Scott said. "I did photography for my high school newspaper, and for the Daily Evergreen as an undergrad. I have a Canon."

"Are you good?" Joe asked, still snapping photos.

"Yeah, I've won a few awards."

Joe sat back on his heels and studied Scott, then he lifted off the camera strap and held it out. "The job's yours," he said.

"Job?" Scott asked.

"Photographing the dig. The artifacts and our progress."

Scott reached out for the camera, looking shocked. "You would trust me with this? Trust me with the photography on the project?"

"You said you're good." Joe said. "I'll take you at your word."

"Wow. I mean, thanks," Scott turned the camera over in his hands. "I won't let you down."

"I'll give you the rest of the gear later—lenses, filters, and more film."

Gabby and Joe resumed digging, while Scott snapped a photo now and then, adjusting the settings on the camera. They didn't need to sift dirt to find these artifacts. Each centimeter of dirt brushed away revealed another sculpted rock.

"There's several points here, clumped together," Joe said.

"What does it mean?" Gabby asked.

"Maybe this was a storage pit," said Joe. "They're piled on top of one another, as if someone put them here for safekeeping."

"How old do you think they are?" Gabby asked.

"Don't know yet. We'll study the soil layers and see if we can piece together the geologic history of the area, and hopefully find some organic material for carbon dating." Joe said.

"Are they spearheads?" Gabby asked.

"Spearheads, scraping tools," Joe replied slowly, "and they could be very important."

***

At the end of the day, after Scott and Gabriella drove off in search of dinner, Joe drove to a 7-11 in downtown East Wenatchee, if you could call the few blocks of old businesses *downtown*. He pushed a quarter into the outside pay phone and dialed Bradley Randall's home number. Bradley answered on the fifth ring.

"It's Joe Running."

"Joe. What's going on?"

"I'm calling with good news. We found several more artifacts already, many of them similar to the first three. It looks like it could be a tool cache."

"Bring the samples in," Bradley said.

"I think you should see the artifacts *in situ* and have a look around."

"Yeah, okay. Let me check my schedule and see when I can get away."

"Thanks."

"And Joe." Bradley said. "Keep up the good work."

Joe drove back to the orchard, excited and doubtful and thrilled and cynical. The artifacts just seemed too good to be true. He changed into shorts and a t-shirt, and jogged up Grant Road, toward the distant basalt cliffs. Nothing like a good uphill run to dampen a swirl of emotion. He had run a lot after Janet left him.

Chapter 5

Carlos paused in front of his pickup's side view mirror to straighten his tie and smooth back his hair, a ritual he performed every Sunday when he arrived at the Gonzales house after Mass. He examined himself critically through a layer of fine dust coating the mirror. He had been a good-looking kid. When he was twenty, the girls gave him the eye all the time. At fifty, he still had a full head of hair, his face hadn't weathered too badly despite a life working outdoors, and he took pride in his thick mustache. He brushed each side with a forefinger.

Carmen opened the door after his first knock. She, too, had a full head of dark hair streaked with gray, pulled back into an elaborate knot. Her curvy figure, round face and dark, sparkling eyes took Carlos's breath away.

Carlos whistled softly. "You're looking extra pretty this morning," he said in Spanish.

She smiled indulgently and held the door open. The simple white house had hardwood floors, sanded and finished by none other than Carlos himself.

"I watched you all during Mass," he said.

"You should be watching the Padre," she scolded.

He ducked past her, risking a pat to her behind. She swatted at him, but he sidestepped and headed through the kitchen and out the back door.

Outside, three men stood around a large metal box set over a pit where a fire blazed. They nodded at Carlos. The next few minutes were spent lighting pipes and cigars.

"How's it going, Carlos?" Rafael asked.

"People snooping around the place. Bad business." Carlos frowned, chewing on his pipe and staring at the flames.

"I hear they're digging up the orchard," said another.

Carlos shrugged. "Digging squares in the ground with little shovels. What are we eating today?"

"Barbacoa. A nice chivo. We put it on early. It should be done by noon."

"Ah, goat. My favorite," said Carlos.

"Are they digging near your land?" Rafael asked.

Carlos frowned. "Yes."

"Bad luck." The men shook their heads. "You're done for now."

"It'll all work out," Carlos said without much conviction.

Car doors slamming interrupted the conversation. A small army of little kids raced around the side of the house and began jumping in front of the men and the fire, as if the earth itself were too hot to stand on.

Three women and two young girls streamed into Carmen's kitchen, bringing with them freshly made tortillas, a pot of beans, and containers of pico de gallo and a spicy cabbage mix.

Later, Carmen peered out the kitchen window and caught Carlos's eye. He winked at her and she smiled back. She and the other women carried out the side dishes as the men began to slice off juicy slices of meat.

Carlos filled up two plates and sought out Carmen. "Time to eat," he said. "Come sit with me."

They sat in lawn chairs beneath a large pine tree, slightly away from the others. "Can I get you a drink?"

"A Pepsi."

He returned with a soda for her and a Corona for himself.

"You have strangers in the orchard?" she asked between mouthfuls. "Scientists?"

"Yes. Those rocks Juan found might be important."

"What will you do with the trees around where the rocks are?"

Carlos shrugged. "Can't spray when we need to, can't thin, can't do anything with people in the orchard. We're going to lose an acre of crop, for sure, maybe more."

"Why is she letting them in?"

He shook his head, took a long pull on the Corona. "Who can say? Claire's under a lot of pressure, trying to get the money under control. How's work going for you?"

Carmen shrugged. "Fine. The usual. Everyone gossips while we pack the fruit. We all get along, and it makes the time go by fast." Carmen took a bite of the roasted goat. "Mmm, delicious."

Carlos stopped eating long enough to pat Carmen on the leg. He leaned in and they sat shoulder to shoulder while they ate. When they finished, Carlos wiped his mouth and cleaned his mustache with his napkin.

"You've been patient," he said softly. "I can see now there's always going to be one thing after another. Maybe there will never be the perfect time for us to get married, and we're not getting any younger."

Carmen set her plate on the ground and turned to him, eyes wide.

Carlos leaned into her. "Will you marry me, Carmen? Sooner rather than later?"

She looked at him for a moment, then smiled. "Yes! I was hoping you would ask while I'm still young enough to walk down the aisle without a cane."

They kissed, a brief, sweet kiss, pulled apart and gazed at one another, until the hooting and hollering and applause began.

"At last!" Carmen's sister stood and shouted to the group. "They're finally going to tie the knot!"

Carlos stood and took a bow, and the whole group burst into laughter.

Chapter 6

Bradley had visited the site and been impressed, taking more samples back for processing. Even with a rush on the lab work, it took three weeks to get the results. Bradley hunched over his office desk pouring over the report. Several artifacts were agate, while two translucent and milky-white rocks, probably scraping tools, which were chalcedony, a quartz. *Works of art*, Bradley thought, happy he'd decided to make the trip to Wenatchee after all. The next page of the report, however, captured Bradley's full attention. Two of the rock tips had traces of bovine blood. Blood! Testing indicated the blood could be thousands of years old. Bradley whistled. He spent the rest of the day in the library, rummaging through books and journals with growing excitement. It appeared a Clovis site had dropped into his lap.

The literature didn't include any Clovis points anywhere near the size of these. The largest point in a Colorado Clovis site called the Drake cache was over sixteen centimeters, about six and a half inches, and the longest from two other Clovis sites, the Fenn site in Utah and Anzick site Montana, maxed out at sixteen centimeters.

By the time he left the library, his hands trembled with excitement. He knew he should call Joe first. Hell, he should drive to Wenatchee and tell him in person. But Washington State University in the far eastern wheat fields of the state had a long-standing rivalry with the University of Washington in Seattle, and Bradley Randall couldn't resist this cherry, no matter how hard he tried.

He buzzed his secretary. "Get me the number for the Seattle Times."

He couldn't help but chuckle at the thought of his counterpart at the U.W. reading about this in Seattle's own newspaper—a Clovis find in Washington state, and guess who discovered it first?

***

Claire woke up with a start. She glanced at the clock beside the bed. Seven. She couldn't remember the last time she had slept so late. She pushed her hair, loose and tangled, back from her face. Outside, a car door slammed. She threw back the covers, padded to the window. Her upstairs bedroom had dormer windows that offered a view to the front of the house and beyond. Several unfamiliar cars were parked along the driveway. She threw on some clothes, ran a brush through her hair and headed downstairs. She stepped outside as a Mercedes pulled into the driveway. A camera-toting, silver-haired man and his wife got out.

She shielded her eyes against the morning sun, wishing for sunglasses. "Can I help you?"

"We're here to see the Indian artifacts," the man said. "We came early to beat the crowd."

Claire stared at them, dumbfounded. The couple looked at her expectantly, then, when she only stared back at them, at each other.

Finally, the woman pointed. "Oh, look, dear. I see some people. Let's go."

Claire turned to look. The woman was right. People were scattered through her orchard like a rash. Blood pounding in her temples, Claire rushed toward the dig site until she spotted Joe.

"What in God's name is going on here? What are these people doing here?"

Joe blinked. "I'm as surprised as you are. They say they read about it in the paper."

"The *Seattle Times*," the Mercedes woman said.

A man plodded toward them, camera hanging around his neck, steno pad in his hand. "I'm with the *Wenatchee World*." He flashed a press card at them. "It sure would have been nice if you guys could have called the local paper first instead of going straight to Seattle. Anyway, I'm here to get the story. Who's in charge here?"

Claire felt a flash of anger. "I can't believe this!" She glared at Joe, anger radiating like a fever, then turned and stomped off.

Bradley Randall showed up at ten.

***

"What the hell were you thinking?" Claire glared first at Bradley, then Joe. The men sat side by side on the couch in Claire's living room. "I trusted you, and this is what I get? I told you I couldn't have people getting in the way. Do you know what happens these days if someone gets touched by spray drift? I end up with a big, fat fine. I could get sued."

"Ms. Courtney, I do apologize for this sudden invasion of your privacy, but you have to understand," Bradley interrupted. "This looks like a major find. We believe the items on your property are relics of Paleo-Indian hunters known as the Clovis people. They are very, very old. If they're what we suspect they are, they could tell us the story of people living at the final hour of the ice age. Can you imagine?" Bradley picked up steam. "If we can pinpoint dates, we'll be able to fill in a pattern of movement of an ancient culture. To study how they survived. Even more exciting, thousands of people will be able to see a tool held by ancient man, used by man living right here thousands and thousands of years—"

Claire held up a hand to silence him. "I get it. I'm the one who called you, remember? Here's my problem. I have nearly two hundred acres of apples and twenty acres of cherries. This is how I make my living, okay? I can't afford another bad year. I need the money. I can't afford to have a lot of people trespassing in my orchard. For one thing, there's insurance. Liability. What if somebody trips and breaks a leg?"

Bradley chewed on his lip, the pate of his head flushing pink. "I'll need to check the budget, but I'm sure we can get financing for security to keep the public out of your way. Insurance is tricky, but I'll check with the university president."

"Good. You do that. But let's get one thing straight, or we call the whole thing off right now." Claire's eyes fixed on Bradley. "This is my place. I call the shots here. I don't like surprises like I had this morning."

"I'm sure we can address all of your concerns most adequately. And," he cleared his throat, eyes darted toward Joe, "although Dr. Running has done a marvelous job so far, I'll be taking over."

Joe turned slowly to look at Bradley.

Bradley continued. "Dr. Running will still be on the project, but a discovery of this magnitude requires experience." He cleared his throat. "I'll take the lead on the project."

The room fell deadly quiet, save for the ticking of the clock. Joe stared, no *glared,* at Bradley.

Bradley avoided Joe's eyes. "Yes, well, I'll consult our people, and have some papers drawn up."

Joe stood, towering over Bradley. He turned to Claire. "I want you to know, I didn't know anything about the newspapers. I've been straight with you from the start."

A knock sounded on the front door, then it opened. "Professor Running?" Scott's voice called. "There's something you need to see."

Joe's gaze lingered on Claire for a moment longer, then he headed to the door with Claire and Bradley close behind. They followed Scott as he trotted through the trees toward the dig, where Gabby knelt next to an open pit.

"Take a look," Scott said.

They all peered into the pit. The bulbous end of a bone lay partly in the dirt. Bradley inhaled sharply, knelt down next to the pit, and reached out toward the object. "Oh my God," he said in a reverent tone. "It looks like an animal bone. A very large animal bone, like a mastodon."

***

The Colvilles arrived the next day.

Bradley had left for Pullman. Joe, Scott, and Gabby were expanding the pit centimeter by centimeter when a truck pulled into the driveway and doors slammed. After a few minutes, Scott glanced up. "Whoa, check it out."

Three Native American men approached—two tall, young men flanked an elderly man—all walking with purpose toward the dig.

Joe stood and greeted them. "I'm Joe Running," he said, hand outstretched.

The elderly man looked up at him, took his hand firmly. "You are the archaeologist from Washington State University who wrote to us. I'm Sam Moses, Tribal Councilman of the Colville Confederated Tribes. This is Chester Somday and Jack Waters."

"It's a pleasure to meet you," Joe shook each man's hand. "Welcome. Please, let me show you around."

He led them close to the pit. "This is Scott Carlson and Gabriella Cortez, graduate students in anthropology at WSU."

"Gabriella, that's beautiful," Sam took Gabby's hand between his own. "I believe it means angel, and you are aptly named."

"Thank you, sir," Gabby stammered.

Sam released her hand and turned to Joe. "Tell us about your discovery."

"Workers were digging trenches to lay irrigation pipe when several of these large, arrowhead-like rocks surfaced," Joe said. "The orchardist, Claire Courtney, contacted WSU, where I'm an associate professor of anthropology. We've just begun a preliminary investigation, but it's a rich find of Clovis artifacts. And just yesterday we discovered a bone, a big one over seventy centimeters long, maybe a mastodon, and it's decorated with etchings. The bone will allow us to carbon date the age of the artifacts."

Sam Moses peered into the pit where several large points lay stacked upon one another. A look of wonderment transformed his face. "The twins," he whispered. "Chester, Jack, take a look."

The two men gathered close and peered into the pit.

"Twins?" Joe handed him a latex glove.

Sam took the glove absent-mindedly, pulled it on, squatted beside the pit and ran a finger along one of the Clovis points. "Dragon slayers."

"Blue Star and Red Star," Chester said.

"Yes." Sam looked up at Joe, breaking into a broad smile. "The legends of our People are born out here, with these tools—the tools of our ancestors. You haven't heard the story of how the Star Twins slayed Spexmen?"

Joe shook his head.

"It's a Wenatchi Tribe legend. After the great wall of water flooded the Wenatchi valley thousands of years ago, a fierce dragon named Spexmen lived in the river, devouring man and beast alike with an insatiable appetite. Then one day, twins were born to the People. And, as you know," Sam scrutinized Joe, "the People don't have twins. The Wenatchi knew the twins were a gift from the stars, and they named them Red Star and Blue Star. As they celebrated, the Salmon People cast a spell over everyone, crept into the camp, took the twins and secreted them away. With the help of Smiyaw—Coyote—they took them to a cave in the Moses Coulee, where the twins lived in the dark. The Animal People came and taught them their specialized knowledge and brought songs of power over the years.

"When the twins matured, they were brought out of the cave into the light. For the first time they beheld their parents who raised them—giant ants. And who was there to greet them? Smiyaw—Coyote. Coyote enlisted their help to free the People from the dragon, Spexmen, and together, they made a plan."

Sam paused. By now, Scott and Gabby had crept next to Joe, and were listening with rapt attention.

Sam continued. "To make weapons, the twins used gigantic points made of the hardest stone around here—stones as hard as diamonds." Sam held his hand out to the pit. "They're called Clovis Points, and they're dragon slayers. From the forest, the boys obtained ironwood, which they used to make long shafts and attached the Clovis Points. Spexmen had two vulnerable points—his eyes and his underbelly. The twins enlisted the help of Sparrow Hawk, then they tracked Spexmen in the river. The twins began tormenting him from opposite sides of the water. One twin would hide on one side of the river, while his twin would taunt Spexmen from the other side. By the time Spexmen arrived to devour the twin he could see, that boy would hide and his brother on the opposite side of the river would call to Spexmen. Back and forth Spexmen swam, hour after hour, until he was angry, hungry, and exhausted. At last, Sparrow Hawk plunged from the sky and stabbed Spexmen in the eye. Then the twins attacked, first piercing the other eye with their spears, blinding the beast. When the fierce dragon reared back his head to spew out flames that would consume the twins, they attacked Spexmen in his vulnerable spot beneath the neck. They killed the beast, freeing man and animal alike from torment."

Gabby clapped. "I love that story!"

Sam peeled off the glove and stood, facing Joe. "These tools show the skill our People possess, as well as affirming local legend. We believe they should be left where they are. Along with these tools are the bones of animals, and possibly the bones of our People." Sam paused. "You're one of us, son. You know we don't disturb our graves."

"No one respects the graves of our People more than I do, Mr. Moses," Joe said. "I assure you, if any human remains are found, all activity will stop. I also welcome you to come and be a witness to the work we're doing here, and also want to reassure you, this is a small-scale, preliminary investigation. After we determine the size and scope of the site, the orchard owner will decide what to do next."

Sam Moses stayed quiet for a long while. "Very well," he said at last. "For now, we give permission for you to continue. You contacted us. You have shown your respect. We will come often and ask you to report to us frequently."

"Thank you, sir," Joe said.

"We'll stay in touch." Sam said. The three men turned and left.

Chapter 7

Spencer Grant clicked on the light of his condo, tired but satisfied. He'd spent the last five hours at a black-tie gala to raise funds for the University of Pennsylvania Museum of Archaeology and Anthropology, which he liked to think of as *his* museum. He had enjoyed himself, drinking champagne and schmoozing with the donors. There had been several matronly but well-heeled women who fawned over him, two of whom whispered '*Robert Redford*' to one another, giggling like schoolgirls, after he stopped by to chat. He smiled as he walked to the next table. How could he *not* feel good? Museum trustees in attendance included a surgeon and her husband, a media mogul and his wife of fifty years, and the rough-hewn self-made CEO of an industrial HVAC company who attended with his daughter and snuck out for a smoke a few times during the evening. All in all, the evening had been elegant, the food sumptuous, and his speech about the significance of preserving natural history from present day to prehistoric a success.

Blessed with sandy hair, blue eyes, and a boyish grin suited more to a surfer than an archaeologist, years of working in the field had, instead of weathering his skin, merely created a ruddy complexion of good health. At five foot ten, he stayed trim by bicycling to work and hitting the gym three times a week. He had sprinkled a number of bicycling jokes in his speech about the bizarre experiences of cycling through car-jammed streets in Philadelphia, all of which brought chuckles and a couple outright guffaws, much to Spencer's delight.

He dropped his keys into a nineteenth century Apache basket on the credenza by the front door and picked up the mail the housekeeper had left in a neat pile. He loosened his tie and unbuttoned his shirt as he headed for the bedroom, shuffling through the envelopes the best he could one-handed, and tossed the mail on his bed to hang up his jacket. When he went back to look through the pile, an envelope from an online information company caught his attention. He subscribed to a weekly bibliography of recent scientific articles. Tired, but curious, he opened the envelope and scanned the text.

He started to toss the pages onto the dresser but stopped. The last citation on the list came from the *Seattle Post-Intelligencer*. A cache of artifacts thought to date back thousands of years had been unearthed in an orchard in East Wenatchee, Washington. Preliminary findings from Washington State University scientists classified the artifacts as belonging to the Clovis culture.

Spencer sat down on the bed. He reread the summary. A new Clovis find. He glanced at the clock. Nearly midnight. Better wait until morning to call the governor. But he needed a favor, and he needed it fast.

***

Hand cradling her coffee cup, Claire was reading the paper when the phone rang. She reached out to the black wall phone, eyes never leaving the page.

"Hello."

"Claire Courtney?" A man's voice.

"Yeah."

"My name is Spencer Grant. Do you have a minute to talk?" Very polite.

Instantly wary, she said, "I have about a minute."

"I'm an archaeologist with the University of Pennsylvania Museum of Archaeology and Anthropology. I read about the Clovis artifacts discovered on your property. I'm very interested and wondered if I might be able to come take a look."

Claire let out a long sigh. "You might want to talk to the Wazzu people," she said.

"Wazzu," he repeated slowly.

"Washington State University. Joe Running is the guy who did the dig. You should talk to him."

"I see. I could, but I would really love to look over the site myself and talk to you about what's happened so far. I've managed explorations of the Clovis culture in the past, so I have some experience with this."

"I'm pretty busy..."

"Please, Ms. Courtney. I know all of this must be very inconvenient for you. You have an orchard to manage, and now you've had this disruption. If news has made its way to Philadelphia, you must have people from all over calling. I ask for part of a day of your time. You name the day and I'll be there. This is very important to me."

Claire blew out a breath. "How about Friday? I suppose you know where to find me."

"Perfect," he said. "Will nine in the morning work for you?"

"Fine. Goodbye." She hung up before he could reply.

***

Friday morning, sporting jeans tucked into black rubber boots, Claire bent over to pick up the irrigation pipe. She had kissed this job goodbye last autumn when she had decided to go ahead and install permanent irrigation underground. No more dragging pipe around, she had thought at the time. She coupled two pipes together, straightened, stretched backwards, hands on hips. The grass had traded in its winter pallor for fresh green in the sun-warmed air. The robins chattered, having returned from wherever they disappeared to in the winter. From the depths of the orchard, a pheasant squawked. She'd have to remind Carlos to tell the guys, *no hunting*.

Along with Grant's phone call, the phone hadn't stopped ringing since the article had appeared in the papers. Reporters and scientists from all over. Some people asking directions to her orchard. She quit answering the phone.

Blinking in the morning sun, she saw a man walking toward her through the trees. She glanced at her watch. Nine. Right on time.

"Ms. Courtney, I presume? I tried at the house, but no one answered."

"You found me."

"I'm..."

"Spencer Grant," then she tacked on, with emphasis, "*I presume.*"

He looked taken aback, then smiled a dazzling smile.

Temporarily blindsided, she realized he was talking. "... and in order to try and distinguish myself from the hordes who are probably bothering you, I've brought a letter." He held out an envelope.

After a moment's hesitation, she wiped her hands on her jeans, took the letter, and turned it over. It was a fancy one, with a seal on the back and a return address of the Office of the Governor of the State of Pennsylvania, addressed to her. She glanced at Spencer and broke the seal, pulled out a sheet of thick stationery. *Dear Ms. Courtney,* it began. The letter said the Governor Robert Patrick Casey Sr. would like to introduce Dr. Spencer Grant, an associate with the University of Pennsylvania Museum of Archaeology and Anthropology. It listed Dr.

Grant's accolades—a world-renowned archaeologist, the undisputed authority on the Paleo-Indian culture, a Philadelphia treasure himself. It concluded with assurance of Spencer's trustworthiness, assuring he brought prestige to any project.

"Ms. Courtney, I know you've been inundated by the press and a lot of curiosity-seekers. Unfortunately, that's often the way these things start out. Everyone is at first surprised and excited..."

"Perdóneme, Señorita Courtney," a voice spoke hesitantly from several yard away.

Claire looked up. *"Juan. ¿Qué pasa?"*

Juan's jeans hung on his bony hips, tethered by a tired leather belt. Behind Juan stood Poe Riddle, the newest member of the crew. Poe had a lanky build, limp, brown hair and a perpetual sullen expression. A scar marred his upper lip left of center, the result of a knife fight or a falling ladder, depending on which story you believed and how many beers Poe consumed before he told the story. When Poe talked, he smacked the air with *yonders* and *reckons*. Poe hailed from Arkadelphia, Arkansas, God's truth. A humid, wet rag of a town.

"A couple sprinkler pipes in the southwest corner burst over the winter," Juan said in a startlingly high-pitched voice. A scrawny mustache struggled to find purchase on his upper lip.

Spencer said, "Juan Rivera? The man who actually uncovered the artifacts?"

"Yes," Claire said.

Spencer reached out and offered his hand. *"Mucho gusto en conocerlo."*

"El gusto es mío," Juan squeaked and shook Spencer's hand, glancing at Claire.

"Sadly, that's about all the Spanish I know." Spencer grinned. "Do you speak English?"

"Si," Juan answered. "Yes."

"What did you think when you first saw the artifacts, the large rocks in the ground?"

Juan glanced at Claire, hesitant. "I've never seen anything like those strange rocks. I thought they might be important, so I told Carlos."

"The foreman," Claire elaborated.

"You were using a trencher?" Spencer asked.

"*Si,* but not very deep. Six inches maybe," he said. "Easy to dig."

"Did you find anything else unusual?"

"No," Juan turned his attention to Claire. "Like I said, a couple of pipes didn't get drained. I can't find Carlos, so I'm telling you."

"Thanks, Juan."

Juan walked away, trailed by Poe.

Spencer turned to Claire. "Will you show me the site?"

"What the heck," she waved the envelope in the air. "Wouldn't want to disappoint the governor of Pennsylvania."

Tarps secured by two-by-fours covered the pits. Spencer moved the wood and pulled back the tarp, then knelt down by the pit and reached out to touch a Clovis point, smiling. Then he spotted the bone. "The mastodon bone with etchings," he whispered.

Claire watched him. He seemed polite and intense at the same time. And handsome. Absurdly handsome.

He turned to Claire. "Where is everybody? I can't believe there's no security. No cover over the pits except a tarp."

"Somebody's supposed to be around," Claire said.

"Sloppy," Spencer muttered. "How long has this orchard been in operation?"

"My grandfather bought this land in the late forties, and along with my dad started planting trees. Grandpa died a few years later, and it took my dad nearly fifteen years to get the farm to the size it is now."

"It's remarkable the artifacts weren't uncovered when planting trees."

Claire shrugged. "If my dad saw anything, he never said a word. He knew better."

"What do you mean? This is a remarkable find. You were smart to recognize the significance of it."

"I'm happy everyone is so excited about it, except me. I'm a businesswoman, Dr. Grant, and I'm afraid this business may hamper *my* business. It's hard enough as it is. The more strangers I have in my orchard, the more complicated it becomes."

"Hey there, Miss Courtney." Scott ambled toward them, sleepy-eyed, his hair a jumbled nest. "The professor went for a run, and I'm keeping an eye on the site." He stopped and squinted at Spencer, then thrust out his hand. "Scott Carlson."

Spencer shook his hand. "Spencer Grant. You might want to keep your eyes open if you're supposed to be guarding the site. People know about the artifacts here, and looters may not be far behind." He didn't smile.

Scott glanced at Claire, ran his hand through his hair. "Yeah, sorry."

The three regarded one another in awkward silence.

"I'm here now," Scott said finally. "Keeping a close eye on things."

Spencer turned to Claire. "May I buy you a cup of coffee, Miss Courtney?"

"I have work to do." She tucked the governor's letter in her back jeans pocket, then hesitated. *What the hell was she about to do?* "My favorite place for coffee is across the new bridge on the north end of town," she said finally. "It's called Apple Inn."

Spencer smiled. "It sounds delightful."

***

"I used to come here with my mom for lunch sometimes," Claire said as she bit into her cinnamon roll. They sat at a table for two surrounded by home-spun crafts, quilts hanging on the wall, and silk apple blossoms in jars decorating the tables. "They make great sandwiches with homemade bread and potato chips," she said, wondering what had possessed her to invite this stranger to one of her favorite places. Maybe nothing more than she had suddenly craved the restaurant's delicious cinnamon rolls, and perhaps a touch of nostalgia.

"This place is charming," Spencer said. "I have to tell you, the flight from Seattle was spectacular. Mount Rainier and the volcanic Cascade Mountain range leading to the Columbia River, then the high plateau to the east. The geological history is laid out like a book—the glaciers scraping the Columbia riverbed thousands of years ago. Herds of bison, caribou, deer, and moose must have roamed the low hills. Imagine the people who must have hunted them."

Claire pushed away a few wisps of hair that had worked out of her braid and curled gently around her face. "You're not eating your cinnamon roll," she said. "Don't you like it? They make them fresh every morning."

"Oh, sorry." He flashed that blinding smile again. "It's just that I'm impressed with the place and its ancient past." Spencer took a bite. "Delicious."

She watched him over her coffee cup. "You're a very important man with your letter from the governor and all."

"I'm not so important," he said. "I hoped the letter might keep you from slamming the door in my face."

Claire wiped frosting off her fingers with a napkin. "What is it you want, exactly?"

"What I want is to conduct an extensive exploration of your Clovis site. I bring with me considerable financial backing and years of experience. I'm not boasting, but I think you should know many people consider me the authority on the type of artifacts we're dealing with here. Furthermore, have you considered yet what you'll do with the artifacts?"

"What do people usually do with them?"

"Artifacts, like those discovered in your orchard, tell the history of mankind. We can learn from them, share them, treasure them. Museums are places where the public and scientists can enjoy them together."

Claire considered him over the rim of her cup. "Like your museum."

Spencer smiled. "In a situation like this one, often the owner of the property donates a portion of the artifacts to a local museum, and a portion to the institution conducting the investigation. If you agree to donate a certain number of artifacts to my museum, we will pick up all costs associated with the digs. Insurance, labor, lab processing. The works."

Claire set her coffee cup down. "I need to explain something to you, Dr. Grant. The history of mankind is," Claire searched for the right word, "noble. But I live in a practical world, and all your lofty plans won't pay my bills."

"Bills must be paid," Spencer said, and sat back in his chair. "I'm asking you to be patient. I need to see more of what's buried in your orchard, but I want you to know I am open-minded and understand your situation."

"Something else," she said. "The archaeologist who did the first dig, Joe Running. If I do hire you, I'd like him to stay on. To be a part of the project. He's young, I get that, so you'd be in charge, but he did a good job, I think."

"Of course," Spencer said. "Whatever you want."

"Let me sleep on it." Claire said.

***

Bradley Randall burst into Joe's office without knocking. Joe, immersed in journals, looked up. He had hardly spoken to Bradley since the afternoon in Claire Courtney's living room. He couldn't trust himself to talk to him after Bradley had taken—no, stolen—the dig leadership away from him without notice, in front of Claire Courtney, no less. Joe didn't trust himself to speak with a civil tongue to the man.

On the other hand, the find had been much more significant than anyone had imagined, so part of him understood that Bradley would want to manage the dig himself, why he couldn't bring himself to trust the rookie. Still, the way he had broken the news had been shoddy.

Bradley stared at Joe with an odd expression. A blush crept up his neck and he seemed to struggle for words.

"Are you okay?" Joe hoped the man wasn't having a heart attack.

Bradley mustered up one word. "Shit."

"What." It wasn't a question. Joe knew something unpleasant was coming.

"Spencer Grant showed up and talked her into hiring him. I should have known it wouldn't take him long to find out. Damn, it burns me. I've had our attorneys and our insurance companies working on this deal. It's already cost the university a big chunk of change, and she calls and says she's hired someone else."

It took a moment for the words to sink in. "Claire? Are you talking about Claire Courtney?"

"Who else?"

Joe stared at the older man. "She hired Spencer Grant?"

"Exactly."

Joe leaned back in his chair, realizing he had just been booted off his first dig. As the words sank in, Joe felt an overwhelming sense of disappointment. He wouldn't set foot on the Courtney ranch again, except as a spectator. Project terminated. He'd been so excited over this first dig, *his* first dig, even if Bradley Randall had taken the reins.

He eyed Bradley, whose red face appeared alarmingly like a man whose artery might blow any second. "You okay, Bradley?"

"I don't give a damn who the authority is," Bradley huffed. "We were first. We did a good job."

"Why, thank you."

Bradley ignored the remark.

Joe gathered his papers. "I'll forward all the lab work and my reports to Claire Courtney and Spencer Grant."

"How am I going to explain this to the board of directors?" Bradley wore a morose expression. "One last thing," Bradley seemed to have a hard time getting the words out. "She asked for you. Claire Courtney. Part of hiring Grant, apparently, stipulated you be kept on as an archaeologist on the project. It will be a pain in the butt to clear your schedule, but at least it will keep WSU in the game."

"Me?" Joe blinked. "Really?"

"Really," Bradley said dryly. "I guess you'll be able to deliver all your paperwork in person."

Chapter 8

Spencer piloted the plane, maneuvering to set up shots of the orchard and surrounding geology. The photographer rode shotgun with Claire in back, peering out the window of the rented Cessna. How different her orchard looked from the air—like a green carpet. Except the southeast corner where flickers of light danced red and silver in the cherry orchard.

Spencer glanced over his shoulder. "What's with the glitter?" he shouted over the noise of the engine, pointing at the color.

"It's an experiment," she leaned forward. "It's like tinsel on a Christmas tree, and it's supposed to scare the birds away so they won't eat the cherries."

When the photographer gave the thumbs up, Spencer turned to Claire again. "Want to explore?"

"Sure."

The small plane banked away from the orchard and headed up the Columbia. They followed the river's course through Wenatchee, past Rocky Reach Dam, and on up toward the small town of Entiat. Claire, nose pressed to the window, tapped Spencer's shoulder then pointed down as they flew over the town.

"Look down through the water, what do you see?"

Spencer squinted downward. "It looks like an old road disappears into the river."

"What else?"

Spencer peered into the river. "Rows of something, maybe, underwater."

"It's old orchards. They flooded the town of Entiat in order to build Rocky Reach Dam." Claire shouted. "They moved the town to higher ground, but these orchards and some houses were flooded. In 1962, my parents took me to see everything before it disappeared under the water forever. After they built the dam, we drove back along the same road. The image of the road disappearing into the water sticks with me to this day. It gave me such a weird feeling."

"It's what I do, Claire," Spencer shouted back. "Explore places from long ago that have been buried – hidden from view.

She looked down at the river again, feeling nostalgic for her parents, Josh, and Keith. Relics of the past, just like Entiat's watery grave.

***

Claire rattled around the kitchen, rummaging in the pantry, listlessly opening the refrigerator door, hoping against hope some edible food had found its way inside. No such luck. She settled for a can of vegetable soup. Her mother had cooked and canned and baked in this kitchen. It had been alive with heavenly smells and laughter during those years. But the room had gradually been abandoned when the cancer seeped through her mother's bones, and despite her mother's best intentions, Claire had never become much of a cook.

She opened the can, emptied it into a bowl and stuck it in the microwave. Outside, as a car door slammed. She went to the front door, opening it just in time to see Spencer taking the porch stairs two at a time.

Sandy hair slightly ruffled, he held one arm behind his back. "Ah, good. You're here."

"I thought you were leaving today."

"I'm on my way to the airport right now." With a flourish, he produced a bouquet of flowers from behind his back. Gladiolas, impatiens, tiger lilies. He held them out to her. "For you."

Surprised, she took the flowers. "What's the occasion?"

"To celebrate the dig. Listen, I've met with the director of North Central Washington Museum, Alex Stanfield. He's eager to meet you. He's agreed to handle all the arrangements for public tours during the dig. The site will be closed to the public except for these scheduled tours." Spencer leaned close to Claire, eyes lively. "No more strangers popping up when you least suspect. Buses will pick people up from the museum and bring them here. There'll be a display at the museum, and after school starts in the fall, Alex will coordinate tours with schools."

Good God, she thought. "I suppose there's no other way, is there?"

"Don't worry. I'll take care of everything." Spencer's voice was reassuring. He glanced at his watch. "I better go or I'll miss my flight. I've arranged to have the concrete cap lifted off the pits first thing when I return." Spencer had arranged for, and paid for, a concrete cap to be poured over the open pits, and chain-link fence to surround the entire dig site. "Enjoy your peace and quiet while it lasts."

"That's a joke," Claire said. "We're starting cherry harvest in a couple days."

"I have to go, and I hate to leave." He dazzled her with a boyish grin, and then he was gone.

Claire went back inside. Flowers. For her? No, he said to celebrate the dig. But why give her flowers? She found a glass vase. They *did* add a nice splash of color. Claire's mom loved flowers, and always kept some in the house. They would pop up in her bathroom, in the kitchen, on the fireplace mantle. Claire had loved those colorful surprises.

She stared at the bouquet and ate her soup. He had scheduled the new, improved dig to begin after the fourth of July. She had plenty to do until then. If she could get a good cherry crop and a good price, she might be okay. The year before she'd had a great cherry crop, but then so did everybody. The market became flooded, the price dropped. The year before, a late-April freeze had killed nearly all the blossoms in the apple orchard. She still wrote a check each month to the bank for the money she'd been forced to borrow.

If everything went belly up, maybe the artifacts would pull her through. Buried treasure, like ancient Egyptian tombs.

Back in '78, the family had made a trip to Seattle—Claire, her mom, dad, and Josh—to the Seattle Center, to an exhibit of King Tutankhamen. King Tut, as Americans dubbed him, had been a young Egyptian king who had died at the age of eighteen, which was freaky. She had been fascinated with the treasures from the tomb—the wooden image of Tut himself, a slinky statuette of some goddess, the gold death mask of Tut, and especially the jar-like coffins which contained Tut's internal organs. "Gross," Josh had said at the time with ghoulish excitement. She also remembered being spellbound by the legend of Tutankhamen's curse—a death curse bestowed on anyone who disturbed his sepulcher. Claire thought of the concrete cap in her orchard, covering the pits like a burial vault, and her flesh erupted into goose bumps. *A goose walked over your grave*, her mom would have said.

***

In the southeast corner of Courtney property, bins sat waiting to be filled with the clusters of cherries that were growing plump. The days were sunny, and the temperatures persevered in the eighties. Perfect cherry-growing weather. Carlos had a picking crew lined up.

The fruit warehouses, or sheds, as the locals called them, likewise had full crews, including teenagers who worked during summer vacation. The larger sheds ran twenty-four hours a day during cherry season, and the teens didn't seem to mind the night shift.

Claire climbed into a 1978 Ford F-9000 her dad had bought used, coaxed the engine to life, and pulled the old flatbed out of the garage. The original shiny red paint had faded to a mellow shade somewhere between orange and pink. The substantial hood sported a large grill striped with horizontal metal, the oval Ford emblem stuck smack in the middle. The truck had well over a hundred thousand miles on it, but they only used it a couple of months a year—for cherries in June, then again for apples in September. During harvest, the truck got a fifteen-hour a day workout.

Harvest meant both Claire and Carlos worked long days, up before dawn and hauling cherries to the warehouse long after the last picker had gone home or returned to the cabins on the property. Cabins. Claire made a mental note. She needed to make sure the pickers' cabins were supplied with the basics. With Joe, Scott, and Gabby in residence, there were three fewer cabins for the pickers, but WSU paid a reasonable rent, where pickers rented the housing for a song. There were also outhouses in the orchard to look after. The previous year, the state had fined a grower a hundred bucks for not having toilet paper in a privy.

Exhausted after a long day, Claire didn't get to bed until nearly midnight. She must have drifted off to sleep quickly, because when the first staccato sounds drummed on the roof, it woke her from the depths of a sound, dreamless sleep. It sounded like someone knocking at the front door. Then the breeze blew through the open bedroom window, billowing the white curtains and carrying with the fragrance of rain. She started to settle back to sleep, but a flash of light pierced her closed eyes, followed by the low rumble of thunder. The drumming grew louder, picking up intensity until it fairly beat on the roof.

Claire's eyes flew open. She sat bolt upright in bed.

Rain! Rain could destroy a cherry crop, washing away thousands of dollars with a single deluge.

She jumped from bed and ran to the window.

"No!" She slammed her fist on the wet sill, then rushed to her closet and began pulling out clothes. She glanced at the clock—two o'clock. There would be no more sleep tonight.

She dressed and made a pot of coffee, paced between the kitchen and the living room, watching the storm, waiting for it to stop. Rain followed by sunshine could demolish a cherry crop. The cherries soaked up the water, and when the sun shone on the saturated fruit, the taut skin ruptured, splitting the fruit wide open. She would be the proud owner of twenty acres of culls. If it rained hard enough, it could damage the cherries without waiting for the sunshine.

About four in the morning, the rain sputtered to a stop. Claire shot out the front door and headed to the spray shed. As dark clouds retreated, a streak of pale pink painted the eastern sky. There wasn't much time. Carlos already had both sprayers hooked to two tractors when she arrived. The sprayer fans would dry the cherries, but Carlos looked grim.

"Damn it, Carlos." Claire couldn't think of anything else to say. She climbed on a tractor, started it, and they each headed down the dirt road toward the cherry orchard. She took a short cut through the trees. Already the sound of sprayers from nearby orchards hummed in the pre-dawn air. Soon the pulsating rotors of a helicopter beat the sky. Claire looked up, jealous. All the growers were desperately trying to dry the fruit before the sun came out. Helicopters were the quickest way, but the most expensive. Some lucky neighbor had hired the work done by air.

They each moved up and down the long rows. She forced herself to maintain a slow and steady speed as the branches trembled under the force of the mechanical wind. By nine in the morning, the sun beat down with full force. Claire jumped off her tractor and pulled down branches, examining the fruit every half hour. There were a few splits, but not many.

At noon, she took a lunch break. She made a cheese sandwich and stepped out onto the porch. Her eyes were scratchy from lack of sleep. Then she went back out to examine the cherries. It looked like their work had paid off. The crop appeared to be saved.

That evening, bleary eyed, she collapsed into bed at eight and fell into a deep sleep. In the early morning hours, she dreamt of an orchard filled with red, ripe cherries, and then the trees began to melt, and they turned into a red river—a river of blood. Then the river mingled with pure, white snow and rolled down a steep mountainside, gathering momentum, streaks of red bubbling to the dirty, white surface. When it finally stopped, a form appeared beneath a thin shroud of snow. Then the snow melted away, revealing the face a man who stared upward, eyes wide but milky white and blind, his mouth open, as if in a scream.

Claire woke from the nightmare, crying hot tears into her pillow. After a while the tears dried, and she turned onto her back, stared up at the ceiling, aching with the horror of it. She forced herself out of bed and rummaged in her dresser drawer until she found the photograph. She studied it, handsome young Keith with tousled brown hair, wearing an infectious grin along with cowboy boots. She stared at it until the photo blurred. Slowly, she replaced it in the drawer, and went to take a shower. Trying to fall back asleep would be futile.

Chapter 9

Joe arrived a day before Spencer and the rest of the crew. He set up house in the same small cabin he had stayed in before, but it had been spring then. Now the summer sun baked the place. Joe opened the door and two windows, but his shirt stuck to his sweaty back while he put away pots and pans, a few dishes and hand towels. He made the bed with fresh sheets, then headed out to pick up a few supplies and get some dinner.

He hadn't had his hair cut during the weeks he'd been there, and it had grown long enough to stick to the salty sweat of his neck. He liked the feel of it.

Before he reached his truck, he caught sight of Claire sitting outside at a table in the shade of pine trees. He stopped, hesitated, then veered toward her. "Claire," he said as he walked up. "I want to..."

Before he could get the sentence out, she held up a hand, palm out like a traffic cop. "It's too damned hot to talk without a cold drink in your hand. There's a pitcher of lemonade in the fridge, and glasses in the cupboard. Help yourself and come on back."

"Can I get you anything? More lemonade?"

She held a nearly full glass of lemonade up in response.

He returned, cold glass already sweating droplets in the moist heat, and joined her. He held his glass to hers. "Cheers," he said.

"Cheers back at you," Claire said as they clinked glasses.

He settled into a chair. "I wanted to thank you for asking for me to be a part of the dig. It means a lot to me. When I found out you'd hired Grant I was..." He searched for the right word. "Disappointed."

"I'm afraid you got the short end of the stick, mostly from your boss over there at Pullman."

Seeing Claire put Joe in a forgiving mood. "Bradley's not so bad. This is my first year at WSU, my first year out of graduate school. To put me in charge of a find like this was a leap of faith he couldn't make."

"You're taking it better than I would. I work for myself for a good reason. I don't much like anybody telling me what to do, and I'm not one for a having a bunch of people underfoot, so we'll see how this whole thing plays out."

"Why'd you call WSU when you found the artifacts?"

"I'm a WSU graduate."

"Are you?"

"Class of seventy-eight, ag major. Came home and been working the farm ever since, first with my dad, then by myself with Carlos after Dad passed. A heart attack dropped Dad to the ground in the middle of harvest, 1979," she said, voice gone quiet. "He smoked, and had just quit the year before, and he sure liked his meat and potatoes. He went fast. Not like Mom, who passed from cancer. That was a lousy couple of years."

"I'm sorry."

"Thanks. How about you? Where'd you grow up?"

"Wellpinit. Spokane Indian Reservation. With my mom and brother, who both still live there. When it was time to go to high school, I transferred to Reardan so I could play baseball." It was so easy to say, like that decision to leave the rez and go to school in town had been an easy one, but it had been anything but easy.

"With your height, I would have guessed basketball."

"I like to be outside. Never had much use for a basketball court."

"What position?"

"Center fielder," he said. "We went to state all three years at Reardan. Then I went off to college at the University of Michigan."

"How'd your team do?"

"My junior and senior year we took first in our division, and second both years in the NCAA Mideast Regionals."

"Impressive," Claire said. "I played tennis in high school, but I wasn't any good at it."

They drank their lemonade amidst the gentle buzz of bees busy at work on this hot summer afternoon.

"Didn't you have cherries to harvest in June?"

"I did."

"How'd it go?"

"Surprisingly good, after a rocky start. We had a good rainstorm that could have wrecked the whole crop. But it didn't."

"You've got a big job to do here."

"For a woman, do you mean?"

Jeez, she could be touchy. "No," Joe said emphatically. "For anyone. I've helped out on my cousin's ranch in Idaho, so I have some idea of what it's like to harvest crops and work all day at hard, physical labor."

She studied him. "Yeah, it's hard work. But I can't imagine doing anything else."

His glass was empty, and he couldn't come up with an excuse to stay, so he stood to go. "Thanks again, for the lemonade, and for keeping me on the project."

She waved away his words as if they were pesky flies. "We'll see how it goes."

***

As Spencer had promised, the new, improved dig began on the Monday following the Fourth of July holiday.

Standing in front of their cabins, Scott watched Gabby through his camera lens, amazed at his good fortune. He was still here, still working with Gabby, the woman of his dreams. He snapped some photos. Click click, whir.

"Save the pictures for the artifacts. I'm a mess." Gabby held her hand in front of her, fingers splayed, like a celebrity spoiling the paparazzi's shot.

He lowered the camera. "You look perfect."

She rolled her eyes. "Joe should be here soon, and the new professor, too. Let's go."

They strolled toward the artifact site.

"Have you been on a dig before?" Gabby asked.

"I did one last summer in Greece. Amazing is the only word to describe it."

"Greece," Gabby repeated in awe. "Lucky you."

"The singular best experience of my life."

"What was the project?"

"Finding sea level changes and shoreline shifts near Pieria. Sunshine, the sea, hanging out in Greece. Living the dream."

"Cool. Why didn't you go back this year?"

"Um, my parents thought it would be good for me to do something local."

"Now here you are," she said.

"It's not Greece, but it's not bad. The company is good." He glanced at her, hoping he didn't sound like a schmuck, but knowing he sounded like a schmuck. "The truth of it is," he fidgeted with the camera as they walked, "my duties were pretty much getting coffee for everybody and errand boy. I never dug an inch of dirt, much less uncovered any artifacts. And they didn't want me taking pictures. That's why this is so cool that Joe asked me to be photographer."

"Maybe this apple orchard is better than Greece after all. Where did you grow up, Mr. Nikon?"

"Bellevue. My dad's a stockbroker in Seattle. He wanted me to go into finance. He nearly shit a brick when I became an anthro major. Threatened to cut me off. But so far, he's still paying the bills."

"My dad would be right at home in this orchard," Gabby said. "He's an ag worker. Mom, too, along with having four kids. My parents are illegals, but I was born in Yakima, so I'm American. So are my sisters and brothers, and every single one of us has already gone to college, is a college undergrad, or is taking AP classes in high school, headed to college."

Scott wasn't sure he'd heard her. "Your parents aren't legal?"

Gabby cocked her head. "Are you embarrassed for me because my parents are migrant workers?"

"Not sure, Gab. This is new territory for me." To his relief, he spotted Joe walking through the orchard. "Dr. Running. Joe!" He called.

"Hey, welcome back, you two." Joe waited for them. "Hope you've had a good summer so far."

"Hi there, Professor," Gabby said. "I've had an awesome summer, and it's about to get better."

They walked to the dig site, to the concrete cap that covered the pits. A few minutes later Spencer showed up followed by four graduate students, three guys and a girl. Scott eyed the guys, all good-looking frat boy types. His heart sank. Competition for Gabby's heart.

"I want you to meet my team," Spencer said. "Mark, Kevin, Frank, Jennifer, this is Dr. Joe Running and . . ."

"Scott," he introduced himself.

"Gabriella."

There were handshakes all around. Mark was a tall blond, next came Kevin who wore wire rim glasses a la John Lennon, and the girl, Jennifer, with glasses and waist that were both thick. But the guy who made Scott nervous was Frank. Frank wore sideburns brazenly descending below each ear, like Elvis in his later years and he was staring at Gabby as if she were a T-bone steak he was about to devour.

Spencer delivered a short speech about the excitement and significance of working on the project, and finished off with directions.

"We'll be keeping a log of every artifact we uncover, along with a detailed analysis of location and depth. A crew will be here any minute to remove the concrete cap. Mark and Jennifer are going to take over the original pits—Pit One and Pit Two. Kevin and Frank are going to start a new pit two meters to the west, and I'm going to have Joe's crew head fifteen meters or so to the east." He pointed off toward the apple trees. "There."

Scott watched Joe's expression turn as hard as the concrete cap on top of the pits.

"That location is out of range of the artifact concentrations we found on the radar," Joe said, voice tight.

"True." Spencer said. "But I'd like your team to work the periphery, to make sure we're not overlooking anything."

Work the periphery? What the hell? Scott knew this guy was sticking them out in no man's land.

"I think it might be a waste of time." Joe said, voice flat.

"Did you survey the area with sonar?" Spencer asked.

"Not that far over, because we had so many hits in this central area, it seemed prudent to explore here first."

"And explore it we will," Spencer said. "And you and your team will begin exploration fifteen meters to the east. Is that clear?"

Joe stared silently at Spencer. Scott glanced at Gabby, who gave him a look that said, *what the hell*?

Joe finally turned and walked away with Scott and Gabby on his heels. When the crane arrived, everyone gathered to watch the concrete cap come off the pits they had so painstakingly dug. The artifacts, *their* artifacts, sat where they'd left them. After the Philadelphia crew jumped down into the pits, Gabby, Scott, and Joe returned to outer Mongolia and got to work.

Carlos emerged from the orchard and walked up to Joe. "Why are you digging here?"

Joe looked embarrassed. "Exploring the perimeter," he replied tersely.

"This was the first place we put underground irrigation pipes two years ago," Carlos talked fast and low. Scott strained to hear. "We had this area dug up, and never saw a thing. We found the pointed rocks, over there." He pointed toward the original pits. "With the trencher."

Joe sighed. "I know, Carlos. I don't have a choice."

Carlos stared for a moment, then turned and left as abruptly as he'd arrived.

***

As the day wound down, Joe and Spencer walked toward Spencer's new trailer, deep in conversation. Scott stood and glanced over at the Philly crew. Despite his misgivings and, face it, jealousy, he decided to take the high road. He walked over to their pits.

"Hey guys," Scott pushed his glasses up. "Almost quitting time. We have beer on ice and you're all welcome to join us for a cold one."

Mark, the tall blond, stood and stretched, hands on his lower back. "Sounds good. Where?"

"There's lots of shade over there, near our cabins." He pointed. "Come on over after you're done."

Scott and Gabby left to grab the drinks. Some of the pickers were staying in the cabins alongside them now, and Gabby exchanged greetings with them with quick, staccato words. "I wish I was bilingual," Scott said as they went inside Scott's room.

"Yeah, they say it's good for your brain," Gabby said. "Guess that makes my brain better than your brain."

Scott packed a cooler with beer and ice, and they carried it in tandem to a stand of fir trees near a tumble of lilac bushes just as the boys arrived with Jennifer trailing behind, looking unsure.

Scott opened the cooler lid. "Who wants a beer?"

"What's the flavor?" asked the one with the John Lennon glasses.

Scott scoured his brain for a name. "Kevin." Scott said with satisfaction. "It's Coors."

"My man," Kevin smiled, reaching out a hand.

Jennifer peeked around the boys as Scott handed out beers. "Do you have anything else?" She asked tentatively. "Like a soda?"

"I have iced tea in my cabin," Gabby said. "Want a glass?"

"Yes, thanks." The two girls headed off.

Frank-with-the-sideburns took a Coors from Scott, popped it open, turned it up and chugged it down in five gulps while Scott stared. Mark and Kevin both chuckled.

"Now that my body knows we're off work and in beer mode, I'll take another." Frank tossed the empty to the grass as Scott handed him a new can.

"You guys live *there*?" Kevin asked, looking skeptically at the cabins.

"Yeah," Scott says. "They're pretty comfortable. There's a kitchen, a table with a couple of chairs, and a bed. The building in the center has bathrooms and showers."

"The Chief stay here, too?" Frank asked.

Scott had just about had enough of Joe getting insulted today. He turned slowly to look at him. "You mean Professor Running?"

"Who else would I mean?"

"Yeah, he lives in a cabin on the other side of the bathrooms. Gabby and I live on this side."

"Speaking of *the Chief*, here's irony for you," Frank said. "We're staying downtown at a motel called The Chieftain, with a big Indian head in full feather war bonnet on top. Christ."

"But it's a nice place with room service," Kevin added.

"Back to these cabins you guys are staying in," Frank said. "I've been seeing a bunch of Mexicans around them lately."

"It's housing for ag workers," Scott said. "Some of them are staying there now."

"I hope your doors have locks. Is WSU so poor it can't afford motels for you guys?" Frank asked.

What an asshole, Scott thought, but remembered that high road. He spoke slowly and deliberately, as if Frank might be stupid. "When I was on a dig in Greece, we stayed in tents near the site. This is the Taj Mahal compared to that."

"You were on a dig in Greece?" Jennifer asked in a breathless voice as she and Gabby joined the boys, each holding a sweating glass of iced tea. "That's so cool."

Frank turned his attention to Gabby, taking another swig of beer. "Gabriell-A," he said, emphasis on the 'A'. "My dark beauty. Where are you from?"

Gabby looked him full in the face. "My family came here from Mexico," she said. "I was born in Yakima, not too far from here."

"Another irony," Frank smiled broadly. "But for a trick of fate, you could be picking apples in this very orchard. You're already staying in the hired help cabins."

"Don't be a dick, Frank." Jennifer said, turning beet red.

Frank lost his smile. "Don't be a cunt, Jennifer."

"Kids, kids, no fighting, no biting," said Kevin, then to Scott and Gabby. "Sorry. We usually have better manners than this."

"You're right, *Frank*." Gabby bit off his name. "I'm one generation away from picking apples in this orchard. And you want to know why I'm a graduate student instead? Because of my parents. They came from Mexico because they wanted a better life for their kids. It may be a cliché, but it's the truth."

Frank shrugged and looked away. The boys downed their beers, the pretense of camaraderie in tatters, then finally threw their empties on the ground. "Thanks for the beer," they mumbled in unison, and headed toward their car.

Jennifer handed her glass back to Gabby. "Thank you so much." Jennifer said. "I'm sorry about them. They can be first-class jerks."

Gabby took the glass. "Then we're lucky you're here."

After Jennifer rushed after the boys, Scott and Gabby stared at one another.

"I thought that went rather well," Scott deadpanned.

Gabby burst into laughter.

Chapter 10

One benefit of working an empty pit with little chance of finding artifacts, was the digging went fast. Joe and his crew were down almost four feet when the soil changed.

"Why is it so gray?" Gabby dug into it with a trowel. "And light, like pumice?"

"It's probably volcanic ash," Joe said. "It's pretty common in this area."

"A volcano? Like Vesuvius?"

"Yup. Glacier Peak volcano is about sixty miles northwest from here. It's erupted many times over the years, starting thousands of years ago. The geologists who did the initial scan here talked about it. They said it was common to find varying depths of ash and pumice in the shadow of the volcano. The Chelan area has deposits more than a foot thick."

The ash layer one side of the pit was neatly defined and nearly a foot deep, while the other side of the pit looked disrupted, as if the area had been disturbed—not uncommon in a developed area like the orchard. Joe scooped ash into a few vials. "I'll send it in to have it tested, just to be sure."

"Professor," Gabby whispered. "They're back."

Joe looked up to see Sam Moses and the same two guys who had been with him on his first visit, Chester and Jack. Spencer's crew gaped at the Colvilles, who marched past them without so much as a glance in their direction.

Sam Moses walked straight to Joe and shook his hand. "How are you, son?"

When they had last spoken, Joe had been in charge. No longer. A shadow of embarrassment swept through him, as if he had let Sam down. "I'm okay, sir. And you?"

"I know about the arrival of the man from back east taking over," Sam said quietly. "I find this development disturbing. But we won't let them…"

"Can I help you?" Spencer hurried toward them. "I'm in charge here."

"Yes, you can," Sam turned to Spencer. "The Tribe is greatly troubled by this project. We are concerned about our ancestors. About what you may uncover here. The number of artifacts indicates that this may be a burial site. Digging here is no different than us going to one of your cemeteries and digging up your grandmother." His mouth set into a grim line. "The Tribe officially asks you to stop all work on this project until we can discuss this matter further."

Spencer didn't miss a beat. "Sir, I am sorry you are offended by this project. No offense was intended, I assure you. The proper permits were acquired for this excavation, and I am within the letter of the law. Additionally, we're on private property. Claire Courtney owns this site and everything on it, and beneath it."

Sam Moses frowned, as did Chester and Jack.

Spencer, apparently unruffled, continued. "This project is, for me personally, among the most exciting I've had the privilege to conduct. The artifacts we're finding are thousands of years old. These aren't your grandfathers, or your grandfathers' grandfathers. These belong to prehistoric man. Clovis people, we believe. These people didn't hunt deer like your ancestors. They killed woolly mammoths. The size of the Clovis points is staggering. Come and look, but don't touch," he instructed, as if Sam was a child who needed to be cautioned.

Sam shot a withering look at Spencer but followed.

"Look at them." Spencer kneeled by the pit. "This was a cache, perhaps, where they kept the tools they used to hunt."

"We are a resourceful people, as these artifacts prove," Moses said.

Spencer regarded him. "I would be happy to meet with you in private and discuss the matter further."

"We would be happy if you stopped work until such a meeting occurs."

Spencer didn't hesitate. "Impossible."

Sam signaled to Chester, the taller of the two with broad shoulders. Chester pulled two cards from his wallet and handed one to Spencer and one to Joe.

"You'll find our contact information," Sam Moses said tersely. "Call me and we'll meet. However, if you continue with this project, we will be forced to take action." Without waiting for a reply, the three men walked away.

"Unlikely," Spencer muttered, then turned to the crew. "Back to work, everyone."

Chapter 11

They were beat. Claire and Carlos pulled the last props from the flat-bed trailer. Each tree had a group of wood props leaning against its trunk which would support the branches as the apples grew larger and heavier.

"I'll put the tractor away," Carlos said.

"Thanks, Carlos." Claire pulled leather gloves off her hands.

Carlos started the tractor and drove away in a cloud of diesel smoke.

A movement caught her eye. Someone was standing near a tree, watching her. It was Poe Riddle, the newest hired man.

"Jesus, Poe," her heart pounded in her chest. "You scared me. You and Juan can call it a day. Same time, same place, same job tomorrow."

"Claire," Spencer called from the opposite direction, walking toward her. Dressed in khaki slacks and a light green, short-sleeved shirt, he looked cool and urbane. When she glanced back to Poe, he was gone.

"I have a surprise. Walk with me." Spencer took her hand and tucked it into his arm.

Claire allowed herself to be pulled along, although it felt awkward to walk through her orchard on the arm of a man. They strolled toward the house.

"I found a wonderful deli in town. I bought mesquite roasted chicken, pasta salad, marinated artichoke hearts, and fresh bread. Have dinner with me. You must be exhausted."

"I *am* hungry," she said tentatively.

"Wonderful. I hope you don't mind, but I moved the table and chairs from the yard to your veranda."

It annoyed her, for some reason, that he had made himself so much at home.

Spencer studied her. "You *do* mind. I apologize. I should never have been so presumptuous as to move your belongings."

"No, it's fine." Claire murmured, staring as they neared her house. The outdoor furniture was neatly arranged on the veranda, covered with a red-checkered tablecloth and food. She couldn't help but be impressed by all the trouble he had taken. "It looks like something out of a magazine." She smiled.

His expression relaxed. "Dinner awaits."

"I need five minutes to clean up."

Upstairs, Claire splashed water on her face and changed her clothes, surprised to find herself hurrying. She walked out the front door in a sleeveless summer dress in a brightly colored print, rummaged from the dark recesses of her closet.

Spencer stood, holding out his hand to her. She put her hand in his.

"You look lovely." He guided her to her chair.

She must have looked as hungry as she felt, because Spencer said, "Go ahead and help yourself while I get the wine."

As she filled her plate, Spencer produced a bottle of Chenin Blanc from an ice-filled bucket (a cherry picker's bucket, Claire noticed—one of several she kept hanging in the garage). He opened the bottle easily, as if it were the thousandth cork he had extracted. He poured a glass for each of them and sat next to her, so they both looked out onto the small, grassy front yard and beyond to the orchard. He held up his glass. Claire did the same.

"To a perfect summer evening. There is no place I'd rather be than right here, with you." Spencer clinked his glass against hers, eyes never leaving hers.

Claire started to drink, then abruptly put her glass down.

"You don't have to do this, you know."

Spencer looked puzzled. "Do what?"

"Wine and dine me."

A slow smile spread on Spencer's face and he shook his head slowly. "You are one tough cookie, Claire Courtney."

Claire didn't know what to say.

"If I am wining and dining you, it's strictly for my own extremely selfish reasons. It's because I find you beautiful and fascinating, if somewhat elusive."

"Elusive? What do you mean?"

"Claire."

"What?"

"Eat your chicken."

Claire devoured her chicken, which fell off the bone like butter. Halfway through the meal she noticed Spencer watching her with the now familiar expression of mild amusement. She sat up straight and forced herself to slow down.

Spencer's expression grew serious. "Did you happen to see the Native Americans who came around today? The Colvilles?"

"No. What did they want?"

"They might be a problem."

Claire stopped eating. "What do you mean?"

"He threatened us today. Told us if we didn't close down, there would be trouble."

Claire wiped her mouth with a napkin. "Why?"

Spencer shrugged. "They want to stop the dig. They accused us of being grave robbers. They say the Clovis people are their ancestors, which is bullshit."

"Can they do anything?"

"Never say never." Spencer sat back. "We have the proper permits. It's your property. Private property. But they can become a major pain." He studied Claire. "If not handled correctly, they could become a problem. If we happen to find any human remains, as exciting as it would be, we could get shut down."

"They don't have any claim on the artifacts, do they?"

"They would argue ownership, but these artifacts, as I explained to Mr. Moses, are far older than their indigenous tribes. These artifacts are ancient, Claire, as you know are thousands of years old for crying out loud. Long before the Colvilles or the Yakamas or the Spokane Tribes ever existed. Don't worry, I've dealt with this before."

"And if I choose, if they're worth anything, I can sell them, right?"

"Yes, Claire. If you like, I could sell a few right now."

"You've sold artifacts before? For the owners?"

"I've bought and sold artifacts many times. Since these points are so large, they should be in demand. Now, let's enjoy our dessert, shall we?" Spencer pulled a couple of slices of cheesecake from a cooler.

Getting wined and dined was not a bad thing. Not bad at all.

Chapter 12

Joe rapped on the door to Spencer's trailer. When the door clicked open a blast of air-conditioned air rushed out.

"Joe. What can I do for you?"

"Come look at this." Joe walked away without waiting for a reply. Spencer sighed, dawdled inside the trailer for a minute, then followed. He found Joe kneeling at the edge of the second pit where Kevin and Frank stood nearly waist deep, surrounded by vertical walls of dirt, rich with artifacts.

"More beveled bone rods," Joe said when Spencer joined him. "I think it's a sled shoe. We agree that the Clovis people stored their spear points, knives, scrapers, all their hunting equipment here, intending to come back. I think they covered their cache with small sleds normally used to haul their belongings and game. These bones must have been used as shoes on the bottom of the sled to protect the wooden runners from wearing out. Look at the bone fragments here." He pointed to some bones sticking out of the dirt. "They'd been gnawed on, maybe by a wolverine."

"Great scavengers of the day." Spencer kneeled next to him. "We found excreted bone fragments close by a few days ago."

"The sled theory explains how the wolverines scattered bones and artifacts as they rummaged for food," Joe said. "By digging a pit, roofing it with a sled, and banking it with loose dirt, they improvised a great way to store their equipment."

"The hunters could have come back season after season," Spencer pondered. "Until the last year when, for whatever reason, they never returned again. It's an idea worth considering." Spencer stood. "The area all around here could be full of artifacts, which is exactly why I put you and your team on the adjacent plots. Keep up the good work."

Spencer walked off. Frank and Kevin glanced at one another, then smirked at Joe.

Joe's excitement evaporated. It was a damned brilliant theory, and Spencer knew it. Yet he continued to treat Joe like the hired help instead of a colleague. Despite the heat, Joe needed to take a run to sweat out his frustration. He headed to his cabin to change.

***

Scott worked methodically under the relentless sun. The temperatures had climbed to ninety by early afternoon. Sweat stained his t-shirt, and his hair stuck in damp curls to his forehead as he dug slowly with a full-sized shovel. No need for a wooden spatula or any of the finer tools in this remote pit. He had found nothing all day. Nada. Zip. He glanced over at the pits where Frank and Kevin were using paint brushes to clean off more wolverine shit filled with bones, while Jennifer and Mark worked on a new pile of tools they had found, shorter and broader, probably scraping tools.

Since their ill-fated attempt at socializing, each group ignored one another, with the exception of Jennifer, who went out of her way to greet Scott and Gabby in the morning and often sat with them at lunch.

Scott's thoughts returned to a recent letter from his parents. They wanted him to come home for a visit. He dreaded visits with his parents. His mother was okay; he could be a panhandler on the streets of Seattle and his mother would still love him and tell him how proud he made her. His dad, on the other hand, expected a lot from Scott. He had paid Scott's way through undergraduate school, and still footed the bills, but he was getting more impatient with his son's direction. One more semester and Scott would graduate, and then he'd be on his own. It would be a relief, actually. An end to the lectures on the futility of archaeology as a career.

His shovel struck something firm. Scott blinked, sweat running down his face. He took off his glasses and wiped his face with his forearm, then replaced the glasses. Gingerly, he scraped at the dirt. He squatted and ran his hand along the shovel mark, brushing away the dirt, revealing something dark and shiny. He frowned. He reached for his tools and grabbed a brush, carefully removed dirt to reveal more of the same dark material. He looked up, searching for Joe and Gabby. Neither was in sight. He laid his shovel down, climbed out of the pit, and went to search for Gabby. He went to her cabin and knocked. No response.

"Gabs, are you in there?"

Nothing. He heard water running in the bathroom building. He walked over, opened the door an inch and hollered inside.

"Gabs!"

"Who's there?" She sounded alarmed.

"Scott. Come look at something."

"I'm taking a cold shower. It's so hot outside."

"Hurry, would ya?" Scott shouted. "There's something you need to see."

She emerged a few minutes later in shorts and a t-shirt with dripping hair. "Where's the fire?"

"Come take a look. Grab your gloves."

She followed Scott out into the bright afternoon sun, stopped at her cabin and grabbed gloves. "What'd you find?"

Scott led her back to the pit and jumped down inside. "Look."

Gabby peered over the edge as Scott brushed away more dirt revealing something smooth and black.

"What is it?"

Scott peered intently inches away from the dirt. "Look how smooth it is. Obsidian maybe?"

He pulled on his own latex gloves and reached out to touch the dark substance.

"Weird." He sounded puzzled.

"What?" Gabby jumped into the pit beside him.

"It's soft, whatever it is."

"Soft?" Gabby pulled a glove on and reached out, touching the black surface gently at first, then poking.

"Careful, don't be so rough."

Gabby raised one eyebrow at him. "This looks like garbage. In fact, it looks like an old plastic garbage bag."

Scott pushed up his glasses and squinted at the material, clearing away more dirt. Maybe she was right. It did look like an old bag, blackish green with a dull luster.

"Thanks, Scott, for dragging me out of a cold shower so I could look at somebody's garbage from 1975."

Scott pulled a Swiss army knife from his pocket, pulled out the blade and sliced a corner of the bag.

"Oh, God," he fell back against the dirt wall of the pit.

"What the . . ." Gabby gaped.

Out through the slit in the plastic stuck the toe of an old boot. Scott held his breath and lifted the corner of the bag, peeking inside. He jerked away, trying not to throw up in front of Gabs.

"There's something, *someone*," he stammered, "wearing the boot."

Gabby screamed.

***

Claire arrived in less than a minute, panting hard, and hooked her fingers through the gaps of the fence. "Is someone hurt?" she called out.

Scott and Gabby looked up with expressions of shock.

The gate to the fence creaked open and slammed shut. Spencer hurried to Scott and Gabby, kneeled, and peered into the pit, talking in a quiet voice to Scott. After a few minutes he stood and backtracked outside the fence and over to Claire. He put an arm around her, pulled her into him and gently guided her away.

"We need to call the police," Spencer said in the same tone and volume that someone might say, *we need to make a cup of tea.* He navigated her away from the dig, toward the house. "We're going to call 911, but we don't need to run. Dead is dead," he said, devoid of emotion.

"Dead?" Claire turned to stare at him.

"Everything will be okay. Trust me, Claire."

When they arrived at the house, Spencer called 911. Withing ten minutes sirens wailed up Grant Road. Firemen and police and EMT's jumped out of cars and trucks, Spencer led them to the dig site, and Claire sat on the veranda, taking it all in, stunned. An hour later a man who introduced himself as Detective Taggert showed up.

"May we talk in the house?"

Claire gasped, and turned to go inside.

"Claire. Are you all right?" Spencer asked, following Claire, who stumbled toward her front door along with the detective.

A deputy stopped him. "You need to stay here, sir."

"Yeah, I'm okay," she managed, embarrassed to discover her throat had tightened.

"Don't say anything to him." Spencer ignored the deputy. "We need to call your attorney."

"My attorney?" she repeated dully.

"You *do* have an attorney, don't you?"

"No."

"Then don't say anything. I'll find one for you."

Chapter 13

"The murderer is always someone close, like a wife or sister or something," Frank said.

"Like you know what you're taking about," Jennifer said sarcastically.

The graduate students huddled in two groups outside of the chain link fence, watching the action. Carlos, Juan, and Poe watched from the shadows of the apple trees.

Another rig pulled to a stop in the driveway and a police photographer hurried through the orchard toward the pit where the body had been found. Spencer and Joe hovered over the opening along with the county sheriff, Ed Grady, and the city cops. A gangly deputy dug while the others looked on.

"Coroner on his way?" Sheriff Grady asked the photographer when he joined them.

"Naw, he's up in Bridgeport and won't be back for hours. They said to take lots of pictures, document everything, and he'll examine the body at the morgue."

"Bridgeport? What the hell's going on up there?" Ed Grady was thin and wiry, thanks in part to heredity, but mostly to a two-pack-a-day smoking habit. He'd been reelected every election for the last fifteen years, which was hard to figure since he didn't have any political clout or friends in high places. Maybe his name just looked familiar on the ballot.

The deputy started to sweat as he dug around the outer edges of the black bag—he didn't appear to share the archaeologists' painstaking methods of unearthing buried objects.

Joe had returned from his run to find the driveway full of emergency vehicles. He hurried to the dig and watched the deputies hack around in the dirt. "I have some tools to dislodge it without damage," he volunteered, and retrieved several smaller shovels and trowels, handing them down into the pit.

As they scraped the dirt away the sheriff knelt, squinting. "It looks like a Hefty bag all right. Heavy duty."

The photographer snapped photos from every angle. Scott also trained his Nikon on the scene until the sheriff put his hand over the lens and told him to get lost before he confiscated his film. Then the sheriff turned to the ambulance technicians, who were watching with interest.

"Okay boys, we'll help you scoop it out careful like. Remember the bottom of the bag is split. Let's not spill or we could have an ugly mess on our hands."

The city cops, in their smartly pressed uniforms, looked at one another and took two steps backwards. The ambulance EMTs dropped the stretcher onto the ground beside the hole. Joe pulled on latex gloves, as did Ed and the deputy. They slipped gloved hands under one side; the EMTs did the same on the other side. With a quick movement, they lifted the body up and out of the hole and onto the stretcher, careful to keep the exposed boot tilted slightly upward. The bag seemed surprisingly light, given the size of the boot protruding from the bottom. The photographer reloaded film and continued snapping.

The sheriff turned to Spencer and Joe.

"No surprise to you folks, but there'll be no more excavating going on around here until further notice. Clear?"

"Yes," said Spencer.

The sheriff grunted before continuing. "All your people here, and anyone else working on this project needs to keep us informed on their whereabouts. My deputy here will take names. We'll be talking to each and every one of you."

The EMTs carried the stretcher away. Spencer followed as they slid the stretcher into the back of the ambulance, slammed doors, and pulled away quietly, urgency no longer an issue.

No sooner had the ambulance left when a shiny, new BMW pulled in and a portly man in a suit climbed out with effort. The attorney. Spencer greeted him and led him inside Claire's house. After twenty minutes or so, the detective and Spencer came outside. The detective drove away, and Spencer walked over to Joe.

"Since we're suspended, I'll call in a security company to guard the place." Spencer said, looking back to the house. "This'll blow over. We hired a good attorney. He's still in there with Claire."

Another truck pulled into the driveway, and Chester, the tall guy who had usually accompanied Sam Moses, came toward Joe, glancing curiously at the police cars.

"Dr. Running. This is from Sam Moses." Chester handed him an envelope.

Spencer frowned and walked away.

Joe tore it open. It was an invitation to come to a business meeting, including date, time, and address. With the dig suspended, Joe had some time on his hands.

"Thanks, Chester. Please tell Mr. Moses I'll be there."

Chapter 14

The coroner stared with interest at the black bag laid out on the stainless-steel table in the center of the morgue. In his early sixties, the coroner's build was slender, most of his hair had disappeared with his youth, and his expression was at once curious and sensitive, the attributes of his trade.

The lighting was excellent and the air chilly, which helped keep odors in check. He tugged on latex gloves, settled a surgical mask in place, and unzipped the body bag, revealing the black plastic bag that had been exhumed in an orchard. The sheriff had called him before the autopsy. "Looks like we've got a homicide on our hands, since suicides and accidents don't usually get wrapped up in a garbage bag and buried," he had said.

The integrity of the bag had been breached twice, one recent cut made with something small, like a Swiss Army knife. An older rupture lined with crusty dirt inside and out was curved. Maybe a shovel blade. He made a note and cut the rest of the bag away.

The original breach in the bag had given insects direct access to the body, and the flesh-eating beetles had done a good job of consuming the soft tissues. Adipocere, a gray, waxy substance made primarily of saturated fatty acids, covered the remaining tissue. That was something you didn't see every day. Conditions had to be just right—a lack of oxygen, warm temperatures, and high levels of moisture—consistent with the soil of an irrigated orchard in the summertime.

Regardless of the poor condition, the coroner noted the remains of a slender body, probably male, with short brown hair, dressed in a plaid shirt, jeans, and boots.

The coroner peered at the head and mouth. He probed the face and found a nasal fracture and a fractured jaw. He peered into the mouth. Dental records were the surest source of identification. The slightly stained teeth appeared to be in early stages of decay. Three teeth were missing: the upper lateral incisor and canine, along with the lower canine. The upper teeth had been gone for some time before the fatal injury.

The coroner placed his hand on either side of the head, rotating it laterally. A small chunk of missing hair revealed a vague mark on back of the skull. Nothing serious.

He cut away the clothes, determined a male gender, and noted broken rib bones with significant splinters of bone poking medially. The ribs, usually a protective cage around the lungs, liver, heart, and spleen, might have become problematic.

An unusual glitter caught his eye near the bottom of the rib cage, where the stomach had rotted away. He picked up some forceps and reached inside, eased out an object and held it up to the light. It appeared to be a man's gold ring, with a large, red stone in the center. How the heck had that ended up in the man's stomach? He placed the ring carefully in a stainless-steel bowl and went back to work.

His best estimate was that the victim might have been in the ground since late October, shortly after apple harvest and around the time the freak snowstorm hit on Halloween. He might have been frozen for the winter, before spring blossomed in the orchard and the fly eggs hatched, grew into maggots, and found a feast waiting for them—a good spring, indeed. It was now July, and it had been hot and humid, and the orchard had been irrigated.

The coroner lifted the hands and examined the fingernails, then stepped back and considered the whole body. The bones that weren't broken were thick and strong. The hair color, the nails, the bones, the teeth, all indicated a man in the prime of life, most likely in his twenties. Only the teeth showed slight signs of decay.

The coroner peeled off his gloves and stepped away from the table. A smoker in medical school, he always missed lighting up at the end of an arduous postmortem. *Ah well.* The line between life and death was thin one, and he didn't want to narrow it even more with cigarettes.

He washed up and shuffled toward his windowless office to type the report.

When he arrived home that night, he'd have to tell his wife that he found the damnedest thing inside a man's gullet. A ring, for pity's sake. And he thought he'd seen everything.

***

Claire and her nattily attired attorney, Mark Wiggins, met the craggy-faced detective, Wayne Taggert, at his office in the Wenatchee Police Department.

The detective handed each of them a copy of the coroner's report and gave them time to read it.

"Does the description sound like anyone you might remember Miss Courtney?" The detective asked. He placed a photo of the ring on the table. "How about the ring? As you can see, it's a ring that would be hard to miss. Like a Super Bowl ring. A gaudy ruby and gold ring."

Claire paused. "Maybe," she said at last, "maybe I've seen that ring." She looked the detective squarely in the face. "Billy. Billy Parker wore one like it. I assumed it was fake."

The detective scribbled on a yellow legal pad.

"Who's Billy Parker?"

"He worked for us for two years, I think. He'd go home to Arkansas for a couple of months in the winter. He didn't come back this year." Then the realization sunk in. "Oh."

"Did Billy have any enemies? Get in fights?"

Claire shrugged. "He got along with everyone, as far as I saw. Nice young man." She hesitated.

The detective eyebrows shot up like a question mark.

"Billy was cheerful," she continued. "Always had a smile. A sunny disposition, I guess you'd say, and kinda cute. The second year he worked for us, he was still a great kid, but became a little more, I don't know, moody, I guess. Some days he'd talk a mile a minute, other days he'd be pretty quiet. Missed a few days of work, but not enough to be a problem. Hangovers, I figured."

"Anything else?"

"If it *is* Billy, what a shame. He was engaged, I think, to a gal in Arkansas. He seemed excited about life."

The detective sat back, made a few notes on a yellow legal pad. "You got any regular workers here? Foreman and the like?"

"Yes."

"Names?"

"Carlos Barbosa, Juan Gonzales, and Poe Riddle."

The sheriff scribbled. "Have them all come to my office tomorrow afternoon at two. I don't suppose we'll have to worry about you going anywhere until this case is closed."

"Where would I go, Detective? I have an orchard to run."

***

That night, a rapping on the cabin door woke Scott from a sound sleep. He fumbled for his glasses and peered at the clock beside his bed—12:15.

When he opened the door, Gabby stood there, wide-eyed. She pushed past him and closed the door, leaning on it.

"I can't sleep," she blurted out. "Every time I close my eyes, I see that damned boot sticking out of the bag." She glared at him, daring him to make fun of her.

Scott, half asleep but waking rapidly, realized with painful self-consciousness he wore only boxer shorts and Gabby had on an oversized t-shirt over short shorts, her legs long and coltish. He stumbled over to the cooktop, rubbing his hair, trying to make sense of the situation.

"Come in and sit down," he said. "I'll make us something. Tea? Hot chocolate?"

Gabby's face brightened. "Hot chocolate sounds good." She fell into a chair while Scott got a kettle of water heating up, then grabbed his jeans from a hook near the bed.

Gabby leaned one elbow on the kitchen table, resting her head on her hand. "Back home," she watched as Scott hopped on one foot, then the other, pulling on his jeans, "the news was full of murders and shootings. They showed dead bodies on TV sometimes. But I never saw anybody dead in real life before. Have you?"

Scott pulled a t-shirt over his head before foraging through a cupboard and retrieving a can of instant cocoa mix. "My grandfather had a heart attack at home. I saw him, his body, before they took him away."

"How awful."

They listened to the water creaking and groaning in the kettle, trying to boil. When it finally worked its way up to a whistle, Scott mixed them each a cup of cocoa and joined her at the table.

"You know what's ironic about this?" Gabby asked. "All this time we've been digging and sifting, I've been hoping to find a skeleton. More than hoping, I actually prayed." She cast her eyes skyward. "Please God, let me find a bony hand holding one of the Clovis points. Let me, Gabriella Cortez, make the history books as the one who unearthed Clovis Man."

Me too," he admitted. "Only my photographs were going to be published in National Geographic."

Their guilty gazes met.

Gabby looked away. "At first, I was so pissed when Spencer moved us, trying to get Joe and us out of the way so his team would dig up all the good stuff. But what if we hadn't been digging where we were. This body—whoever it might be—might never have been found. I wonder who it is. How did it get buried in a garbage bag in an orchard? What if he died in one of these cabins and got drug outside? He could have been murdered right here."

Scott covered her hand with his. "Don't scare yourself, Gabs. You're not alone here. The police will figure it out. We're safe. There's too many people around."

Gabby took a drink. "You keep cocoa in your kitchen," she said, not moving her hand away from his. "How sweet."

Scott grinned, grateful Gabby had come to him at this hour, although a smidgen of guilt crept in. It wasn't right to take pleasure at somebody's death, even if it drove Gabby to his doorstep in the middle of the night.

Chapter 15

Joe found the address from Sam Moses's invitation—a one-story office building with a *Colville Confederated Tribes* sign. A few cars were parked out front, and a mobile home sat across the parking lot, fronting a couple acres of sagebrush and jumbles of cottonwoods. Across the highway, Lake Chelan glimmered in the sun.

Joe knocked and tentatively opened the door. "Hello. Anybody here?"

Chester appeared in the foyer. "Come on in. Give me a minute."

Poster-size historical black and white photos of Native Americans adorned the walls: a photo of a Native man in full feather headdress; a group of Native women dressed in beaded buckskin standing next to ponies; a group of men and women standing before a group of teepees in a terrain looking very much like the acreage in front of this very building.

Chester reappeared and led Joe down a narrow hallway to an office brightened by a large window facing the lake. Behind an impressive desk and nearly swallowed by a leather chair sat Sam Moses.

"Thank you, Chester," Sam said. He motioned for Joe to sit down. "Thanks for coming. We're waiting for one more then we'll get started. Can I get you something? Coffee? Water?"

"I'm good," Joe said, sitting. "Thanks."

"What Tribe are you, Joe?"

"Spokane. I grew up outside of Wellpinit."

"We're neighbors, then," the old man said just as a knock sounded at the door, and a woman entered.

Joe stood, trying not to stare as a striking woman stepped inside. Everything about her was angular, from high cheekbones and straight nose, to square shoulders, narrow hips, and long legs. She wore her black and shining hair in a shoulder-length blunt-cut parted on the side. Her dark blue business suit fit nicely.

She reached out a hand. "Shawna Ross."

Joe suppressed the urge to wipe his palm on his jeans before shaking her hand.

"Joe, Shawna is the Tribe's lead attorney. Shawna, Dr. Joe Running. He's the WSU archaeologist working on the Clovis dig."

Her eyes traveled the length of him, from head—only a few inches taller than her own—to toe.

"Thanks, Grandfather. Dr. Running. A pleasure to meet you." She held his hand firmly and smiled.

Joe looked from the woman to Sam Moses as he sat. "Grandfather?"

The old man beamed. "Yes, Shawna is my granddaughter. Have a seat, both of you." He turned to Joe. "I hear there's trouble on your project, Dr. Running."

Joe waited until Shawna settled into her chair before he sat down. "I'm afraid we've dug up a body."

Sam and Shawna glanced at one another.

"One of our ancestors," Sam whispered.

"No. This body was wearing boots and buried in a plastic bag."

"What?" Shawna stared.

"We're all pretty rattled."

"A murder then. Our prayers go out to the unfortunate soul." Sam said, then abruptly changed the subject. "You must be unhappy not to be in charge of the project anymore."

"Grandfather, please," Shawna shot a look at Sam. "My apologies for my grandfather's bluntness."

"It's okay." Joe wondered if it ever *would* be okay. "Sure, I'm disappointed, but Spencer Grant is a Clovis expert. I can't blame Claire Courtney for hiring him."

Shawna and her grandfather exchanged glances again.

"We have something to ask of you," Shawna said. "Try to keep an open mind. May I have your word this conversation is confidential?"

"Okay," he said, uneasy.

Shawna crossed her legs and leaned forward. "We think Claire Courtney may be tempted to sell the artifacts. Artifacts are big business, as you know, Dr. Running."

"Joe."

"Joe. Take the Anasazi sites in Utah. Looters dig for pots and whatever else they can find to sell them on the black market. An Anasazi pot in good shape can bring as much as $50,000. A monolithic ax found in Mississippi went in New Orleans for $150,000. It's no secret these items bring big money."

"Spencer Grant has sold artifacts before," Sam Moses added. "All we want from you is to keep your eyes and ears open, and report to us."

"Claire Courtney has been suffering financial difficulties for a number of years," Shawna went on. "She may be tempted to sell, and it's likely Spencer Grant would help her. We believe all the artifacts belong to the Colville Confederated Tribes. We're planning to go to court for possession, and we want to make sure the artifacts are safe in the meantime."

"How do you know Ms. Courtney's financial situation?" Joe's uneasiness grew.

Shawna gave him a cool gaze. "We do our homework."

"You want me to spy on Claire Courtney."

Shawna spoke, voice smooth. "Not spy, Joe. Simply observe. You can help put our suspicions to rest. We're not out to get anyone. We're trying to find the truth. And to preserve the integrity of our culture. You'll be compensated, by the way."

Nothing about this conversation felt right.

Shawna studied him. "You're uncomfortable with this. There's no need to be. It's all on the up and up." She stood, leaned over the desk, and retrieved a business card. She wrote on the back of it.

"Take this. The office number is on the front. My home number on the back. Think it over and call me." She paused. "Any time. You can always get a hold of me."

"The fact that you hesitate is good," Sam said. "You're a man of integrity and you're not sure what we're asking of you. All we want is, if anything seems off, if you see something unusual, let us know," Sam said. "Think about it."

Chapter 16

Carlos, Juan, and Poe stood in the reception room at the sheriff's office, looking as out of place as flies on a wedding cake. Carlos stood stiffly, Juan hitched up his jeans and glanced around the room, while Poe scowled at the floor.

The secretary, a woman in her late fifties with parchment paper skin and carrot-red hair ignored them while she attacked the keys of a typewriter. The office had seen better days. A dingy path was worn in the linoleum floor and the edges curled.

The phone on her desk buzzed. "The sheriff will see you now," she said without looking up.

Carlos opened the door and the three men shuffled single file into the office.

A haze of cigarette smoke hung in the air despite an open window in the back of the room. Sheriff Grady sat in a large wooden chair that was covered with an embroidered pad tied to the seat and back, obviously sewn with care, maybe by some grateful female citizen, or perhaps his wife. With a cigarette dangling from his narrow bottom lip, the sheriff frowned at a pile of papers as he leafed through them. The men stood side-by-side silently for a full minute before Grady spoke.

"Coroner says the body's that of a young Caucasian man," Grady's eyes darted to the three to measure the impact of his words.

Carlos's grip tightened on his hat and he said nothing. Juan stared at the sheriff, and Poe's upper lip twitched.

"Cat got your tongue, Carlos?" the sheriff squinted through the smoke.

"Have you asked me a question?" Carlos looked the sheriff full in the face for the first time, eyes tired.

"Damned right I asked you a question, smart ass. A dead white boy is found in the orchard where you're foreman. What do you know?

"Only what Claire told me."

"Only what Claire told me," the sheriff mimicked. "You pretty tight with the boss lady, huh, Carlos?"

A cloud of anger passed over Carlos's face. "I've worked for the Courtney family for a long time," he said in measured words.

Grady stared at him for a moment, then stubbed the cigarette in the ashtray in several jabs. "I don't care if you was her wet nurse, muchacho. If I find out you knew something about this and didn't tell me, your ass is mine. Comprende?"

"I understand," Carlos said grimly.

"How about you two? You know of anyone who's gone missing?"

"No sir," Juan squeaked out.

The sheriff froze, then smiled. "What's your name, boy?"

"Juan Gonzales, sir," Juan piped.

"Lordy, you got the voice of a girl." The sheriff laughed. "Any balls in them jeans?"

Juan gazed at the floor.

"And you," he turned to Poe and the smile evaporated. "You see anything? Heard of anyone who disappeared lately?"

Poe presented a face of stone and shook his head slowly.

"Speak up, boy!"

"No, sir." Poe's drawl came out as *no sah*. "I reckon not."

The sheriff fixed his gaze on Poe. "Lawdy, what we got here? Where you from, boy?"

"Arkansas," Poe said, and stared the sheriff defiantly in the eye.

The sheriff shook his head, then reached down to the side drawer on his desk, a big old wooden scratched-up monolith of a desk. A drawer screeched open and the sheriff pulled out a small paper bag with the word "Evidence" printed on the side, along with some scrawling handwriting. The sheriff dumped the contents into the palm of his hand. A man's ring. He picked it up gingerly between his thumb and forefinger and held it out toward the three men, sweeping the ring slowly from left to right, then back again. "How about this here gold and ruby ring. Looks expensive. Seen anyone wearing this?"

The three men stared stonily at the ring. No one moved. Color crept up Juan's neck.

"You know something, girly?" The sheriff shoved the ring in front of Juan's face. "You know where they found this ring? In the victim's gut. How the hell did this ring get into a man's gut?"

"Maybe he swallowed it?" Juan's voice came out in a squeaky whisper.

"Don't be a smart ass, boy. Of course, he swallowed it, but why?" The sheriff pushed the ring in front of Poe. "Why would a man swallow a nice ruby ring? You in the market for a ruby ring there, Poe?"

"No, sir."

The sheriff waited, looking from one man to the next, settling on Carlos, and dangled the ring in front of Carlos's face. "I know you got yourself a girlfriend, muchacho. Carmen Gonzales. Old gal lives out in Sunnyslope."

Carlos stiffened.

The sheriff smiled at his reaction. "If I hear you or your boys here been holding out on me, we're going to have to start watching the old Gonzales place pretty close. Make sure nobody's drunk driving on Sunday after fiesta. Checking everybody's papers for illegals. You know."

"Uh, Carlos," Juan's squeaky voice sounded shaky. "Did..."

"Billy," Carlos said flatly. "Maybe Billy Parker had a ring like that."

"Yeah, maybe," Juan chirped.

Poe's eyes narrowed.

Sheriff Grady grinned and set the ring on the desk. He sat back and lit another cigarette.

"Come on," he prodded. "Let's hear it. Tell me all about this Billy fella who swallowed a ring."

Poe didn't tell the sheriff shit about Billy. A cold, darkness gripped him when he heard Billy was dead—unmistakably, flat out dead—and he couldn't shake it off. He thought he might puke on the sidewalk outside the sheriff's office, but managed to hold everything in. He needed a beer, but first he needed to find a pay phone and make a call he dreaded.

***

He wandered a few blocks downtown to a tavern he'd been to before. A fake lighthouse leaned out over the sidewalk on South Wenatchee Avenue, in front of the Lighthouse Tavern. Dimly lit inside, even at four in the afternoon, a guy could get a steak for $5.99 with a baked potato smothered in butter, sour cream, and bacon, and the beer was plentiful and cheap.

Poe found a spot at the bar and ordered a beer.

A couple of stringy-looking fellows played pool in the corner of the room as Poe hunched over his beer. *Billy, Billy, how can you be dead?* Afraid he might cry into his beer, he gulped it down.

Three 20-something burly farm boys wandered in, sunburned and sweaty, and bellowed an order for three Budweisers at the bartender, then settled into a corner table.

After the burly boys had been served, Poe signaled the bartender for another. The visit to the sheriff's office weighed heavily on him. The ruby ring in the stomach of the dead guy, who happened to be his cousin, Billy Parker, tormented him. How did a ring end up in Billy's stomach? He prayed Billy hadn't suffered, but he must have. Only twenty-four years old and dead. Murdered and buried in some God-forsaken orchard up north and no one cared a spit.

The bartender set a new beer before him and took away his empty. Poe took a deep drink and thought hard. He would have to step forward, he knew, in order to get Billy home to his mama. He'd had to call her with the horrible news, and she'd fallen apart, screaming and crying and carrying on until he finally said he had to go, and hung up.

He didn't know how he would get Billy, or what was left of Billy, back home. Billy's mom hadn't been any help. He reckoned getting Billy home would involve money and paperwork. Poe had some cash stashed away, but he had no idea how much it cost to get a body shipped. Maybe he could get Billy turned to ash and ship him home in a box, UPS.

Poe and Billy grew up together, had lived just a couple of blocks away from each other in a ramshackle section of Arkadelphia. The girls loved Billy. His dimpled good looks came from his mother, who still maintained a shadow of cute on her increasingly wrinkled face beneath a graying pixie cut. Full-bloom adorable, Billy was and had been his whole life. Both boys had brown hair, but where Poe's hair hung in stringy strands, Billy's hair, although cut short, was thick and wavy, even if his hair hadn't seen soap for a week. His rosy cheeks and dimples reminded folks of Sunny Jim of peanut butter fame.

While still in short pants, they'd played stickball, or kick the can, or whatever other game they could figure out in dirt yards on humid afternoons. They'd spent most of the summers splashing around the shores of the Ouachita River, but they never learned to swim proper so never ventured out past shallow water. One June when school finished for the year, the Riddles and the Parkers—five families, ten adults, and twenty-three kids—took the bus together to Emerson, over an hour away, to attend the Purple Hull Pea Festival & World Championship Rotary Tiller Race, an annual gathering for fans of purple hull peas and abnormally fast garden tillers.

Poe and Billy went through school together until they quit after the ninth grade. Billy's grades weren't much better than Poe's, which was to say dismal, but where the teachers glared at Poe, they beamed at Billy, admonishing him to try harder next time—they knew he could do it. Poe didn't hold that against Billy. Best buddies they always had been, and always would be.

After quitting school, they'd tried to get on at Blakely Mountain Dam, the best place to work for miles around, but their ninth-grade education couldn't get them through the door. They worked the cotton fields alongside the darkies after giving up on school, drinking hard every night and chasing girls. Career opportunities were limited in Arkadelphia. Tired of hot, humid summer days no longer dedicated to splashing in the river and back-breaking work, they decided to follow in their daddies' footsteps and head northwest to pick fruit. Back then, the men had followed the fruit every summer until Poe's daddy had fallen off a ladder and broke his arm. He was never the same after that. He had started drinking more, shrunk in size, and eventually just quit breathing. Billy's daddy died a couple of years later after coughing his guts out for the better part of a year.

Just a couple of years before, Billy had found the girl of his dreams, Brenda. Raven-haired Brenda wore thick, black eyeliner and white lipstick. Petite yet curvy, Brenda fancied halter tops and bell-bottom jeans.

It took a lot of talking to convince Billy to leave Brenda behind for work, but Poe talked Billy into joining a few other boys in the spring of '85 to leave for California to work the strawberry fields near Watsonville. Billy promised Brenda he'd be back soon, bringing enough money to get married and buy themselves a little place to call their own. He almost convinced her to try to start a baby together before he left, but Brenda's mama hadn't raised no fool.

Strawberry picking wasn't exactly a bowl of cherries. It was as back-breaking work as picking cotton. Poe and Billy pooled their money and bought a dilapidated Subaru coupe with nearly 300,000 miles on it, and drove to Sacramento to work the almond harvest, and then to pick apples. Poe wanted to keep moving north. Billy wasn't much interested at the time. He liked the weather in Sacramento and heard the cold crept in during apple harvest up north. But Poe convinced him to go, and they made the long trip to Wenatchee in central Washington state. The Courtney ranch hired Billy, but Poe missed the cut, so he found work at an orchard in Cashmere, about twelve miles west of Wenatchee. He and Billy found a run-down place to live in East Wenatchee on Cascade Avenue—a long, wooden building painted brick-red with five apartments that rented out to migrant workers, all men.

Every morning they climbed into the Subaru, Poe dropped Billy off at the Courtney ranch, then drove to Cashmere. At the end of the day, Billy caught a ride home or walked the long miles back to the apartment.

After that first harvest, they returned home to Arkadelphia, and spent the winter months happy with their families. Billy spent most of his time with Brenda, and by the time Poe and Billy returned to Wenatchee, Billy had officially proposed. Brenda had squealed, planted kisses all over Billy's rosy-cheeked face, and fervently said yes.

They'd only been back in Wenatchee a few months when Billy bought a car, an old BMW. Poe had no idea where the money came from. Once Billy bought his own car, he came home to the apartment later and later after work. Some nights he didn't make it home at all. Then Billy moved into another apartment in the same building when one emptied out, saying it would give them each some elbow room. Then one day, Billy showed up wearing a gold ring with a red stone smack in the middle. Poe quizzed him about it, but Billy said he'd been saving his money, and bought the ring.

Poe was ready to go home to Arkansas for the winter, but Billy said he still had work and wanted to wait a month or two before heading south. Poe should have known right then that something was up. Billy didn't want to go home to Brenda? That was just messed up.

When a big snowstorm hit at Halloween, Poe was ready to go home. But Billy didn't show up at the apartment for three days, and Poe couldn't leave without him, or at least knowing Billy's whereabouts. Poe went to the Courtney ranch and talked to Carlos and asked, "Where's Billy?"

Carlos had shrugged and said Billy had picked up his last paycheck the day of the snowstorm, and he hadn't seen him since.

On a whim, Poe asked, could he take Billy's spot for the next few months?

"Not sure how much work we'll have," Carlos had replied slowly.

Although Poe longed to go home and see his mama, he needed to find Billy, so he pressed the issue. "I could really use a few extra dollars, Mr. Barbosa." The name stuck in his craw. Back when their daddies were coming northwest to pick fruit, most of the hired help hailed from Arkansas or Oklahoma. Slowly but surely the Mexicans were taking over, and it galled him to work for one.

"And I'd like to stick around and wait for Billy, when he shows up." Poe thought he saw Carlos's eyes shift away.

Then Carlos stared Poe straight in the eye and said, "We can keep you on for a little while. No promises."

Now that Billy had been found—tragically dead—Poe ached for home. He didn't like being in a place where he didn't know anyone. In Arkadelphia, everyone knew everyone, and their mamas and daddies and cousins. Not so in Wenatchee. Mostly he felt invisible, which served a purpose sometimes.

He took a gander at the three farm boys in the corner of the bar as they guzzled their third beer. If they heard the way Poe talked, he'd be dead meat. They'd make fun of him and eventually bat him around like a pinball. But his business wasn't finished here. He may not be able to get Billy's body home, but he owed it to Billy's family to figure out how his cousin wound up dead.

Chapter 17

While the dig was on hiatus, Joe received a note in the mail from Shawna Ross inviting him to dinner. The beautiful handwriting listed a Manson address. Saturday night. Seven. No RSVP. Apparently, she assumed he would show up. He expected she was right.

By the time Joe made the forty-mile drive up Highway 97, the midnight blue shirt he had put on so carefully after his shower was wrinkled and tired, despite the air conditioner blasting on high.

Joe glanced at the address on the dinner invitation. Loop Avenue, it said, but to Joe, all the roads in rural Manson seemed loopy, built around rambling property lines and crooked boundaries, circling orchards settled long before city planners and real estate developers. He kept driving north, and finally he spotted Loop Avenue and, thank God, her house. A steep driveway led to an impressive home with a majestic wood prow over a striking wall of windows that faced the lake. A side door opened as he parked in front of a three-car garage, and there stood Shawna, wearing khaki shorts and a faded pink top tied at the waist, revealing a couple of inches of long and lean torso. He climbed out of the truck, wondering if he should have brought flowers or something. He was pretty rusty at this.

"Hi. Come on in." She led him through a mud room into a large kitchen.

Joe thought of his own, humble apartment in Pullman as he looked at the stainless-steel appliances, gleaming countertops, and tile floor.

"Home sweet home," she said. "What can I get you to drink?"

"Coffee, tea, water."

She raised her eyebrows. "Teetotaler?"

"Yeah."

"No problem." She got him a glass of sparkling water and poured herself white wine. "Cheers." They clinked glasses.

He followed her into the living room and stood before the wall of glass as sunlight danced on lake water backed by rugged mountains.

"How was the drive?"

"Good," Joe answered. "The roads up here are confusing."

"Manson's an old orchard community. It's only been in the last couple of decades that the tourists found it. How's everybody doing, Claire and Spencer and the lot? It must have been awful to find the body."

"Scott uncovered it. We're all pretty shook up."

"Any idea who it is?"

"Not that I know. Apparently the body had been there a while. Claire and Carlos and some of the hired men were being interviewed today, but I haven't heard anything." He worried about Claire for a moment, then realized Shawna had asked him a question. "I'm sorry. What?"

"Where'd you get your degree?"

"University of Michigan on a baseball scholarship."

"Baseball? Were you good?"

"I did all right. How about you? Where'd you get your law degree?"

"I started with an economic degree from Stanford, then went to Gonzaga for law."

"That's impressive. You could have practiced law anywhere. What brought you back here?"

"Grandfather, for one thing. As long as Grandfather is around, I'll stay here. Then, we'll see. I've been mulling over a few ideas. I feel like I have an obligation to my family. To my People."

She talked about her grandfather, but never mentioned her parents. Perhaps they had something in common there.

"I hope you're hungry," she said, taking her wine toward the kitchen. She pulled a plate from the fridge and set it on the kitchen counter. "Appetizers. Wild rice cake with mushrooms and pesto."

Joe perched on a stool at the counter and took one. "Looks delicious."

"The menu tonight is all indigenous food."

Joe grinned. "For me growing up, indigenous food at home was Spam with box macaroni and cheese." He popped a rice cake in his mouth.

She laughed. "You can't underestimate a good can of Spam. But tonight, dinner is cornmeal and seed crusted walleye. I hope you like fish. We're also having sweet potato mash, and kale salad with squash and black beans. For dessert, blueberry sorbet. I made it all myself."

"You're an over-achiever, I'm guessing."

She paused, tossed him a mischievous look and said, "I'm a woman of many talents, Joe Running."

Joe swallowed the rice cake hard, and although the air conditioning was running just fine, he began to sweat.

He calmed himself down and made it through dinner—a delicious dinner—in one piece. Afterwards they wandered back to the living room and watched the orange glow of the sunset as the first star popped out in a darkening sky.

"What will you do with the dig shut down?" Shawna asked.

"I'm headed back to Pullman tomorrow, with the sheriff's permission." He walked over to a dream catcher on the wall, strung with netting and delicate feathers suspended in the center. He touched the feathers. "This is beautifully made," he said.

She moved beside him. "My dream catcher," she said softly. "I've had a recurring dream since we met, and I can't get it out of my mind."

"Something to do with artifacts?" Joe was heating up again, and having trouble breathing.

"On the contrary," she murmured, stepping into his arms. "Nothing old and stuffy."

Joe had never kissed a woman so close to his own height before and it was effortless. No stooping. From head to toe, their bodies pressed against one another. A perfect match.

As much as he enjoyed the kiss, the touch, *her*, he took a step away when their lips parted, walked to the front windows again and stared out. Any man in his right mind would have let the moment carry on. He watched her expression reflected in the glass. She looked surprised. Maybe disappointed? He couldn't help but smile, and he turned to her. "A lovely home for a lovely woman. Thank you so much for inviting me. Did you say something about dessert? Blueberry something?"

She studied him, expression curious. "Sorbet."

Joe enjoyed the moment, the feeling of being wanted, the joy of anticipation. He decided to take things slow. Very slow. "Sounds perfect."

Chapter 18

Claire watched herself in the dresser mirror as she brushed her hair. She was primping, she realized, before going downstairs to Spencer. She replaced the brush on the dresser, thought about changing into something nicer than jeans and cotton shirt, decided against it on principle, and headed downstairs.

Spencer seemed to be studying the rock fireplace. He turned when Claire came in.

"This is exquisite," he said. "River rock, isn't it? From the Columbia?"

"Yes. I'm impressed. My father did all the work himself."

"It's beautiful. People pay a fortune for work like this nowadays. And this mantle is a work of art."

"Also Dad. Made it from a burl of redwood. He was a renaissance man. Would you like a drink?"

"Yes. I would love a martini."

She laughed. "Beer or whiskey is all I have."

Spencer grinned. "I'll take a whiskey."

She had to retrieve the whiskey from the study, which was a little embarrassing, then take it to the kitchen to make the drinks. She handed Spencer his. "Hope you wanted it on the rocks."

"This is perfect. Thank you."

It was Claire's turn to examine the rock fireplace as if she hadn't seen it for a long time.

"Your man, Carlos..." Spencer began.

"My manager Carlos?" Claire interrupted.

"Your manager...has he worked here long?"

"Since I was ten. Used to be people didn't come and go much around Wenatchee, not counting the ag workers. When I was a kid, migrant workers came from the south, usually Arkansas and Oklahoma. Later, Mexico. Today it's mostly Mexicans, and many of them settle down here with their families. Wenatchee's a place where people live generation after generation."

"Carlos doesn't seem very happy about the dig,"

"He's not."

"Why not?"

She wasn't sure she liked his line of questioning. "It feels like we've been invaded, if you want the truth. With WSU, with Joe, it was all preliminary. Maybe nothing would come of it. But you, you're big time. This is quickly becoming serious business and attracting too much attention. Another thing, the dig is too close to Carlos's house. He's worried about a deal we've been working out for quite some time."

"A deal?" Spencer's voice had an edge to it.

"Carlos wants to buy the house he's lived in all these years, along with the cherry orchard, and part of the apple orchard near his house. And I've agreed to sell it to him. Hell, I'd give it to him if I could afford to."

Spencer stiffened, but Claire didn't notice. "He has a woman friend, Carmen. They've been waiting until Carlos gets the land and house, then they'll get married. I've tried to talk Carlos into marrying her now. Why wait? Neither of them is getting any younger. Carlos has been putting away some savings for quite a while, and during these past few years when money's been tight for the orchard, he's taken credit instead of money for pay."

"You mean, you owe him money that will apply to the purchase?"

"Yeah."

"How much?"

Claire stopped short. He was getting pretty nosy. "It's really none of your business."

Spencer put his drink down. "Do you have any of this deal down on paper?"

Now he was getting pushy. "It's none of your..."

"Claire, listen to me. You need to be the owner of the artifacts. Do you understand? If this dig turns out to be as big and important as I think it's going to be, you need to be the sole, legal owner. If there are papers, IOUs, things could get...complicated."

Things already felt complicated. "There's no papers. Nothing signed. It's an agreement we have."

"A verbal agreement."

"Yeah."

Spencer exhaled. "It shouldn't be a problem then. It's bad enough the Tribes think they own anything that's buried. The last thing we need is an ownership dispute. Can you settle this with Carlos?"

Torn between being annoyed and doing the right thing, she said, begrudgingly. "Maybe."

Spencer visibly relaxed. He glanced toward the kitchen. "I don't suppose there's anything cooking in there for dinner."

"I don't suppose there is."

"Please, let me take you out. I need a guide to explore this wonderful valley of yours."

She wasn't so sure.

He stepped up to her. "You hired me, remember? I'm here to help you. I've been through all this before. Trust me, will you?" He smiled, looking boyish and handsome at the same time, and her heart did a little flip. He leaned down and kissed her softly on the mouth.

It had been so long since she'd been kissed it felt weird. Foreign.

When their lips parted, he pulled an envelope from his back pocket and placed it in her hands and enfolded her hands in his own.

"What's this?"

"A gesture of good faith." He released her hands. "Open it."

The envelope wasn't sealed. She pulled out a check and stared at it, incredulous. "Twenty thousand..." her voice trailed off.

"Twenty thousand dollars. I sold two points, ten grand a piece. And my buyer is interested in more of whatever we find."

Claire stared at the check, dumbfounded.

"You did say you wanted to sell. I figured the cash would come in handy sooner rather than later." Spencer peered into her eyes. "Happy?"

Had she said she wanted to sell? They'd talked about it, but this—all this money—was shocking. "I didn't know it would be so fast. So easy."

"I'm connected." He smiled. "Now, I don't know about you, but I'm famished. Where shall we go?"

"I'm a little freaked out here." She needed to be alone, suddenly. To breathe. "Maybe some other night."

He left, begrudgingly, and she had to admit part of her wanted him to stay. That kiss had been startling, and nice. She could get used to kissing him.

That night she lay awake for a long time. Twenty thousand dollars of easy money. She didn't sweat for it, work for it, break her back for it. The check fell into her lap because some weird rocks turned up in her orchard. It didn't feel right.

She fell into a fitful sleep and woke in the wee hours in a fever. The dream had come back, always the same cursed nightmare. His face—his beautiful face—swallowed in a river of snow.

Fully awake, she turned on her side and faced the window. A slight breeze fluttered the curtains but died before it reached her. She checked the nightstand drawer for the envelope. Still there. She finally fell back asleep and awoke to the morning sun pouring in. She slid open the nightstand drawer. The envelope hadn't gone anywhere. Coffee. She needed some serious coffee. She dragged herself out of bed.

Downstairs, she filled the coffee carafe at the sink, and when she turned to pour, something caught her eye. The back door. The glass pane nearest to the doorknob was broken and glass lay scattered on the linoleum floor. She froze, stared, mind blank. Should she call the police? Or check out the house? She put the carafe down, backed away and crept out of the kitchen. The house barely breathed. She ducked into the study. Everything looked okay there. She tiptoed toward the living room, and her breath caught in her throat.

Suspended from the fireplace mantle, the very same mantle she and Spencer had admired the night before, something was hanging on a hook—the way they used to hang Christmas stockings.

A head! The severed head of a dog. No, not a dog. A coyote. A sob choked her. She backed away, headed to the front door, shot outside, down the stairs, and into the orchard, towards Carlos's house.

She banged on his kitchen door. "Carlos!"

Carlos opened the door, coffee cup in hand. "What? What is it?"

"In the house. Someone broke into the house and..."

"Are you hurt?"

"I'm okay. Above the fireplace," she panted from the sprint through the orchard and the shock. "Come look."

Together they took off towards the house. She had left the front door open. Carlos plunged inside, but Claire couldn't make herself go back in.

Just then Spencer's car pulled into the driveway. "Claire!" he called, smiling. But when he got close enough to see her face, he stopped. "What's wrong? You look like you've seen a ghost."

"Inside. Carlos is inside."

Spencer frowned, then disappeared inside.

Claire heard talking but couldn't make out what they were saying. A good five minutes passed, then Spencer came out first, his face gone pale.

"I've called the sheriff," he said. "This must have happened during the night. Did you hear anything?"

"Nothing."

"Thank God you're all right." Spencer took Claire's hands in his. He lowered his voice. "Did they rob you?"

"No. I still have it." She stepped backward, pulling her hands from his. "I wish you hadn't called the sheriff."

"I had to call him. Someone broke into your house. They could have hurt you."

Carlos came out and the three of them waited until the sheriff arrived. The second the sheriff car appeared, Carlos vanished. Spencer greeted Sheriff Grady and led him in the house. They were gone for quite some time, and when they came back out the sheriff grabbed his car radio, talked for a few minutes, then returned to Claire and Spencer.

"Damned if I'm going to keep a rotten coyote's head around for evidence. Looks like it might have been dead a couple of days before the head came off. No blood to speak of. We'll get photos then take it to the dump, pronto. House is empty, no other damage I can see, except the kitchen door. We'll dust for prints." The sheriff poked a cigarette in his mouth and lit it.

"Any idea who might have done this, Sheriff?" Spencer asked.

Grady squinted up at him through a swirl of smoke. "You'd be in a better position to tell me." He turned to Claire. "I hear you had some visitors from the reservation."

"They came to protest the dig," Spencer said. "They say that whatever we find here belongs to them."

"Did they make any threats?"

Spencer spoke slowly. "They were threatening in their manner, but they didn't specifically make threats."

The sheriff shook his head as he pulled a small scratchpad from his shirt pocket and scribbled notes, cigarette dangling from his lip. "I'd get the window fixed today, and get new locks if I was you, Miss Courtney," he said, tucking the notes back into his pocket. "We'll increase the patrol around here, but the county's big and we don't have enough deputies."

Another sheriff car pulled in. "That'll be Carl, the photographer, and Willy with a fingerprint kit. If you'll excuse me, I'll show them around."

"Sheriff," Spencer stopped him. "Time is money, and I have a lot of people waiting to get back to work."

"Between a body in a garbage bag and a coyote head decorating the fireplace, this ain't exactly what I would call a healthy work environment, Mr. Grant. Oh, excuse me, *Doctor* Grant. Now, I don't have a lot of hope we're going to find much on this one, but we'll give it a few more days. You folks hold off until you hear from me."

"Very well, but if we're not going to be working, I need to go back to Philadelphia for a few days."

The sheriff sighed, and pulled the notepad out of his pocket again, along with a stubby pencil and handed it to Spencer. "Phone number, in case I have any questions."

***

Oblivious to the drama of the coyote head, Gabby slept in. At eleven, she emerged from her cabin in cut-off jeans and a tank top, stretched, and spotted Scott sitting in a folding chair in front of his place, cleaning his camera. She wandered over. He pushed his glasses up and smiled.

"Hi," he said.

"Hi yourself."

Scott replaced lens covers and tucked the camera back into its case.

"Here we are, supposed to be on a great archaeological dig, and what are we doing? Nothing," Gabby said.

Scott seemed about to speak, then thought better of it.

Gabby prodded. "What?"

"Nothing," Scott said.

"Come on, you were going to say something. What?"

"What do you think of the new crew?" He cleared his throat. "Jennifer seems nice."

"I keep getting them mixed up, except Jennifer. Mark, Kevin, Frank, they all talk the same, have attitude, like they're the hot shots and we're country bumpkins."

"Frank's the one with sideburns. Whoever's left over is either Mark or Kevin." Scott took off his own glasses and wiped them on his t-shirt.

"I'm bored," Gabby stated as if it were a revelation. "How long are we going to sit around here and wait?"

Scott cleared his throat. "Would you like to do something."

"Yeah. What?"

"I don't know, go sightseeing?"

"What are we going to look at around here? Apple orchards?"

"There's a couple of dams on the river with visitor's centers, and I read about a place called Ribbon Rock where you can see stripes of old volcanic lava in a cliff."

Gabby stared. "Earth to Scott. I am already bored. Let's do something fun."

"Like what?"

"You're from Seattle, right?"

"Bellevue, actually. A suburb."

"Why don't you take me home to meet Mom and Dad?" Gabby faced him, hands on hips.

Scott hedged. "Naw."

"Why not?"

"For one thing, the sheriff said we were supposed to hang around."

"It's not like we're suspects or anything. Come on, you can show me around Seattle. We can ride the ferry and go up the Space Needle. Go to Pike Place Market. We can leave a note for Joe."

Scott peered up at her. "Okay, but I don't want to see my parents. If they find out we're not working right now, Dad will stick me with a job at his company or something."

"Seattle, here we come. Take your camera. I want pictures."

Chapter 19

Poe returned to the Lighthouse Tavern after work, a place that was beginning to feel familiar, a small comfort. This time he picked a small table in the corner, where he could watch all the comings and goings with his back against the wall, like the gangsters used to do in the old movies.

As Poe nursed his second beer, in walked a burly Mexican with a permanent horizontal fold of skin between his eyes, a nose that looked like it had been broken at least twice, and a gold front tooth. He walked up to the bar and ordered a beer. He never so much as glanced at Poe, but when the man pulled out his wallet and laid the money on the counter, Poe froze. On the man's hand sat a gold ring with a ruby in the center, like the one they found in Billy's stomach.

The man took his beer, which looked like a child's sippy cup in his large mitt of a hand, and ambled over to a table, where he drank his beer and watched a guy and gal playing pool. The man drained his beer in short order, then stood and glanced around. His eyes settled on Poe for a fraction of a second, then he turned and walked out.

Poe paid his tab and left, blinking at the bright afternoon sunlight. When he could see again, he spotted the man walking casually along Wenatchee Avenue, heading south. Poe climbed into his Subaru, waited until the man put some distance between them, then began to follow. The man walked about a mile, then turned up a side street and headed toward a sprawling brick building with plenty of windows. A large sign at the entrance said Washington State Employment Security. Poe stayed back, parked and turned off the engine, watching. A couple of young Mexican boys approached the man. They couldn't have been more than sixteen. Something changed hands, then the kids walked away laughing and talking. The scenario played out several times over the next forty minutes, sometimes one guy approaching, other times two or three, mostly Mexicans. There would be an exchange, and when the men left, they never went back to the employment office; they would always walk away and get into cars or just keep on walking.

Finally, the large man took off, walking south along a busy road that ran behind the office building. Poe followed at a distance, driving slow. The man then took a left onto a quieter side street and climbed into a parked car—a Camaro. The Camaro sported a chain-framed license plate. A line of dingle balls hung above each window. The engine roared to life.

Poe waited a few beats after the Camaro drove away, then followed. The Camaro took the bridge across the Columbia River and headed east on highway 28, picking up speed until Poe's shaky speedometer read seventy. The speed and course remained steady for a solid thirty minutes until they came to the farming community of Quincy. The Camaro slowed down through town, then on the other side, took a right onto a narrow, paved road. Poe followed nervously, keeping his distance. Then the Camaro took another right onto a dirt road.

Poe pulled over, watching as the Camaro kicked up a trail of dust. What to do now? He couldn't very well follow. He'd stick out like a sore thumb. He sat for a while, pondering his options. Before he decided what to do, a column of dust came creeping toward him, down that same road. Poe started the Subaru and pulled out onto the country road, but when the car spitting dust intersected the paved road, it turned his way, closed the gap between them in a matter of minutes, pulled around him and stopped. Poe braked and two men jumped out of the car and came toward him. They each carried a handgun.

Poe instinctively put his hands up. One of the men opened the driver door, waving Poe out with the barrel of the gun. Poe emerged from the car, hands in the air.

The man asked something in Spanish.

Poe weighed his options, gut churning in fear. "I'm Billy's cousin," he choked out.

"*No conozco* Billy," the man growled.

"Billy Parker," Poe said louder, as if it might help the moron understand English.

The two men glanced at one another, then motioned for Poe to follow them, gun pointed steadily at Poe's head, while the other man drove. The car whipped a U-turn and drove back to the dirt road, turned in and purred along, raising a cloud of dust behind it until it pulled up to a double-wide mobile home. Two other men, including the big man Poe had followed, stood outside, glaring, with shotguns in their hands. A black Jeep Cherokee sat parked in front of the mobile home.

The driver grabbed Poe by the upper arm and pulled him outside. Poe gritted his teeth and kept his hands in the air. One of the shotgun guys opened the door to the mobile home, and blue smoke wafted out into the dusty air. The driver pushed Poe inside.

It took Poe a minute to adjust to the dim light once the door closed behind him. The air smelled of cigarettes, stale pizza, and beer. The mobile home might have been new, with fake wood paneling and plush furniture, but everything looked dirty. Crushed beer cans and paper plates of food in varying stages of decay covered the countertops. The sink overflowed with dirty dishes. Heaping ashtrays teetered on the arms of chairs.

On the couch sat one of the biggest men Poe had ever seen. He must have weighed four hundred pounds. His belly spilled out from beneath a once-white undershirt, cascading over the top of green boxer shorts. He reminded Billy of a gigantic frog, puffed up with self-importance.

The guy who had dragged him inside released Poe's arm and patted him down. Poe had nothing to hide.

"Quién eres tú?" the fat man asked.

"I don't talk Mexican," Poe replied.

"Name," the fat man said.

"Poe Riddle. My cousin's Billy Parker. He's dead," Poe struggled with the words. "Dead'n buried in an orchard."

The fat man glanced at the two other men, and back at Poe with a blank expression.

"If you knew Billy, maybe y'all might could tell me something." Poe started to sweat. This had all seemed like a good idea in the cool safety of the tavern, but it didn't seem like such a good idea anymore.

The fat man began to laugh, a belly laugh. Poe noticed the fat man wore a ring, too. He shifted uneasily until the laughter died down and the fat man grew serious again.

"How'd you come here?" the fat man asked in strongly accented English.

Poe squirmed, pointed to the ring. "Y'all have rings like Billy's."

The fat man looked incredulous.

Sweat began to soak Poe's t-shirt.

The fat man frowned. "We don't know no *Billy*. Get out."

Poe turned to go, the hair on the back of his neck prickled with fear. He forced himself to walk slowly out the door. Outside, no one made a move to get into the Camaro, so Poe began to walk down the dirt road, bracing himself for the rat-a-tat-tat of bullets that would hit him in the back any second. Instead, a birdsong—the song of a meadowlark—gave him courage and he continued, staring straight ahead. After an eternity he climbed into his car, made a U-turn and drove back along the road. He glanced in the rearview mirror as he turned onto the main highway and headed west and let out a long breath. Still in one piece, with not even so much as a scratch, he let out a long breath.

It had been stupid to come here.

He pondered on Billy as he drove back to town. Billy must have been mixed up with these bad Mexicans. Drugs, most likely. It explained a lot.

When Poe and Billy first arrived in California, and then Washington, they had hung around together a lot, having beers after work, playing pool at the local tavern, hunting for food to remind them of home—only to discover nobody ate grits in the Northwest. Billy rambled on about Brenda, and how he needed more money, enough to send some home to his mama and sisters, but also enough to buy presents for Brenda, and still save money so they could get hitched.

Billy started missing their beers after work. Then came the ruby ring, soon followed by the well-used but still cool BMW, until Billy finally quit hanging out with Poe. How could he have been so blind? Billy fell in with bad guys. Why hadn't he seen it at the time? Then Billy went and got himself murdered.

Poe's heart had once been soft, like Billy's, but it had been growing harder with each passing day since Billy disappeared. By the time Poe turned his car into the driveway of his apartment, his heart felt as petrified as the old bones dug up in the orchard so close to Billy's body, shoved in a garbage bag and stuck in the ground.

Chapter 20

The sheriff gave the okay for the dig to resume a week later after coming up with nothing on the coyote head or the murder investigation. Nada.

Joe emerged from his cabin and inhaled the fresh morning air. He crossed the commons and rapped on Scott's door, and then Gabby's.

When they gathered outside, Gabby gazed at Scott. "Like Scott's 'do?" She ran her hand over Scott's hair. His mop of curly hair had been buzzed right down to a crew cut.

Joe reached up to his own hair, growing slowly but steadily to his shoulders.

"It looks great."

Scott stole a glance at Gabby, and grinned. "It feels great."

"We went to the San Juan Islands," Gabby chattered as they started toward the dig site. "We rode on a ferry, and that's when the breeze blew Scott's hair out of his face and he looked so great I talked him into getting a haircut. I love the San Juans. I can hardly wait to go back. We went to Friday Harbor and rode bikes everywhere. We had the most awesome fish and chips."

"Sounds fun."

"It's a different world over there," Gabby went on. "Sea creatures and rabbits and fish and it's not hot like here. I loved it."

"I've heard it's a beautiful place," Joe said. "By the way, something landed on my desk that you two might be interested in. A grant for graduate students to work on a Pompeii project next summer."

"Pompeii, as in Italy, Vesuvius, Pompeii?" Gabby asked.

"One and the same. I'll get you a copy of the application if you're interested, and I'm happy to write a recommendation for each of you."

"Holy cow!" Gabby gasped.

"That'd be great," Scott said.

Spencer was waiting just inside the chain-link fence. "Joe, Scott, Gabby, welcome back."

"How was Philadelphia?" Joe asked.

"Busy. I've talked to the sheriff and a detective about the body."

Gabby cringed, her smile evaporating.

"There were no dental records, and the corpse was in bad shape, but they think it may have been a worker here at the orchard because of a ring Claire and her crew recognized. Odd thing though. They found the ring in the guy's stomach."

"His stomach?" Scott grimaced. "How bizarre."

"The guy apparently had worked here for a couple of seasons. The sheriff gave us the green light on the dig, but there's still a detective asking around. By the way, Claire had some trouble."

"Trouble?" Joe looked alarmed.

"Someone broke into her house and left a mess. A coyote's head. Hanging from the mantle."

Gabby drew her breath in sharply. "Who would do such a thing?"

"My guess would be the Colvilles." Spencer glanced at Joe.

Joe stared at him hard but said nothing.

Gabby didn't show the same restraint. "The Colvilles? Why?"

"You've all seen exactly what I have. The only negative reaction to this project has been from the Colvilles."

"How'd they get into her house?" Joe asked.

"Broke a window out of the kitchen door. I'm having a locksmith come out and change all her locks. This has all been quite a strain on Claire, so we're changing the game plan. No more tours, no more reporters. We're going to tighten things up around here."

Spencer greeted his Philly crew as they stepped through the gate.

"Yeah, you guys go dig the artifacts, and we'll go dig up the south forty," Gabby muttered under her breath as she and Scott walked toward their pit. "Maybe find another corpse."

***

"Want a Coke?" Scott walked up to Gabby holding two sweating cold cans.

The afternoon sun beat down as Gabby climbed out of the pit and picked half-heartedly through the dirt on a screen. She worked in the pit adjacent to where the body had been found, and her eyes kept returning to the indentation where the body had lain.

"Hey, thanks," she said. "And thanks for the last couple of days. I loved the San Juans. *Loved them.*"

"I had fun, too. When it's not raining, you can't beat the west side of the state. Some pictures came back already. Want to see?"

"Sure."

They walked over to the shade of an apple tree and sank to the grass. Scott pulled an envelope from his shirt pocket. Inside were photos of Gabby on the ferry, Gabby riding a bike, Gabby walking a beach.

"These are all of me," Gabby complained, not altogether unhappy. "You'd think I took this trip alone by looking at these pictures. You need to show me how to use your camera."

"That's the end of the San Juan shots," Scott flipped through the stack. "Here are some pictures of the dig. I need to sort these out and give them to Dr. Grant."

He hesitated at a shot of the dark garbage bag, the boot protruding at a sick angle.

"Jeez, Scott," Gabby said, subdued. "You took a picture of the body."

"I thought the cops were going to break my camera."

They looked at two more similar photos in silence, then Gabby held up the next print.

"What's in this picture?"

"It's the obsidian scraping tool Jennifer uncovered the day before the body."

"I never saw it."

"I thought they were going to leave it *in situ*. Give me a second." Scott stood and walked back to the dig, to the pit where Jennifer was working.

"Hi, Scotty." Jennifer looked up, grinned, and pushed her glasses up on her nose. "I like your haircut. Did you have a nice break?"

"Yeah. How about you?" Scott squatted next to the pit, holding the print up and looking in the pit.

"The guys took off for the lake, but I stayed at the hotel and read three books."

"Sounds fun," he said abstractly.

"Looking for something, Scott?" Spencer joined them.

Scott stood. "I was just looking at some photos of this pit I took before the break."

"And?"

"I'm not seeing the scraping tool that's in the photo."

"May I?" Spencer held out his hand, and Scott handed him the photo.

Spencer studied it, uttered a non-committal, "Huh." And handed back the photo. "What are your plans after graduation?"

Scott shrugged. "I'm not sure yet."

"Photographers are a dime a dozen, but an archaeologist who can document his work with high quality, publishable photographs is always in demand." Spencer smiled. "Keep up the good work."

Chapter 21

Joe sat in the tribal office across from Shawna. She wore a charcoal gray suit with pinstripes; the jacket clung to her contours nicely. Joe tried not to stare.

"How are things going on the dig?"

"Fine. Good." He cleared his throat. *Get a grip*, he scolded himself. *You're not a sixteen-year-old boy*. "We found five more points, probably spearheads. It's got to be a weapons cache, it's such a concentrated site. Everything's stacked neatly, like they were put away for safekeeping, like the owners expected to return. Some artifacts are scattered around, probably from scavengers searching for food and finding the bones."

"Bones?"

"Yeah," he leaned forward. "Bone tools made of mammoths bones. Decorated even."

"Nothing resembling human remains? Ancient ones, I mean."

"No. Most definitely not but, there is something else." He had her full attention. "Somebody broke into the Claire's house one night while the dig was on hold and hung a coyote's head over the fireplace."

"What?"

He hesitated, debating whether or not to tell her the rest of it. "Spencer told the crew it might have been the Colvilles."

She inhaled sharply, stood, paced, and turned back to Joe. "See? We've officially protested the dig, now we'll get blamed for everything that goes wrong."

"Any idea who did it?"

Anger flashed over her face. "You think we did it?"

"No. Of course not. Spencer's closing the dig to the public, for security."

"We're locked out now."

"You won't be locked out. I'm not for hire, but I'll let you know anything that's appropriate for public disclosure."

"Thank you. I'll make sure we have someone there. Chester and Jack can trade off during the day and I'll get some night shift guys, too." She picked up a pencil and made a note. "By the way, I'm leaving for Olympia tomorrow. I'll be there off and on for a while working to legalize Native casinos. You know," Shawna tapped the pencil on the desk, "we, and I mean all Native Americans, were knocked on our asses in the 1800s. It took us 150 years to pick ourselves up and brush ourselves off, until we finally caught onto the *new* American way of life— capitalism. Nevada has casinos. Why can't we? You'd think the government would be happy we're finding a way to be self-sufficient. Instead, they're trying to cripple us by not allowing casinos on reservations. Do you know why?" She pointed the pencil at Joe.

Joe shook his head.

"Because we're in competition with the state lottery and the new horse track in Seattle. Do you know who plays the slots, Joe? Old ladies on tour buses. They're still going to buy their state-sponsored lottery ticket when they leave here. We're organizing petitions to get an initiative on the next ballot. We're working with the system. We're getting better at playing it the Anglo way."

She stepped around the side of the desk. Beneath her short skirt, long, shapely legs begged for attention. Joe kept his eyes firmly on her eyes.

She glanced at her watch. "It's getting late. Why don't you come to my place for dinner? I have some steaks we can barbecue."

"Sure," he said too fast. "I'd love to."

He followed Shawna to her house, stepped out of the truck and took in the view. Over the lake, thunderclouds billowed in a darkening sky. The lake churned as a wind began to blow, hard and steady.

He followed Shawna inside.

She put her purse on the counter then opened the fridge, pulled out a bottle of mineral water and handed it to Joe. She poured herself a glass of white wine and took a sip. "Let me go change. Make yourself at home."

When she returned, she was barefoot, wearing a summer dress.

"I'll make the salad if you barbecue the steaks," she said.

They stepped out a side door from the kitchen to a deck. "Here's the barbecue."

Joe glanced to the west where the clouds continued to build. "Might be rain coming with those clouds."

"We'll play it by ear." Shawna sipped her wine, watching him. "What makes you tick, Joe Running?"

He shrugged. "I like what I do, and I know how lucky I am to have figured that out pretty early in life. What about you?"

She smiled, cat-like. "I have ambitions."

"Such as...?"

"I've decided I want to be CEO of CTEC."

"CTEC?"

"Colville Tribal Enterprise Corporation. A hundred-million-dollar business. The casinos, when we get them, will be a part of it. CTEC has a sawmill, a construction company, a house and boat rental business, a wood treatment plant, three grocery stores, and a credit union." She ticked each item off on her fingers. "And we're developing Wapato Point, keeping the land but we're planning to build condos, houses, and a restaurant."

"That's quite a corporation."

"It is. And my goal is to be the first woman CEO of CTEC."

"Impressive."

"What about you? You have a dose of ambition yourself, *Doctor* Running."

"To a certain point. I'm working toward a full professorship, and I'd like to lead fieldwork. Come by the dig sometime and I'll show you around."

"I'd love to. Maybe I'll come for the next protest. *Peaceful, but Persistent* is our motto."

Joe perked up. "Another protest? When will that be?"

She smiled. "It's more fun if it's a surprise." She finished her wine. "I better get the salad going."

They both stood. She looked him square in the eye and stepped into his arms. He kissed her—long, slow, relaxed.

"I'll get the steaks," she said as they parted, and walked back inside, smiling.

Joe gazed up at the sky. Thunderclouds were getting serious. He started the barbecue. Better get the steaks cooked fast.

***

They sat at the kitchen counter and ate the steaks and salad. Joe couldn't but help notice Shawna was on her third glass of wine. He pushed away thoughts of his mother. After they finished eating, he picked up their dishes and headed for the sink. Somehow, Shawna ended up right behind him, and when he turned, she stepped into his arms for another long, slow kiss. She took him by the hand and led him out of the kitchen, down a short hallway, and into her bedroom.

So much for taking things slow, he thought.

Outside, the evening had turned black, and the throaty rumble of thunder boomed in the distance as rain began to drum the roof. But Joe didn't notice.

Chapter 22

Claire stood on the veranda, barefoot in shorts and a t-shirt, and watched the clouds build. The air was still, the orchard an uncanny quiet. Carlos had gone to visit Carmen. Spencer and his crew were back at their hotel. Joe had left in the afternoon, and Gabby and Scott were nowhere to be seen. The evening harkened back to pre-dig solitude. The lone howl of a coyote echoed off the basalt cliffs in the distance. Images of the severed coyote head hanging on her mantle came to mind, and she shivered, despite the heat. She had deposited the twenty-thousand dollar check that afternoon. While it plumped up her bank account quite nicely, something about it felt off.

She poured herself a whiskey on the rocks and left the bottle on the patio table, along with a bucket of ice. She settled into the cushions of a large wooden chair, protected beneath the veranda roof, and tucked her feet beneath her, as alone and content as an oyster. The sky rumbled overhead and a spattering of raindrops, fat and heavy, hit the ground. She watched the rain and thought about Spencer. Sometimes, when she saw him for the first time in the day, her stomach flipped, and she felt giddy. But the feeling faded quickly, leaving an empty space, and she didn't know why. She really didn't know Spencer, but figured he was a pragmatist. He knew her financial situation and had proven he was willing to make this entire inconvenient project worthwhile. Maybe, just maybe, this whole business might help save her orchard.

She nursed her drink, lost in thought, and when it was gone, poured another, fishing out a couple of ice cubes from the bucket. Too lazy to get up and go inside, she relaxed into the warm, whiskey glow. Sometime after her third drink, she drifted off to sleep.

An intense rain pounding on the veranda roof startled her awake. She blinked at a night gone impenetrable black. With great effort, she unfurled herself from the chair. She hadn't left any lights on inside the house, but she could navigate the place blindfolded. She gathered her glass and the near-empty bottle of whiskey and shuffled inside, stopping to lock the newly installed deadbolt behind her. Once in the kitchen, even without turning on the kitchen light she saw something that stopped her dead, heart in her throat.

The back door was open.

Before she could make sense of it, a sound froze her blood. A dry staccato sound, like old bones rubbing together, loud, came from under the table, very near her bare feet. The sound was horrifying familiar, one she had heard often on summer hikes through dry and rocky terrain. It was, without a doubt, a rattlesnake.

Her whole body turned cold, and both the glass and whiskey bottle slipped from her slack grip. The bottle hit the table and came to rest, but the glass fell to the floor and shattered.

The rattle-hiss ratcheted up even louder. Claire stumbled backwards, groped for the light switch, and flipped it on. She shaded her eyes from the stabbing glare and blinked. Beneath the table, inches from where she'd been standing, a rattlesnake coiled in the striking position, tongue flicking, head bobbing and weaving at one end, rattles raised and quivering at the other. She couldn't see the fangs, but she knew they were there, tiny hypodermic needles backed by a reservoir of poison.

What the hell was a rattler doing in her kitchen? She stumbled back to the front door, fumbled with the deadbolt, and ran outside, off the veranda and into the rain, instantly soaked. The shocking cold of the rain snapped her out of panic and sobered her up a little. She had no clue what time it was. *Think. Think.*

Bright lights swept over the house as a truck pulled into the driveway. Joe's truck. Joe rolled down the window and leaned out, engine still running. "Everything okay?"

"Hell no!" Claire shouted.

Joe killed the engine and trotted over to her.

"What's wrong?"

"There's a rattlesnake in the kitchen." She was trembling.

He took Claire by the shoulders, leaned down and searched her face. "Are you okay? Did you get bit?"

She shook her head. "I'm fine, but it's still in there, for God's sake. I'm going to grab a shovel. Wait here." Claire took off toward the garage, returned in seconds, and pushed the shovel into Joe's hands. "Kill it with this."

Joe looked skeptical, but went inside. She followed him back inside and into the kitchen.

The snake had moved out from under the table, gliding sideways in S-shaped undulations.

Joe raised the shovel. The snake reared back in the strike position and hissed, jaws gaping so wide they looked unhinged. Joe took a swing. The blow landed smack in the middle of the long body. The rattler lunged, rattling furiously, cold-blooded eyes fixed on Joe. Joe brought the shovel down again, blade on edge, and struck just below the head. He drove the shovel down hard. The rattler's body whipped and writhed, striking Joe in the leg.

Claire inched past Joe to the counter and grabbed a butcher knife, fell to her knees and began hacking at the snake's tough flesh behind the shovel, adrenaline shooting through her like fire. The dry surface of the rattles smacked Claire's arm as she pushed and sawed until the steely flesh split. The head fell away from the body, both the head and body writhing separately, as if still alive. Claire, breathing hard, stood and the knife clattered to the floor.

"You're hurt." Joe said, staring at her bleeding knees.

Slowly, she followed his gaze to her knees. "It's okay. It doesn't hurt."

"We need to make sure no venom got into those cuts. I'll take you to the emergency room."

"No," Claire insisted. "Absolutely not."

Joe hesitated only a second. "Then go take a shower and wash your knees with soap. We'll need to see if you have any glass in your knees. Or we go to the hospital."

Claire began to tremble and hugged herself. "Somebody put it in here," she said. "Look. The back door's open." Claire hadn't yet replaced the shattered window from the coyote head break in, merely covered it with plywood, and this time someone had chopped through the plywood to turn the new deadbolt lock. First the coyote head. Now this. Someone was trying to scare her, and they were doing a damn good job of it.

"I'll call the sheriff," Joe said.

"No," Claire insisted. "This is my house. Do not call the sheriff. Do you hear me? I'm not going anywhere, and nobody's coming here. I'll take care of this myself."

"I'll clean up here. After your shower, we'll have a look at your knees."

Claire disappeared upstairs. By the time she returned the rattler was gone, the glass swept up, and the aroma of freshly brewed coffee filled the kitchen.

"Coffee smells good," she said, wet hair tumbling over her shoulders. She wore shorts and a cotton shirt rolled up to the elbows. She held out tweezers, a bottle of rubbing alcohol, a magnifying glass, and a bag of cotton balls.

"I pulled out a couple small pieces of glass already," she said.

Joe took the supplies. "Have a seat." He poured her a cup of coffee as she lowered herself into a chair, bending her knees gingerly as she sat. Joe knelt in front of her and peered through the magnifying glass at each knee, carefully touching her skin with his fingertips, probing for glass.

Claire glanced at the clock. It was just past two. "You were out late."

Joe glanced up at her, then returned his attention to her knees. "In some native cultures," he said as he worked, "a rattlesnake is a symbol of violence and revenge." He eased out a sliver of glass.

Claire winced. "No shit." She brushed aside her damp hair. "You used to be around all the time. Not so much anymore."

"I'm not in charge of the dig anymore." Joe ran his hand over her knees. "Can you feel anything? Any small pieces I missed?"

She could feel the smooth warmth of his hand on her knee, the *nearness* of him. He seemed to sense what she was thinking, and his expression turned tender, then he stood abruptly.

"I'll replace the plywood tonight, but you'll need to get it fixed. Or better yet, buy a new door of solid wood."

"Why is someone doing this? Who would do this? Spencer blamed the Colvilles for the coyote head, and I'm sure he will for this, too. What do you think?"

Joe washed his hands, poured himself a cup of coffee and sat across from her at the kitchen table. "I don't see it."

"You like them, Sam Moses and his group." Claire studied him.

"Yeah. I think they're honest people. This isn't something they'd do. They're more likely to sue you than scare you, in my opinion. But maybe it's easier for people like Spencer to believe the Indians are attacking."

"Who else then? Someone who wants the dig to stop, obviously. Other than the Colvilles, who?"

"Like you, I only have questions, no answers. By the way, you should know the Colvilles will be back to protest the dig. Peaceful and persistent," he quoted Shawna. "I'm not sure when."

"Great," she said, tone bitter.

He hesitated. "Do you have any family around? Does your brother ever come visit?"

Claire frowned. "What?"

"Your brother. The first time I was here we looked at the pictures in your study of your family. You said you had a little brother."

Claire stared at him for a long time. "No, Josh doesn't come around."

"I don't see my family much either," Joe said.

"It's not that." If she weren't still a little drunk, and if it wasn't the middle of the night, and if he hadn't just killed a rattlesnake and picked glass out of her knees, she might have told him to mind his own business. Instead, she took a deep breath. "Josh and I did a lot together growing up. We hiked and biked and skied. We hung out."

She cleared her throat. "I met a guy, Keith, when I was twenty. We dated for a year, then we got engaged. Like you, Keith wore cowboy boots. When I first met you, wearing those boots..." She choked up. "I loved those damn boots on him. Anyway, the three of us skied together, Josh, Keith, and I. Hit the mountain first thing in the morning every Saturday and Sunday in the winter."

She stopped talking and wasn't sure she could go on. "We took a trip over a long weekend in February '77 to Revelstoke, BC, for backcountry skiing," she finally continued. "My idea. My stupid idea."

Her voice cracked and she felt cold, as if ice had bored its way into her core. She set her jaw stubbornly and went on. "We went snowcat skiing, hired a Thiokol to drop us off at the top of the mountain. It had snowed a ton and we were all so psyched to ski untouched powder. The problem..." her voice broke, "... the problem was, there had been a big dump of snow in the days before, and they said later, the slab of snow didn't bond to the layer beneath. As the three of us skied down in this unreal powder, something—maybe the Thiokol—broke the slab off above us and started an... an..."

She couldn't go on.

"An avalanche," Joe whispered.

Claire stared straight at Joe, tears streaming down her cheeks. She was crying and she didn't know when she'd started. "Yeah. I had stopped to catch my breath and the guys skied a hundred yards or so ahead of me. I heard it, a low rumbling sound. I looked up and saw this mushrooming cloud of powder and a wall of snow coming straight at us and I screamed. The edge of it came down in front of me, but the guys were straight in its path..."

Claire swiped the tears away with the back of her hand. "I tried to dig them out. We all carried radios and avalanche beacons, and I called the cat on my radio, but by the time the rescue team showed up, they were both...gone. My parents' happiness died that day. Mine, too. Not much later Mom died from cancer, then a little while later, Dad of a heart attack."

Joe looked stricken, and for a second, she thought he might lean in and take her in his arms. Instead, he stared with gentle, dark eyes. "I'm so sorry," he whispered.

She'd never told that story to anyone before. "Yeah." Claire wiped her nose on a napkin. She was glad he didn't try to tell her how brave she was, or that everything would be all right. "God, I'm wiped out."

"Are you okay?" Joe reached out and touched her hand.

She nodded.

"I'll fix the door. Do you have any plywood? A hammer and nails?"

"Garage."

Joe, reluctantly it seemed, stood and took his cup to the sink, then grabbed the shovel and headed outside. He returned with a scrap of plywood and hammered it over the gap in the kitchen door. "Tomorrow, a new door. Solid wood. I'm happy to help with it." He held up the hammer. "I'll put this away on my way out. You know where to find me if you need anything."

"Joe." She followed him to the front door. He stopped and turned. They were close—so close she could have reached out and touched him. "Thanks."

Chapter 23

"A dinner at the governor's?" Claire squinted at Spencer from where she kneeled in front of the tractor, changing the tire. "I can't think of anything I'd rather not do."

"I'm sure you received an invitation. Have you read your mail lately?"

She stood, wiping her hand on her jeans. "Why am I invited?"

"The Office of Archaeology is throwing a party in honor of our project at the governor's mansion, with the governor. Find your letter, young lady."

"So, I'll have to dress up?"

"A nice cocktail dress will do."

"Like I have a cocktail dress," she said sarcastically. "Take Joe. Me? I don't see the point."

"WSU's financing a small part of the dig, so it would be appropriate if Joe came along," Spencer said slowly. "They invited you because you're the owner. None of this would be possible without you reaching out to me."

"I reached out to WSU. You reached out to me." Claire squatted down by the tire again, avoiding his gaze. "By the way, something happened last night."

"What?"

"Someone broke in again. Came through the back door again, this time hacking out the plywood. They dropped a live rattler into the kitchen."

"What?" Spencer's face went pale. "A rattlesnake? My God, are you hurt?"

"Nope," Claire grabbed a wrench and tightened the lug nuts on the tire. "But I have to tell you, I'm getting pretty tired of this. Obviously, somebody's trying to intimidate me, and frankly, it's working. I'm thinking about calling off this whole thing. Maybe we should rebury everything and call it good."

Spencer bent down and looked her square in the face. "You're joking."

She sat back on her heels and returned his gaze. "This whole thing has been a pain. I'm tired of tripping over people on my land every time I turn around, and tired of animal parts and poisonous snakes getting dropped off in my house. I don't want to go to some dress-up dinner in Olympia, and I don't want to have tribal sit-ins in my front yard, which I understand is coming up on the agenda."

"What are you talking about? Who told you that?"

"Joe's been talking to the Colvilles, and they're planning a protest."

Claire gave the lug nut one final turn, stood, and wiped her hands on a rag.

"It must be the Colvilles," Spencer said quietly.

"Whoever it is, I say *uncle*. Enough is enough."

Spencer took a low, deep breath and let it out slowly. "I wasn't going to tell you this right now. I wanted to wait, maybe talk about it over dinner one night, when we had time."

"What are you talking about?"

"The museum, *my museum*, is very interested in this find. So much so, there's a good chance we can purchase it."

"Purchase what?"

Spencer swept his hand out in a broad gesture. "Everything, Claire. We're willing to offer you a very, very good price for the dig site, your orchard, your house, which would make a great Clovis museum. Your money troubles will be over."

It took a minute for the implications to sink in. Sell her place?

"This is unofficial, so far," Spencer continued, "but the figure we've been throwing around is close to five hundred thousand dollars. With some good financial planning, you'd be set for life."

Five hundred thousand? *Holy shit.* She turned to put away the tools.

"Claire?"

With her back to him, she held up one hand, signaled him to stop talking. "I'll think on it. And the governor's dinner, too. I need some time to think."

She climbed on the tractor and drove away.

***

Later that afternoon, Sam Moses returned to the dig along with Chester and Jack. As Joe walked to meet them, his thoughts turned to Shawna. A mixture of bliss and guilt rattled around his heart as he neared her grandfather.

Joe and Sam shook hands. "Good to see you again, sir." Joe said.

"You, too, son." Sam smiled.

Spencer rushed over to them. "I'm sorry, but the dig is closed to the public," he called out, stopping slightly in front of Joe.

Sam turned slowly to Spencer. "Exactly. As long as the dig stayed open to the public, we were able to monitor it freely. Now that it's closed, we'll station security people to watch over things, starting out with Chester here." Sam Moses reached up and put his hand on Chester's large shoulder. "In fact, you may find Chester useful to you. He has some experience keeping out unwanted visitors."

Spencer looked irritated. "May I remind you," his voice remained steady, "not only do we possess the proper permits, but we are on private land in the United States of America where we could dig this place up with a backhoe, if we wanted, and be perfectly legal."

Sam Moses's expression hardened. "You may have your permit, but we have our attorneys working to block this project. We *will* station someone here during this dig. If you don't agree, we will call in the Yakamas and the Puyallups and every other Northwest tribe to visit your site in protest every day. We will make your life miserable until the day we shut you down."

Spencer opened his mouth, then closed it again. His jaw gyrated for a moment or two, then he gave a thin smile. "Of course, we appreciate help with security."

Joe exhaled. Spencer missed his calling. He should have gone into politics.

Sam turned back to Joe. "Keep up the good work. If you need anything from us, just ask Chester."

Spencer looked doubly annoyed as Sam and Jack departed, leaving Chester behind to keep an eye on things.

Chapter 24

Spencer, Claire, and Joe met in front of Claire's house for the long drive to Olympia and the dinner at the governor's mansion.

Spencer showed up in a black dinner jacket, trousers, a black bow tie and cummerbund, and black-laced oxfords—all retrieved from his last trip home to Philadelphia.

Joe's life path had not yet taken him into the foray of black-tie affairs, so he scavenged together some black slacks and a light gray shirt, but necessity forced the purchase of a jacket and a classic gray tie. Luckily, he still had the black, leather lace-up shoes he had bought for graduation and used for job interviews.

Claire had been forced to go shopping at the local fancy shop, Webb's. The sales ladies talked her into a teal cocktail dress made of satin, with short sleeves (they gushed over her sculpted arms), a modestly scooped neckline, and gathered at the waist. It fell slightly below the knee, which consequently forced the purchase of gray pumps. What choice did she have? Wear her rubber boots? The ladies had oohed and awed enough to make Claire feel semi-confident, but when she walked out of the house in the harsh noon sunlight, she simply felt ridiculous.

Joe volunteered to drive Spencer's rented Buick, and Claire rode shotgun while Spencer sat in the back and buried his nose in journal articles written by officers of the regional archaeology society, prepping to meet the authors at the Governor's mansion. Joe concentrated on driving, and Claire shifted in her seat nervously, dreading an evening full of politicians and stuffed shirts in a grandiose setting.

Eventually, their route left rural Washington for the big city. Traffic thickened accordingly, and by the time they pulled onto Interstate 5 it was bumper-to-bumper traffic. Even so, they made it to Olympia early. Joe suggested they drive around a bit and see the sights. Spencer grunted and continued reading.

"Why not?" Claire said.

Joe drove to the Capitol and pulled the Buick into the circular drive in front of the domed building and gardens of red roses and rhododendrons.

The Temple of Justice building was across the street, and a few men and women in suits, carrying briefcases glanced at watches as they poured out of the front door and descended wide, marble steps.

Joe stopped the car and Claire noticed him staring hard. She followed his gaze and saw a woman and two men talking. The woman was hard to miss—tall, raven-black hair, dressed in a form-fitting jacket and skirt. The two men with her, they looked like Native Americans, were dressed in dark, expensive-looking suits.

When the trio reached the bottom of the steps one of the men waved and walked away. The woman and man turned the other direction, moving along the sidewalk a few steps, then stopped and turned toward each other. The woman reached up and straightened his tie, then leaned forward and kissed him. The man's free arm circled her narrow waist, pulling her to him. The man kissed her back, hand sliding down from her waist, resting on the curve of her buttocks. He patted her there, then they broke the embrace, and the woman slipped her arm into his as they resumed walking. It all happened fast, but Claire heard Joe gasp. She glanced at him. His expression had changed. He had a funny look on his face.

"Are you okay?" Claire asked, but Joe didn't respond. He pulled the car back onto the street, gripping the wheel, staring straight ahead. He didn't say a word as they drove to the governor's mansion, an impressive Georgian-style building surrounded by impeccable gardens and evergreen trees. Joe pulled into the driveway and a valet took the keys.

"Everybody ready?" Spencer asked as they exited the car.

"I guess," Claire said with caution.

Joe was silent.

"Here we go," Spencer said, and they all headed inside.

***

Spencer said he had a few people he needed to find. "Will you two be all right on your own?"

Claire ignored the condescending remark and waved him away. She turned to Joe, but only saw the back of him as he wandered away without a word. "So glad I came," she muttered, and set off to explore.

She found a ballroom and a large dining room on the first floor, and wandered, wide-eyed, through a living room with a huge fireplace and French doors leading to a covered porch. She peeked into some kind of small dining room. Afraid she had overstepped her bounds, she found her way back to the ballroom that was filling with people and stood, marooned in the hubbub of the reception, hating the feel of pantyhose on her legs and mad at herself for giving in to the pressure to be here. A waiter stopped with a tray of drinks, offered her a choice of champagne, white or red wine, or something from the bar. She picked up the nearest glass of champagne and took a gulp.

A large man with a red face headed for her, smiling broadly with a highball in his meaty hand. Claire moved away quickly to avoid contact. Deftly cutting between chatting couples and avoiding collisions with the hired help, she asked directions to the ladies' room from an innocuous-looking woman in the hallway, who pointed the way.

She strolled down a hall, examining artwork and feigning interest in any inanimate object until she spotted Joe. He was leaning on a balcony railing, gazing down onto an atrium full of rhododendrons, some blooming red and orange. Joe was oblivious to her presence until she leaned on the rail next to him.

"Hey there," she said. "You're missing the party."

He barely glanced her way. "So are you."

She shrugged. "For me, this is a one-shot deal, but this is your career. Spencer said you could meet a lot of important people here. People who could help you professionally."

His eyes remained steady on the atrium and he didn't respond.

Claire regarded him. "What's wrong?"

"Ms. Courtney?" A pale man stood near her shoulder.

Claire turned. "Yes."

"I'm Patrick Ware, president of the Pacific Northwest Archaeological Society. It's a pleasure to meet you."

They shook hands. He reminded Claire of her childhood dentist. Pale, polite, and placid.

"We're honored you're here. Some of our members have taken the museum tour of your dig and found it absolutely fascinating." He held onto her hand until Claire delicately extricated herself from his grip.

"Have you met Joe Running?" Claire asked. "He's working with Spencer Grant on the dig. In fact, he did the preliminary investigation."

"I know who you are, Dr. Running. It's a pleasure to meet you face to face."

Joe seemed to rouse himself and shook the man's hand.

"May I get you another champagne?" Patrick Ware plucked Claire's now-empty flute from her hand and set off to find a waiter.

"Certainly, you may," she said after him, then turned back to Joe. "Is everything okay?"

Joe shrugged absently. "I don't like these things."

"Welcome to the club."

Joe didn't respond.

Patrick Ware returned to her side, fresh champagne in hand. "Oh, Dr. Running. I should have brought you something."

"I don't drink," Joe mumbled and walked away.

Claire plucked the flute from Patrick's hand, eyes on Joe as he left.

"I have to tell you, Ms. Courtney, the Clovis Dig is the most exciting event since I've been president of the society."

Claire decided to play ball. "Really? Tell me more."

***

Spencer gathered his troops together, nudging Joe out of a corner and interrupting Patrick Ware's monologue to Claire. "You'll have to excuse us, Patrick, but the governor is waiting."

Claire set her drink on a nearby table as Spencer took her by the elbow—he already had Joe's elbow in hand—and propelled the two toward the main ballroom.

"You'll like the governor," Spencer said quietly. "Despite being extremely wealthy... he inherited the Weyerhaeuser timber fortune, you know... he's very down to earth. They say he feels uncomfortable in fancy clothes, fancy cars or whatever. Some say he felt guilty about inheriting a fortune shortly after a plane crash killed his mother and sister."

"How awful." Claire felt a wave of empathy.

A small group surrounded the governor, but Spencer gently nudged their way through the crowd, then waited for a lull in the conversation. "Allow me to introduce myself, sir. I'm Spencer Grant."

The governor smiled. "I've heard all about you, Dr. Grant. Welcome to Washington." The men shook hands.

"Governor Gardner, may I introduce Dr. Joe Running, the Washington State University archaeologist who conducted the preliminary investigation on the Clovis site."

"Sir," Joe towered over the governor. "It's an honor."

"The honor is mine," the governor said warmly as they shook hands.

"And this is Claire Courtney, owner of the orchard where the Clovis artifacts were found."

Claire felt the blood creeping up into her cheeks as the governor took her hand.

"Ms. Courtney, what an exciting treasure you discovered. Thank you so much for sharing the find with the archaeologists, your community, and the state. It's very exciting."

"Thank you, sir," she stammered. "What a beautiful home you have."

Governor Gardner leaned in. "It's not really mine," he said in a stage whisper. "They let me stay here as long as I keep working."

Claire blushed, and those within earshot laughed.

He continued. "This Clovis find is really one of the biggest archaeological events in our state. It's the talk of the town."

"I'm so glad." Claire tried to look pleased.

"Thank you all for coming," the governor said. "Please enjoy yourselves."

***

Spencer steered them into the enormous dining room filled with long tables covered in white tablecloths, centerpieces of riotous-colored bouquets, place settings with tall wine glasses and more cutlery than Claire knew what to do with. Place cards with each guest's name directed them to their assigned seat. Spencer, Joe, and Claire were placed within shouting distance of the governor, with Claire seated across the table from Joe, two archeological society board members, and Spencer. Patrick Ware sat to her right and a buxom older woman to her left, the vice-president of the society, Claire soon heard. Patrick introduced more society board members, who greeted Claire then turned their attention to Joe and Spencer, eager for details of the dig.

Claire didn't mind, because the first course of food eclipsed everything. There were oysters on the half shell and smoked salmon, sautéed scallops, along with jumbo shrimp. Claire felt insanely ravenous. She polished off the seafood in time for a tomato basil soup, which tasted heavenly, followed by a fancy salad, grilled salmon with creamy dill sauce, and green beans. Her world shrank to the exquisite tastes and textures of this one, spectacular meal. Except.

Except somewhere between the salad and the salmon, Claire noticed Joe. As she savored the flavor of salmon and dill, Joe picked at his food, questions from the society board members falling on deaf ears.

"We also had ancient animal scat and wood tested. We believe the inhabitants used the wood to make sleds." He paused dramatically and lowered his voice. People paused and leaned in. "I was going to save this until my paper was officially published, but I want to share it with you tonight." Spencer looked around. "The evidence we're uncovering overwhelmingly supports my Sled Shoe Theory."

Joe sat up straight, his head pivoting toward Spencer.

"I believe the Clovis people stored their hunting tools in a pit and covered everything with small sleds they used to haul food and other supplies," Spencer lectured. "By digging a pit, roofing it with a sled, and banking it with loose dirt, they improvised a damn good way to store their hunting and living tools until they traveled back to the region and needed them again."

Joe frowned as he stared at Spencer, who continued his oration.

"We found bones fragments that had been chewed on and excreted, probably by wolverines, great scavengers of the day. You see, the sled theory explains that after the hunters left for the last time, for whatever reason, wolverines scavenged the bones and scattered artifacts as they rummaged for food."

"Brilliant, Dr. Grant," someone said.

"Fascinating," said another.

"Spencer and I arrived at the theory separately, yet simultaneously," Joe blurted out, sitting bolt upright in his chair and looking intently around the table. "Once we realized we were coming to the same conclusions, we discussed the theory at great length." All heads turned toward him. "The hunting tools, the sled runners, the excreted bones, all painted the full picture of these great Clovis people and their ingenious way of life." Joe looked directly at Spencer.

Spencer gave a tight smile.

"Bravo," someone said, and a small round of applause erupted at their end of the table.

"Additionally, and I haven't had the opportunity to tell you," Joe leaned forward and smiled at Spencer, "WSU geologists analyzed a soil sample. The sample contained ash from the Glacier Peak volcano, known to have erupted and blanketed the state with ash 13,000 years ago. That confirms the results from the organic material radiocarbon testing."

Another small round of applause broke out, and Spencer looked annoyed.

"Dr. Running, what about the Native American protests?" another asked, all eyes on Joe.

"The local Tribes are worried Claire's orchard might be a burial site, but the odds are pretty slim. Only one discovery of Clovis human remains has been found in the U.S.—those of a one-year-old boy found at the Anzick site in Montana. You see, Native American burial grounds are sacred, and they believe the Clovis people are their ancestors."

"What about you?" Patrick Ware asked Joe. "What do you believe?"

Claire sensed Joe's unease as he looked at all the faces around him. All forks and knives had stilled, at least at their end of the table.

"I believe it's time for dessert," Joe said, as chocolate mousse arrived.

A twitter of laughter broke the tension.

By the time Claire licked the last delectable bit of mousse from her spoon, Joe was schmoozing with the best of them. She was proud of him. He seemed to have gotten over the funk he'd been in earlier.

Spencer, on the other hand, seemed irritated at something. After this lavish feast, Claire couldn't imagine what could possibly be bothersome.

***

Spencer and Claire both fell asleep as Joe drove home, much to Joe's relief. It was late, and they wouldn't get back to Wenatchee until the wee hours of the morning. He was grateful not to have to make small talk, consumed, as he was, with the image of Shawna kissing another man, consumed by the familiar way the guy put his hands on her. It had knocked the breath right out of him. He had never felt more foolish in his life. For God's sake, they had slept together just weeks before! She's the one who led him to her bed. Granted, they hadn't seen one another since then, but even so...

At that precise moment he realized how stupid he'd been—a complete ass. Isn't that what they say when you make assumptions? He'd assumed that Shawna was attracted to him, and had been flattered. He'd assumed they were beginning a relationship—possibly a long, serious relationship. She was smart and ambitious and attractive, and dedicated to her grandfather. What's not to like? One painful moment revealed how wrong his assumptions had been.

After he had seen *the kiss*, he'd hardly been able to function at the governor's dinner. The only thing that had snapped him back to reality was Spencer taking all the credit for the sled theory at the dinner. The sled theory was *his* theory, not Spencer's, and he wasn't about to let that distortion slide.

Once he had snapped out of his torturous trance, he had chatted with not only members of the archaeological society, but the director of the State Department of Archaeology and Historic Preservation—people who might eventually champion funds for projects. He had done what he had gone to the damned dinner for—met important people from the state who were interested in the Clovis cache.

He gripped the steering wheel as the headlights illuminated the twists and turns of Blewitt Pass. What was it with women, anyway? First Janet had broadsided him. He'd waited a long time to date anyone in college after that little episode, and when he'd finally started going out again, after two or three dates he'd stop calling before any kind of serious relationship could form. He didn't need to get kicked in the teeth twice.

And then came Shawna. All lessons from the past had vanished when he met her. They seemed so right for each other. They had so much in common.

By the time he pulled into Claire's driveway he had beat himself up to the point of exhaustion. When he returned to his cabin and dropped into bed, he convinced himself that he was making a mountain out of a mole hill. What was the big deal? It's not like they had a long history together.

Still, when he went back to work the next day—and every day after that—the pain lingered, until it eventually faded into a dull ache.

Chapter 25

"They're the mammoth bones with decoration on them, right?" Gabby held the slide viewer up to the kitchen light, squinting.

"Right," said Scott. "Very precious."

Scott had knocked on Gabby's cabin door after dark, arms full.

She had opened the door, chewing on her toothbrush. "Pretty late, isn't it?"

He pushed through the door, ignored her surprised expression, and set the items on the kitchen table. "I've been working on something I want to show you."

"What?" Gabby set her toothbrush down and picked up a hand-held slide viewer and looked at boxes of thirty-five-millimeter slides.

Scott gave her a long, hard look. "Whenever I had a set of photographs developed for the dig, I also had a set of slides printed to keep. Paid for the slides out of my own pocket."

"Why?"

"Because these are one-in-a-million artifacts. Something to show my grandkids. Anyway, I looked over a copy of the artifact log and started comparing artifacts to log entries. I think I found some missing."

"Missing?" She sounded dubious.

"Look at the slide in the viewer. It's Feature Three. There are two of the beveled rods there. One is on top of the other one, but the one underneath is a centimeter or so longer and has some different markings on it. Do you see it?"

"Yes."

"I've gone over the log and found one twenty-five centimeter, decorated, bi-beveled rod of mammoth from feature three at this coordinate. But not two. I've gone over the logs about ten times. There's also a few points I can't account for."

Gabby lowered the viewer. "I don't get it."

Scott leaned close to Gabby's face. "These things are worth money."

"Let me get this straight." She frowned at him. "You think someone is stealing artifacts."

Scott shrugged. "There have been a lot of people around the dig at one time or another. Who knows?"

"How will we figure out who?"

"Keep our eyes open, my dear. I'll take twice as many pictures, and we'll try to keep track of all the artifacts. If someone working on the dig is stealing, we should be able to figure out who."

The next morning, Scott knocked on Spencer's trailer door, feeling a bit like a kid going to the principal's office. He had no idea why Spencer had summoned him.

"Come in," Spencer invited.

Inside the cool dimness of the trailer, Scott waited for his eyes to adjust. He had never been inside Spencer's headquarters. He glanced toward the back, where books, maps, and journals covered a bed. A compact living space included a couch of flowered upholstery, and a small television sat on a countertop. The kitchen included a small table with bench seating where Spencer sat, tabletop buried in papers.

"Scott, thanks for coming. Come here and sit." Spencer waved him over.

Scott slid into the seat on the opposite side of the table.

"Finishing up paperwork," Spencer indicated piles of detailed drawings and descriptions of the artifacts. "You've done a great job with the photography. Top notch."

Things were starting out well. "Thank you, Dr. Grant."

"I'm submitting some of our materials for publication, mainly professional journals to start with," Spencer chatted easily. "Eventually, we'll move into mainstream periodicals, and I'd like to do a book on this project also. Your photographs are going to be an important part of the book and articles."

Scott couldn't believe his ears. He pushed his glasses up. His dream of an internationally published photo spread seemed about to be realized. "Wow," was all he could think of to say.

Spencer continued. "I noticed you've been looking over the artifact log a lot lately."

Scott's heart dropped.

"Is everything okay?"

Scott cleared his throat. "Yeah, sure. I've just been comparing photos with the log."

"Excellent," Spencer smiled. "You're a step ahead of me. In fact, that's why I asked you to drop by today. I go over the log each day, but it's always a good idea to have a couple sets of eyes on organization and cataloging, and since you're our photographer, who better?"

"So, I guess I may as well mention," Scott said slowly. "I couldn't get everything to match up the way it should. In particular, there's a photo of one bi-beveled rod, but I can't find it in the log, and can't find it, the bone itself, I mean, anywhere. And some points seem to be gone. At least four, maybe five."

Spencer sat up and leaned forward. "There's no room for sloppy record keeping on a project. Let's get this straightened out now."

"Sure, Dr. Grant."

"Bring me the photos and the discrepancies in the log, okay?"

Scott shrugged. "Sure, I'll go over it one more time to be sure."

"If artifacts are missing, I need to report it to the sheriff and file an insurance claim. Once again, good work."

"Okay, uh, thanks." Scott didn't quite know what to say. "See ya," was all he could come up with right before he bolted out the door.

***

As the shadows lengthened into evening, Gabby knocked on Scott's door. She waited, and knocked and waited, before exhaling a loud sigh and turning back toward her own cabin. For the last several days, instead of working side-by-side, she had only caught brief glimpses of Scott through the trailer window, head-to-head with Spencer. Just when she was starting to like the guy, he pulls a disappearing act. Hand on her own cabin door, she spotted him walking slowly toward the cabins.

"Scott." She retraced her steps and stood at his door.

"Hi, Gabs." He looked tired.

"Hi yourself. You look like something the cat dragged in."

"I'm beat."

"Come in. Let me make you something to drink. How about lemonade?" She started for the small fridge.

He flopped into a kitchen chair. "I'll take a beer."

"I'm fresh out." She sank into the chair opposite him. "How's it going?"

He rubbed his face with both hands, then frowned at her. "I'm sorry to say," he lowered his voice, "between you and me, I was right about the missing artifacts."

Gabby's heart fluttered. "You're kidding."

"I wish I were. It gets worse. So far, there's at least three Clovis points we can't account for. Dr. Grant made me swear not to tell a soul. So here I am breaking a promise. He said they've sent some artifacts to the lab in Philadelphia, but not the decorated bone and a couple of points."

"You and I are partners," she scooted her chair to his side, gingerly removed his glasses and smoothed a hand over his short hair. "In fact, I've been missing you."

"You have?"

"Yes, I have."

"Guess what."

"What?"

"My photographs are going to be published in the Smithsonian."

"What?" She was thrilled for Scott, but at the same time, was already missing the goofy guy he had been. He seemed to be growing up before her eyes.

"What's wrong? Aren't you happy for me?"

"Of course I'm happy for you! It's just that, things seem to be changing. You and I used to work together, now you're working more with Spencer than with Joe and me. You and I used to have dreams about becoming famous and successful. Now your dreams are coming true, but I'm stuck digging in empty pits."

He stood, stepped behind her, wrapped his arms around her waist. "My dreams are coming true," he whispered into her hair. "You're missing me."

"For real?"

"For real." He turned her around and kissed her.

She kissed him back.

He pulled away, squinting at her. "This wouldn't be a groupie thing you have for me, because I'm almost famous?"

"Scott."

"Just a thought. Never mind." He kissed her again.

Chapter 26

A week after suffering through the cocktail party and dinner at the governor's mansion, Joe sat in a lawn chair outside the pickers' cabins, reading, when Claire walked up.

"Bradley Randall called," she said. "Wants you to give him a call back. You're welcome to use my phone."

They walked up to the house together.

"Kitchen phone, study phone, take your pick," Claire said when they arrived.

Joe went to the study where he had first seen the three Clovis points, where the photos of a young, pigtailed Claire hung on the wall, along with the photos of Claire with her now-deceased brother and fiancé. He stared at the photo, thinking how horrible that must have been for Claire, losing them so tragically. He dialed Bradley's office number.

"Your landlady's looking for you," Bradley said without preamble. "Said your place reeks to high heaven. Wants you to get over there ASAP and see what in God's name is stinking up the place."

"Stinks?" Joe repeated.

"First, she wanted to make sure *you* were alive. She hadn't seen you around for a while and thought you might be decaying on the living room couch. I assured her you were alive and breathing. She says if you don't come home and get rid of whatever's making the ungodly smell, she's calling the police. I'm assuming you'll be arriving tomorrow, so drop by my office when you're done. Now, I have to go. I'm taking the kids and their mom to some play."

***

Joe drove to Pullman the next day. When he walked up to his apartment, the smell hit him before he turned the key in the lock. He batted away flies that seemed as eager to get in as he. He pushed open the door and took a step back as the fetid air rushed out. Something smelled dead. Leaving the door open, he put his hand over his face and walked inside, flipping on lights, opening shades, and heading through the sparsely furnished living room, down a short hallway to his bedroom, where he pulled open a dresser drawer and groped around inside for a handkerchief. He covered his mouth and nose and tied it behind his head.

He dropped to his knees and peered under his bed. A few dust bunnies gaped back, but mercifully the space was devoid of corpses. He turned back toward the living room, where everything seemed normal. He walked into the kitchen.

He took tentative steps toward the refrigerator, thoughts of Claire's coyote head and rattler on his mind, and carefully pulled open the fridge door. No light came on, and the temperature inside felt warm. He hadn't been home for some time, so the sparse contents of the fridge consisted of a mayonnaise, mustard, and pickles. No great loss.

Then he opened the freezer. The smell hit him with nauseous ferocity. Oh, God. Inside the freezer, rotting, were steaks, at least two T-bones, a couple of pounds of hamburger, and the clincher, a nice filet of sockeye salmon.

He retreated to the electrical panel in the hallway and opened the gray metal door. The breaker to the fridge was tripped off. He flipped it back on and returned to the kitchen. The familiar hum of the refrigerator once again filled the small room, joined by a high-pitched voice. "Joe? You in there?"

His landlady. "In here, Faye."

"I'd rather you came out here," she squawked.

Joe went to the front door. Faye reminded him of a friendly old bird as she stood in her crooked stance in the doorway.

"Can't blame you there." Joe untied his handkerchief.

Faye had worked for the university for over thirty years, first in custodial, then moved her way up to the mail room. Managing the apartments supplemented her modest retirement check and Social Security. "What in God's name do you have in there? It stinks to high heaven. Almost called the cops."

"The breaker tripped on the fridge. I had some meat and fish in the freezer."

"That'll do it," she agreed. "One year, a wildlife biology major rented a place. He was partial to picking up roadkill and putting it in his freezer to study. Same thing happened. Fridge quit. The roadkill rotted. Took about a year for the stench to work its way out of the place."

"I'm sorry, Faye. I'll make sure it's clean before I leave."

"Good. Don't you be putting the rotted stuff in the dumpster now. I don't need it to smell outside like it does in here."

"I'll go directly to the landfill."

"They won't be too happy to see you either." She turned to go, then hesitated. "I was worried it might be you stinking in there. I haven't seen you around much lately."

"I'm working on a project, a Clovis find, in East Wenatchee."

"Do tell. Clovis shmovis, it's all Greek to me. Good luck cleanin' up."

Joe took a deep breath of semi-fresh air and re-tied the hanky over his face. He left the door open, went back to the kitchen, where the stench nearly took him to the toilet bowl, but he swallowed hard and held his ground. He pulled out the garbage can from the cupboard and found some latex gloves. He began to gingerly pluck out the packages of rotting meat, dropping them one by one into the garbage can. First the steaks, then the burger, and when he lifted out the salmon, he froze.

"What the hell..." He couldn't believe his eyes.

There, in his freezer, behind the rotted fish, lay three Clovis artifacts, two bifacially flaked scraping tools and one twenty-five centimeter decorated bi-beveled mammoth bone.

***

"Bradley..." Joe began, standing in Bradley Randall's office, trying to calm himself down, to lower his blood pressure by force of will.

Bradley sat behind his desk—buried in paper—looking haggard. "Martin Smith," Bradley began, referring to the President of WSU, "is working my ass off. He keeps expecting me to turn in these blasted reports, including your expense accounts on the dig. How's it going? You enjoy the governor's dinner? You could have invited your boss, you know. I could have used a trip to Olympia. Good PR, anyway. I'm saving all the clippings and making sure the boys upstairs hear about all the accolades we're getting."

How was he going to tell Bradley what he'd found in his freezer? He still couldn't believe it himself.

"Cat got your tongue? What's wrong?"

Joe dropped into a chair in front of Bradley's desk and raked his fingers through his hair. "I don't know what's going on."

"What are you talking about?" Bradley stopped rifling through his paperwork and stared at Joe.

Joe stared back. "I just came from my apartment. The smell the landlady called about, the fridge somehow tripped the breaker and the freezer had meat and fish..."

"Fish, that's the worst."

"When I emptied the freezer, I discovered…there were…I still can't believe it."

"What? What can't you believe?"

"Bradley. There's artifacts in my freezer. From the dig."

"In your freezer? Why?"

"I don't know why. I didn't put them there. There's a couple of Clovis points and a mammoth bone, in my freezer, and I have no idea how they got there."

Bradley stared at Joe for a long time, then stood and walked to the window. "I'm confused," he said at last. "This is confusing. Did you bring them here to study and forget to bring them into the lab?"

"No," Joe said.

"Well, take them back then, or bring them into the lab," Bradley turned toward him.

"The important thing is, how'd they get there?" Joe stared at Bradley. "How did they find their way to my freezer, then have the refrigerator die to create a stink?"

Bradley turned back to the window, studied the landscape. "This whole thing is fishy." He turned to look over his shoulder. "No pun intended. Maybe someone's trying to make you look bad, make it look like maybe you stole the artifacts."

"Who would gain?"

Bradley faced him. "I can think of two possibilities. First, the Colvilles. They're trying to stop the dig however they can."

Joe shook his head slowly, thinking of Shawna and her grandfather. "I don't see it," Joe said slowly. "*Peaceful but Persistent* is their motto. They're taking legal steps to stop the dig, but I very much doubt they'd do something like this. Especially to me." Joe started to say *because they like me*. But he remembered Shawna's kiss, and said, "Sam Moses is a Colville Tribal Councilman. We have respect for each other."

Bradley considered Joe for a moment. "Next on the list is Spencer Grant."

"Come on, Bradley. He's beyond suspicion."

"Grow up, Joe. He's annoyed we're still part of *his* project. He's done everything he can to make you quit. He put you and your crew far away from the cache, where chances were slim to nothing that you'd find anything. I think the best thing to do is say you brought them here for lab work and forgot to sign them out.

"I can't say I took them without signing them out. That would be a lie."

"Don't be a Boy Scout. How *did* those artifacts get into your freezer? Bring the artifacts into the lab. I'll back you. Say we were running tests. I'll log them in myself for a week ago, or however long it would take for meat to start to rot and stink inside a freezer."

"Someone, whoever planted them there, will know the truth. We can't risk being liars, Bradley. Sooner or later, the truth always comes out."

"Not always," Bradley said. "Not that I'd know..."

***

Joe didn't leave the artifacts in the lab. He wrapped them up in a couple of old newspapers and placed them gently in his truck to return to the Courtney orchard. Before he left town, he took the smelly meat and fish to the dump, then went home and cleaned the refrigerator and freezer about a dozen times, until the stench faded away. He stopped by Faye's apartment on his way out of town.

"The fridge up and running again," he told her. "It's clean and it's empty, so there shouldn't be another problem."

"It's working now, is it?" Faye looked thoughtful. "I figured it had gone belly up."

"Just a tripped breaker. Must have had some kind of surge."

"Right," Faye said. "You take care, Joe."

***

A midnight moon cast a pale glow on Claire's house as Joe pulled into the driveway. He took the bundle of artifacts straight to his cabin although the vague aroma of rotted meat clung to them. Exhausted, he went straight to bed, but slept fitfully.

The sun had been up for over two hours by the time Spencer and his crew arrived on site. Joe stood in the shadows and watched, treasuring the crisp, morning air before the inevitable heat suffocated any trace of coolness.

Spencer waved at the crew as they headed to the dig site, then went inside the trailer. Joe grabbed the artifacts. Time to face the music.

"Come in," Spencer called when Joe knocked.

He entered the small, stuffy place and quelled the urge to open a window.

Spencer turned from making coffee. "Joe. What can I do for you?"

Joe laid the bundle on the small table, peeled back the newspaper, and waited.

Spencer finished his coffee making and turned. "What are these?" He sounded surprised. "You found something in your pit? Why didn't you leave it *in situ*?"

"These artifacts were in my freezer in Pullman." The words sounded bizarre, even to his own ears.

"What exactly do you mean?" He had Spencer's full attention, now.

"I mean, the manager of my apartment building called my office to report a bad smell coming out of my apartment. I drove home and found my refrigerator had stopped working. The breaker had tripped. There was meat and fish in the freezer, and they rotted, thus the smell. When I cleaned out the freezer, I found these three artifacts inside. They're from here."

Spencer watched Joe, and slowly walked over to the table, stared down at the scraping tools and mammoth bone. He stared at them for a long time, then walked to a shelf, picked up the dig log, flipped through a few pages, and stopped. Looked up at Joe.

"These have been missing for several weeks. Did you sign them out?" Spencer asked cautiously. "Because if you did, I have no record of it."

Joe shook his head. "I have no idea how they were in my apartment. No idea whatsoever."

Spencer stared at him. "How is that possible?"

"Your guess is as good as mine." Joe thought his answer sounded flippant, but he felt anything but glib.

Spencer glanced down at the book again, then closed it. "This is serious, Joe. I filed a theft report on these very artifacts. We have photos showing where the mastodon bone—the one etched with a design—was *in situ* one day, gone the next."

"I can't explain it. Unless... unless someone put them there. Broke into my apartment, put them in the freezer, and tripped the breaker."

Spencer stared at him, silent for a minute, then laughed out loud. "Come on, Joe. Don't be dramatic. If you took the artifacts to Pullman and forgot to sign them out, so be it. But don't make it out to be someone else's fault."

Joe felt the heat rise to his face. "I don't lie. I didn't take them. I found them in my apartment, and I know nothing about how they got there."

"Joe," Spencer said. "You're pushing me into a corner here."

Joe's mother had told him more than once that he was his own worst enemy, a goody two shoes. And now, maybe for the first time, he figured his mother had been right about something.

Chapter 27

Two days later, Joe got up early, dressed and made coffee. He couldn't shake the conversation with Spencer. He knew he had sounded crazy. The whole thing *was* crazy. Halfway through his first cup a knock sounded on the door. Reluctantly, he opened the door. It was Claire.

"You up?"

"Yeah." He stepped outside.

She flashed a piece of paper at him. "Have you seen this?"

He took it and skimmed through the message. It was a letter from Sam Moses saying tribal members planned on visiting the dig in the afternoon for a peaceful protest.

So, today's the day.

"I don't know which is more annoying," she said. "Snakes in the kitchen or a demonstration in my orchard. I'll tell you what I'm going to do today. I'm spraying. I'll spray from one end of this orchard to another with full head gear and the sprayer on full blast so I won't hear or see a thing. And don't worry, I'm putting on a nutrient application, so I won't poison anybody with pesticides, and I'll stay away from the dig." She took the letter back and folded it, shoving into her jeans pocket. "But they don't need to know that. Tell them I'm spraying something that will make them go blind." She started for the spray shed, waved goodbye with her back toward him.

He wanted to follow, to hide in the soothing, green recesses of the orchard. Instead, he watched until she disappeared.

***

The protesters arrived in the heat of the day—high noon. They showed up in an old school bus, tattered pickups, and a hodgepodge of automobiles. Nearly a hundred people, mostly Native Americans—Colvilles, Wenatchis, a few Yakamas, and some Caucasians, including a few hippies, poured into the place like a flood. There were babies and octogenarians. Children peeked from behind their elders, playing hide-

and-go-seek in the crowd. People carried signs that read, 'May the Creator Protect Us from This Evil Deed" and 'Why Do You Hurt the Wenatchi Indians?"

Not far behind the protesters, reporters and photographers arrived not only from the local paper, but from Seattle, Spokane, even the Associated Press. Sam's PR staff did a good job getting the word out.

Joe noticed a few deputies standing nearby, and Spencer frowning at the gathering crowd from behind the fence. Chester left his post to join the protesters.

Joe hung back. He couldn't help but scan the crowd, searching for Shawna. She was nowhere to be seen.

After everyone had gathered, Sam Moses stepped forward to the chain link fence near Spencer. Sam began in a loud, commanding voice, eyes locked on Spencer. "My people. Let us say a prayer."

The men in the crowd removed cowboy hats and baseball caps. Everyone bowed heads. Even the children held still.

"Creator, we ask for Your blessing this day," he began. "We ask You to erase the shame that has been put on our race. Some people believe we came over a land bridge, but we know this story is false. We grew up here, out of the ground. How can strangers come from across the country and dig up our people and their belongings, to put items on display and keep something they don't own? We never go into their cemeteries to dig up bones and put them on display. Our hearts bleed."

The crowd breathed a collective sigh of sorrow.

Sam wore a somber expression. "If I traveled to Arlington Cemetery, and dug up the remains of John Kennedy, and took them to my teepee to study, I would be arrested."

The crowd murmured in agreement.

"We protest this dig," he spoke loudly and firmly, "Amen."

The crowd echoed.

Sam turned to face Spencer. "We ask you, Spencer Grant, to stop now. Bury the dead. Let the souls of our people rest. Quit disturbing our sacred ground."

Sam stopped, peering hard at Spencer, brow wrinkled. "Are you wearing something beneath your shirt?" he asked.

Spencer took a step back, face flushed red, and he crossed his arms in front of his chest. Joe hadn't noticed before, but there seemed to be some bulk beneath Spencer's shirt.

"Is that a bulletproof vest?" Sam's sounded surprised. "Do you have a bulletproof vest under your shirt?"

Spencer didn't answer, didn't deny the allegation.

"You do, don't you?" Sam turned to his crowd, expression incredulous and asked in a loud, dramatic voice. "Did anyone come here to shoot Dr. Grant, or any of these people digging up our ancestors?"

Snickers came from some of the protesters, angry denials from others.

Sam turned back to Spencer. "You insult us with your distrust. With your fear." Sam looked around until he spotted Joe. "Dr. Joe Running," he called. "Please." He waved him over.

Reluctantly, Joe walked over to join them, Sam on one side of the fence, Spencer and Joe on the other.

"Dr. Running, are you wearing a bulletproof vest?" Sam asked loudly, theatrically.

All eyes were on him. Joe pulled his shirt from his jeans and slowly unbuttoned it. Opened the shirt to show his lean torso, bare skinned.

Sam turned back to Spencer. "Your colleague thinks we're safe, yet you do not. Why?"

Spencer's jaw worked hard, as if there were words he longed to say, yet knew he could not. He said nothing.

Sam's face changed, looking almost surprised, as if a new idea had come to him.

"What other misunderstandings do my People have with you, Dr. Grant? These rocks, these bones you dig up every day belong to us. Will you give them to us?"

Spencer said nothing, didn't move.

"Or will you take them with you to Philadelphia when you leave? Or maybe," Sam frowned, "will you sell these artifacts, Dr. Grant?"

Spencer glanced back to his crew behind him. The four Philadelphia students stared wide-eyed. Scott had his arm around Gabby, and they stood off to the side. Then Spencer looked right at Joe, pulled himself up to full height and scanned the crowd of protesters.

"I'd rather die first." Spencer's voice boomed. "I respect your beliefs. I have spent my life studying ancient cultures. I bring only honor to your people, not shame. This site is a Clovis cache of tools and weapons. This is not a cemetery. No human remains have been found." He hurriedly added, "No human remains from the Clovis culture. Indeed, our excavations uncovered a murder. A man who would have otherwise been forgotten and lost forever, dead and buried secretly, with no honor."

Poe Riddle stood in the shadows of the orchard, watching. He perked up at the mention of his cousin, but everyone's attention scattered as another sheriff car pulled up. It was Sheriff Grady. A murmur went through the crowd as he strode toward Sam and Spencer, joined by his deputies, hands poised near holstered guns.

Spencer's speech increased in intensity. "I am a friend to the Native Americans. This is no graveyard. This is a shrine to the ingenuity of ancient mankind."

The sheriff stopped in front of the fence beside Sam Moses. Joe watched as the sheriff seemed to bask in the dramatic effect of his arrival. Then the sheriff pushed sunglasses down his nose and squinted at Spencer.

"I'm going to have to ask you to unlock the gate."

Spencer glanced at the crowd. "I'd rather not, Sheriff. This is private property. These people might think I'm inviting them in. They could jeopardize our project."

"Fine," Grady said and pointed at Joe. "Then send him out. Joe Running. I have a warrant for your arrest."

Joe's heart dropped to the ground where it lay exposed for all to see. The oxygen was sucked from the air leaving a smothering vacuum.

Sam Moses blinked in surprise.

The crowd's murmur gathered momentum. Photographers and reporters came to life, snapping pictures and moving close to catch every word.

"You're being charged with the theft of artifacts from this property," the sheriff said loudly. "You have the right to remain silent..."

Spencer fumbled with the key, snapped open the padlock and swung the gate open. A deputy rushed forward and handcuffed Joe's wrists behind his back. Two other deputies turned to face the crowd, making sure no one tried to charge the gate.

Numb, Joe glanced over his shoulder. Scott and Gabby stared, looking stricken.

The deputy pushed him out the gate. Joe locked eyes with Sam Moses. The old man stared back, eyes gone hard as obsidian. The deputy propelled Joe through the crowd to the cruiser, pushed the top of his head down, and folded him into the back seat.

Joe gazed out the window at the crowd. A hundred stares—curious, angry, confused. Ice coursed through his veins and blood pounded in his ears obliterating all sound, as the car pulled away from the crowd, u-turned, and headed to town.

***

The water drummed a hollow beat within the tank as Claire washed out the sprayer. She pulled the hose out of the tank and splashed cool water over her face and neck. In the distance, someone called her name.

Gabby and Scott were running toward her, Gabby easily three lengths ahead, long legs pumping. They reached the tractor wide-eyed and panting.

"What's wrong?" Claire asked.

Scott found his voice first, words tumbling over themselves. "They've arrested Joe. They say he stole artifacts."

"I know he wouldn't do it," Gabby added.

"They arrested him," Scott repeated.

"We have to get him out," Gabby said. "Can you put up bail? He'll need a lawyer."

Scott looked stricken. "I think... I'm afraid it's my fault. I've been taking pictures and I found some artifacts missing. I showed Dr. Grant and he reported them stolen."

Claire stared at them as if they were speaking a foreign language.

"Come on!" Gabby said. "Let's go!"

Chapter 28

Joe's breath came in shallow gulps as he eyed the brick building of the county jail as the sheriff's car pulled inside the garage. The deputy took him by the arm and pulled him from the cruiser, then pushed him into the building. His shirt fluttered as they walked, still unbuttoned from proving he wasn't wearing a bullet proof vest.

He recalled reading about near-death experiences where someone's spirit floats above their body on a hospital operating table, observing, as if watching a stranger. That's how he felt now, detached, watching from afar as he was searched, fingerprinted, and given green coveralls, the designated color for a minimum-security inmate, with a matching green wristband. In the space of ten minutes, Joe transformed from a respected college professor to a criminal.

***

Claire called the bail bondsman, but by the time she, Gabby, and Scott arrived at the county courthouse next to the jail, Joe had been released. The clerk said Joe had already been bailed out by, he picked up a paper and read aloud, "The Colville Tribal Enterprise Corporation."

When Claire arrived back home, Spencer was waiting for her. She thanked Gabby and Scott, then waved Spencer inside.

She waited until they reached the living room, until she was standing in front of the mantle where the coyote head had hung, then turned to face him, hot with anger. "You had Joe arrested."

"I know it's difficult," he said quietly, "But he had the artifacts at his apartment in Pullman. He told me himself. They were missing for weeks. He must have stolen them, then had a change of heart."

"Why? It doesn't make any sense. He'd have nothing to gain by taking them."

"You know the artifacts are valuable," Spencer's said.

"Yes, I know they're valuable. *You* sold them for me. But Joe? Why would he steal them to sell? He's starting out. He's building his career.

He has a good job. No way would he risk it all for money. Not to mention, he's Native American. You think he would betray his own people?"

"Your naïveté is one of the many traits I find so endearing," Spencer said tenderly. "But the facts remain. Joe was in possession of stolen artifacts. I had no choice but to report him to the authorities. Our insurance company insisted upon it, for one thing, since they were already processing the claim."

"Circumstantial evidence." Her voice cracked.

Spencer gripped Claire's shoulders, leaned down and looked her in the eye. "Listen, I like Joe. He's a good scientist and he's done a fine job here, until this. How can you explain three artifacts disappearing and turning up in his apartment in Pullman?"

"Somebody broke in, like they did here."

"Two very different scenarios. Someone tried to scare you, and I'm guessing that someone was in the crowd of protesters today. But Joe is a different story. Claire," he said softer. "$500,000 is at stake for you. The museum board is considering making you the offer, and once they do, my museum and I can save you from going under. I know you're barely hanging on. We can take the best care of the artifacts. We'll treasure them and display them both here and in Philadelphia. But Joe needs to go. I can't trust him. He's resented me since the day I set foot on the place."

"He's not the resenting type," Claire snapped and stepped out of Spencer's grasp.

"How could he not be resentful? He'd been in charge. When you hired me, which was the smart thing to do, it knocked him down a notch. I know you felt bad about replacing Joe, but now it's time. It's time to let him go."

Claire turned her back on him. "No."

"Okay, how about this," Spencer changed tack. "I'll drop the charges and we let him resign from the dig. We'll let him walk away, pride intact. We'll say the arrest was a mistake. A miscommunication. But he has to go."

Claire thought she might be sick.

"It'll be okay," Spencer soothed. "Joe will be just fine, you'll see. He has his whole career in front of him. I'll go now and let you think things over."

Long after Spencer left, she stood rooted in place, feeling like she'd just ruined a man's life, and not quite sure how it had happened.

Chapter 29

After Sam and Shawna bailed Joe out of jail—something he would never have imagined happening in a million years—he followed in his pickup to Manson. They went inside the Colville building, into Sam's office, and closed the door. Sam sank into the chair behind his desk and Shawna sat on the desk while Joe stood.

"Goddamn," Sam Moses said. "They set you up. They got you good."

"Don't worry, Joe," Shawna said. "We have attorneys. We'll fight the bastards."

"Who would have thought up stealing artifacts and planting them in your apartment?" Sam Moses said reverently, as if it was the smartest and most unexpected plan in the world. "Makes you look bad. Really bad."

"Grandfather, you're not helping." Shawna gave Sam a hard look.

"Can someone explain this to me?" Joe asked. "Why would anyone set me up?"

"To get rid of you," Shawna said. "It has to be Spencer. He thinks you're one of us, and he doesn't like us and our claim to the artifacts. He knows we'll take him to court, and he's afraid we'll win."

"You don't get to be a man in his position by breaking into people's apartments and planting evidence," Joe argued.

"Maybe the same person who broke into Claire Courtney's house did it," Sam suggested. "Somebody with a grudge."

Joe sank into a chair, the weight of the events sunk in, exhausted him. "This is the end of my career."

"It's the beginning of your career, Joe." Shawna said firmly. "They haven't won, and we won't let them. Do you hear me?"

"You need some rest," Sam said. "There's a trailer out back. We keep it for staff. You can stay there for as long as you like. And don't worry, son, we'll get you out of this mess."

"You can stay at my house," Shawna offered.

"No," Joe said too fast. "Thanks, but I'll take you up on the trailer until I figure out what I'm going to do."

"I'll get you settled," Shawna said.

"What timing," Sam mused as they left. "In the middle of a damn good protest when they pulled that one."

***

Shawna let Joe into the trailer. "The bed is made, there's some food in the kitchen. Help yourself to anything."

"Thanks," he said.

She stepped up to him, reached out to touch his shoulder. He pulled back and avoided her eyes.

She cocked her head. "Other than the obvious, is something wrong?"

Joe said nothing.

"We're friends. Remember? If you're embarrassed, if you're afraid I think you took those artifacts, you're wrong."

It seemed like a stupid time to bring it up, but he couldn't help himself. "I saw you coming out of a building near the Capitol the night of the governor's dinner."

"You did?" She brightened. "Why didn't you say hi?"

"Because one of the guys you were with, you and he..." Words failed him.

Shawna looked at him expectantly for a moment, then her expression changed to, *aha*. "You saw James kiss me."

Joe said nothing.

She smiled gently at Joe. "Because I kissed James doesn't change how I feel about you."

Joe looked skeptical.

"James and I have known each other for a long time. We're friends, and sometimes we... get more friendly. We have an understanding, I guess you could say. No strings attached. I like you, Joe. A lot. I have since the day we first met."

"And you don't see anything wrong with starting something with me while you're involved with..."

"James."

"Yeah, James."

She took a step toward him. "James and I are friends. End of story."

"Listen," Joe said stiffly. "It's been a long day."

"Sure. I'll be back tomorrow." She stopped at the door, turned, and smiled. "Keep an open mind, about everything, okay?"

***

Joe didn't sleep. The events of the day played themselves over and over in his mind as he lay in the small bed, hands behind his head, staring at the ceiling. He couldn't escape the facts. His career had collapsed into shambles, although it had barely taken off. His relationship with Shawna had existed only in imagination. What was left?

Joe was up and showered, but not rested, when Shawna knocked the next morning. "I come bearing coffee," she called through the door. "May I come in?"

Joe let her in.

"Coffee, black, for you," she handed him a cup. "Mocha for me." She held up her cup. "I won't ask you how you slept. Spencer Grant called this morning."

"What did he want?"

"He said he's dropping all charges. He wants to talk with you. He left a number."

"Dropped the charges?" Had he heard her right?

"They never should have arrested you. We should file a lawsuit."

Just like that. First someone upends your life and you find yourself behind bars, then they change their mind. But the damage, the wreckage the arrest left behind, was enormous. "I need some time to think," Joe said at last. "I'm heading to Pullman today."

"Let me send along a couple of our guys to take a look around your apartment."

"Look around? For what?"

"We have security people who are very well trained. Your apartment, as far as I'm concerned, is the scene of a crime. Let them look things over."

Although exhausted, with a brain like Swiss cheese, Joe had to hand it to her. She was persistent. "You're a bulldog."

She grinned. "I've been called a lot of things, but never a bulldog. I won't give up on you, Joe. *We* won't give up. Grandfather, the Tribe. Someone wanted to get rid of you. Probably Grant, or maybe the murderer of the poor guy you dug up, or the person or people who put the coyote head and the rattler in Claire's house. Whoever did it, we'll figure it out."

***

It seemed like a thousand years had passed since he'd been in Pullman. He drove to his apartment, followed by the two Tribal guys Shawna had sent. He unlocked the front door and turned to the guys. "I'm going to the university. Lock up before you go," Joe said.

The security guys chuckled.

Joe set out toward the university with long strides. As he climbed the stairs to his office, he remembered vividly the first time he had taken these stairs—the first warm, realization of how much he liked this little town.

Joe called Spencer from his office. The conversation was short, and Spencer didn't bother with pleasantries.

"You have one option," Spencer said. "You can voluntarily leave the project. If you don't, we'll pursue an investigation into the missing artifacts."

"I understand, and I'll think about it."

"Think fast, buddy," Spencer said, and that pissed Joe off.

Joe hung up and went to talk to Bradley. He found Bradley at his desk looking nearly as tired as Joe felt.

"I told you to bring them here to the lab," Bradley lectured before the door closed behind Joe. "I worried this would happen. Where did your honesty get you? Where did it get *us*? I've been trying to explain all this to Martin. You do remember Martin Smith, the president of WSU, don't you?" Bradley's voice cranked up in volume. "He called me last night to find out what the hell was going on with you. I have a meeting with him and the admin team later today. Frankly, what's happened is impossible to explain."

"You and I know I didn't take the artifacts," Joe said quietly. "I just talked to Spencer. He said if I leave the dig, they won't prosecute. Frankly, I've lost my taste for the whole project. I'd like to return to the classroom."

"The classroom?" Bradley sounded incredulous. "Joe, this is deep shit we're walking in here." Bradley stood, walked to his office window, looked out and cracked his knuckles. "The way things stand, you'd be lucky if they let you mow lawns on campus. Christ, Joe. I'll do everything I can, but right now it looks bad."

Joe stood in stunned silence.

"Officially, you're on paid leave for the foreseeable future," Bradley said. "It may be a while before they figure out what to do with you. We'll need to know where to send your checks, for as long as admin decides to keep you on the payroll. What are you going to do now?"

That was the million-dollar question, wasn't it? He said the first thing that came to mind. "I'm going to Idaho."

Chapter 30

By the time Joe returned to his apartment, the guys were gone. Black smudges of dark swirls and ridges dotted the cupboard doors and the countertops. They'd dusted for fingerprints throughout the apartment. Joe gathered some clothes and shoes, but had nothing to pack them in. His lone suitcase and backpack were in his cabin at the orchard, so he put everything in plastic garbage bags and threw them into his truck. He'd call Faye his landlady later, once he decided what to do in the future.

Joe drove out of Pullman and never looked back. He knew he should stop and see his mother, but what could he say to her, to his brother? His life on hold, he'd figure out everything down the road. For now, he couldn't think about it. For now, all he would think about was getting to Idaho. He drove with the window down, feeling like he'd suffocate if he couldn't breathe in the fresh air. He stopped in Baker City, Oregon, and bought a few groceries and a toothbrush. He drove past mile after mile of sagebrush, then over rolling hills folding back onto themselves. Fields of wheat stubble gave way to the occasional farmhouse, where wind-sculpted trees hovered over simple homes that were outnumbered and outsized by lumbering barns. Gun-metal gray grain silos pointed skyward like rockets on launch pads. Away from the farms, antelope dotted the landscape, delicate, aloof, and serene.

He never once turned on the radio. He didn't want distraction. He preferred the voice in his head that beat him up between long bouts of feeling sorry for himself. Six hours into the trip he crossed the border into Idaho. About the time darkness and fatigue overcame him, he arrived at the outskirts of Boise and found a small motel off the freeway.

After a shower and picking through convenience store groceries, he slept a dreamless sleep. The next morning, he took the freeway again, heading southeast. Five hours later, he pulled off at the Pocatello exit.

Chapter 31

After Joe's arrest, un-arrest, and abrupt departure, Spencer assigned Scott and Gabby a new pit, one adjacent to the original pits. Then he left for another trip to Philadelphia.

"He threw us a bone," Scott said to Gabby after Spencer left, as he stared down into the artifact-laden pit.

"But he left us to the wolves," Gabby said, staring at Frank-with-the-sideburns, who Spencer had left in charge. "Look at him," Gabby whispered, looking at Frank as he kicked back in the shade of a tree, clipboard in hand. "Self-important prick."

"Don't waste your energy. Ignore him."

"This whole thing sucks. At first, I wanted this summer to last forever. Now I can hardly wait to go back to school. Except now it sounds like Joe won't be there."

Scott leaned in close. "What about me? I'll be there."

Gabby tapped the end of Scott's nose. "Thank heavens. Otherwise, school would be as intolerable as this place."

Mark and Kevin joined Frank in the shade and the trio resumed an ongoing backgammon game.

Gabby watched them in disgust. "They're taking a break. Let's take a break."

They climbed out of the pit and Gabby ran to her cabin, returning with two cold bottles of water. They found a shady, grassy spot on the other side of the dig, away from the backgammon game.

Jennifer popped over with a Coke. "May I join you?"

"Pull up some grass," Scott said.

"What?" She looked confused.

"Sit."

"Oh." She plopped down, facing them. "I know you two aren't very happy about Dr. Running. It's all very confusing."

Gabby sat up a little straighter. "He didn't do anything wrong."

Jennifer shrugged her shoulders. "Frank said you guys go back to school pretty soon."

"Yeah, we start the third week in August," Scott said.

"We don't go back until late September. Dr. Grant's going to bring in some older people to take your places. I'll miss seeing you around." She eyed Scott and smiled.

Gabby scooted a little closer to Scott and held his hand. Scott looked surprised, then grinned.

"Oh," Jennifer sounded disappointed. "Do you two have a thing?"

"Yeah, we have a thing," Gabby said.

Jennifer sighed. "Story of my life." She stood and turned in time to see Claire drive through the orchard on a tractor pulling a flat trailer piled with wooden props. "She works all the time." She turned back to Scott and Gabby. "I'm going to get my PhD. I'm going to teach anthropology in a nice, cool classroom."

Gabby put her head on Scott's shoulder and smiled.

Jennifer looked resigned, then plodded back to her pit.

***

Carlos had just finished placing the last wooden prop beneath a tree limb sagging with the weight of nearly ripe apples when Poe appeared.

"Can we talk?" Poe asked.

The detective and the sheriff had finally figured out the dead Billy and the living Poe both hailed from Arkansas. They'd called Poe in for questioning, and he admitted he knew Billy, but said they never worked at the same orchard at the same time, which was the truth. Now it was Poe's turn to ask the questions.

Carlos led Poe to his house and poured them each an iced tea. They sat at the kitchen table, facing one another.

"My cousin Billy. What do you know?"

Carlos had known this conversation was coming. "Nice kid. Hard worker. He said he was saving money to marry his fiancée. I told him I was putting away money too, to marry Carmen."

"What else?"

Carlos took a deep breath. "After that first year, I'd see Billy talk to the other guys, but when they saw me, they'd stopped talking. Some days he would talk, talk, talk. Other days he'd drag himself around here like he had a hangover. I wondered if maybe Billy had fallen in with the wrong people. I wondered if he was selling drugs, maybe."

Poe's eyes went flat. "Then what?"

Carlos shrugged. "Then nothing. He disappeared." Carlos's eyes shifted away from Poe.

Poe sat silent for a few minutes, then said quietly. "If you know more that you ain't said, you'll be sorry."

"I *am* sorry, Poe. I'm sorry Billy's dead. But I've told you what I know."

Poe drained his glass, stood, and walked out.

Carlos sat for a long time in the cool shadows of his house, wondering if Billy was going to rise from the dead and destroy everything.

Chapter 32

Two Years Earlier, July 1985

Billy Parker recalled the day he stumbled upon the Mexican Mafia as plain, dumb luck. One afternoon when Poe wasn't around, he'd been having beers after work with a couple of Okies and two Mexicans, all who lived in the same apartment building, sitting on apple boxes in their shaggy yard, when a car pulled up. A 1981 Cadillac Eldorado. A skinny Mexican guy wearing new jeans and a smooth, white t-shirt climbed out.

"Buenos días," he greeted the men. "Hey, Billy."

Billy squinted at the guy. "*Hola*, Pedro. Help yourself to a beer."

"*Gracias*." Pedro walked to a metal bucket filled with ice and beer. A metal bottle opener hung from the bucket on a string, and he popped the cap off and took a long swig.

"You ain't been around the orchards lately," Billy said.

"Found something better," Pedro said in broken English.

Everybody chatted and drank and laughed for a while, then Pedro took a deep gulp of beer and said quietly, "Anybody want crack?"

The men glanced at one another, suddenly wary. "I'm out of here," one of the Okies said as he stood, drained his beer and left with the other Oakie, followed quickly by the two Mexican guys.

"*Pollos*." Pedro made a clucking sound like a chicken. "You chickenshit like your *amigos*?"

Billy regarded the man. "You sellin' drugs?" Billy's eyes drifted over to the Cadillac.

Pedro ignored the question and walked to the Caddie, patted the car. "You like?"

"I reckon it's a nice ride," Billy said. "You buy that with drug money?"

Pedro laughed, opened the trunk, grabbed a brown paper sack, and held it up. "I have something in here you might like."

Billy had been drinking whiskey since he was ten, sneaking sips out of the bottle he found in the kitchen cupboard, then later, with Poe, stealing the occasional fifth from the liquor store. He had waited until he was seventeen until he took his first toke of pot. He had liked the lazy haze of marijuana, and smoked some now and then, but he could take it or leave it. He'd tried mushrooms once, but they made him throw up. He wasn't so sure now that he wanted to try something new.

"Will it make me sick?" Billy asked. "I hate to barf."

"No, no. The opposite of sick. It won't hurt you. It's something new called meth. It's mellow, man. You'll feel good.

Billy wasn't convinced.

"Listen." Pedro joined him. "Let's go inside. I'll give you a free sample. The reason I'm doing this is I need some extra money. You ever need more money?"

"Who doesn't?"

"Try this, and I'll explain how I made enough money to buy my sweet ride."

Billy admired the Caddie again. "Free, right? You're not trying to sell me anything."

"Absolutely free."

Despite his better judgement, Billy led Pedro inside.

Pedro pulled out a pipe and filled it with small blue-white rocks, offered it to Billy and flicked a lighter over the bowl.

Billy hesitated, then leaned in and inhaled. There was an easing back in his body, like when the ocean recedes right before a gigantic wave hits the beach. Then a title wave of euphoria washed through Billy. "Wow." He gazed at Pedro in a hazy state of wonder.

Pedro grinned. He held up his hand and showed off a flashy gold ring inset with a red stone. "This is what they give you when you go to work selling this shit. It's real gold, man, and a genuine ruby."

Brenda would love to have a genuine ruby ring. A movie of him and Brenda crawled into his head, a blur of him driving up in a deep-throated car, pushing a ring like that on her finger, maybe smoke stuff like this with her. Then they'd strip naked and crawl into bed together. He got hard.

Pedro interrupted his fantasy. "El hombre necesita a alguien que hable inglés."

"Huh?" Billy squinted at Pedro.

"Gringos got money to buy shit. The big man needs a gringo to sell to gringos, somebody who talks English. I'll take you to meet the man. But you gotta be cool. These are tough guys."

"I'm no salesman." Billy stared at Pedro's ring.

"I'll teach you everything you need to know. Think about it. I'll come back tomorrow and we'll talk some more. Got to go right now. People to see. Money to make."

Pedro packed up his pipe and the little rocks and left. The roar of the Caddie's engine seemed to call Billy's name.

When Pedro returned the next evening, Billy had come to a decision. He was here to make money, and working in the orchards wasn't exactly making him rich. He was curious—how much money could he make as a salesman? He could keep working full time and sell on the side. It might be worth the risk and get him home to Brenda faster. God, he missed home.

"Okay. I'll meet these guys, and maybe try to sell some stuff. But if I don't like it, I'm out."

"Easy money, man. You won't be sorry."

***

Billy's orientation into *the business* took place at midnight at the intersection of two dirt roads out in the countryside near Quincy, a farm town thirty miles away. Pedro arranged it, but the man in charge wanted Billy to come alone. Billy borrowed his cousin Poe's dilapidated Subaru, drove the highway to Quincy, then squinted in the darkness searching for road names at the edge of wheat fields until he found the junction. He got out and stood, trembling and scared, waiting in the pitch-black until a car thrummed toward him. He gulped a deep breath and tried to calm down.

Soon a black Jeep rolled to a stop, headlights blinked off, the back door opened, and the car sighed with relief as a man close to 400 pounds climbed out. They called him El Gordo, Billy would find out later. The fat man lumbered up to Billy accompanied by two guys as thick and wide as refrigerators.

Billy swallowed, tried to stand tall, dwarfed by the three giants. He squirmed under El Gordo's gaze as the man looked him over for a long time, then said in broken English, "You want to work for me?"

"I reckon," Billy chirped.

"You scared, little man?" the huge hombre asked.

Billy didn't much cotton to being called *little man,* especially by this monster. He'd never been called *little man* before. Back home the girls called him *cute*. Hell, Brenda stood only five foot two, so she stood on her tippy toes to kiss him. That said, it wasn't the right situation to split hairs.

"Listen, little scared man. I gotta trust you. You mess up, we'll hurt you bad. Maybe kill you. *Comprendes*?"

"Yes, sir."

"Why you want to work for me?"

"I have a fiancée, and I could use the money."

"*Cual es su nombre*? Her name?"

"Brenda."

El Gordo paused for effect, then spoke real quiet. "If you mess up, I kill you first, then we find Brenda and kill her. *Comprendes*? Still want to work for me?"

Billy's veins filled with ice. Hell no, he didn't want to work for this lard ass, but what could he do now? He pulled himself up to full height, all five feet six inches, and said, "Reckon so."

The fat man stared at him for a long while, then nodded once. "Done."

Then, in a weird, midnight ceremony, the fat man pulled out a ring—a ring of gold with a ruby in the center, and one of the refrigerator guys shoved it on Billy's finger.

"We married, *hombrecito*," El Gordo breathed. "You my bride."

The minute the Jeep pulled away, Billy turned and threw up into the dirt alongside the road. After he recovered, he took a piss on a sagebrush one-handed, holding out his left hand with the ring to admire it, before climbing back into the Subaru and heading home. Getting rich might be tougher than he had first imagined.

Chapter 33

Joe drove past the Idaho State University campus, took a left, and pulled into Albertson's grocery store, a place where professors and cowboys shopped side-by-side. Smooth-skinned girls sporting diamond-studded nostrils held doors for farm women weathered by years of work in the blistering sun. Joe ached with the similarity between Pocatello and Pullman. Cow town, college town. Irrigation, education.

Joe bought a sandwich, bottled water, and a newspaper. He sat in the parking lot eating and reading the paper. A cougar sighting on university grounds the week before had everybody shaken up, the paper reported. The cat was spotted on Red Hill Trail on the edge of campus. It wasn't a huge surprise to the locals, since mountain lions seemed to have an occasional affinity for the place. But still, it upset the college kids and faculty, and the wildlife guys had to be called in. They treed the feline trespasser and shot it with a tranquilizing dart, then relocated it out of town so everybody could breathe easy again.

Joe finished lunch and pulled out of the parking lot, surprised by the heavy traffic. Then he remembered it was the weekend of the Shoshone-Bannock Festival. He knew it well. They crown a festival queen, hold an old-timers and a junior rodeo, have relay races, stick games, and host a Native American softball tournament. As a teenager, Joe had played in the softball tournament.

The festival meant all the motels would be booked, and Joe wasn't quite ready to head out to the ranch where he had spent so many summers. He needed a day or two to think things over, to figure out what he was going to tell Tuff Kellerman and Tuff's mom, Esther. Finding a place to stay seemed a minor problem in his whole, messed-up life right now. He could sleep in his truck, if need be. He cruised up and down busy streets, studying the hot and dusty town until he took an on-ramp to Interstate 15 heading north and drove ten minutes to the Fort Hall Indian Reservation exit. He pulled into a shopping center called The Trading Post and the Teepee gas station, where he filled up.

He drove past the Clothes Horse, whose window mannequins wore traditional Native American beaded leather alongside denim. Next came a restaurant called the Oregon Trail and a bingo hall. At the Trading Post grocery store, he parked and went inside. An Indian girl, maybe eight-years-old, gazed at him from behind the counter. She tossed a gap-toothed smile in his direction.

An older woman shuffled from the back room to ring up an order for a couple of elders. Joe picked out some bottled water and iced tea from a cooler and carried it to the counter.

The woman smiled at Joe, dimples punctuating round cheeks.

"You here for the festival?" she asked.

"Yes," he said.

"Know how to get there?" she asked.

"Yeah, thanks."

"You from around here?" The woman rang the items as the eight-year-old stared with unabashed curiosity.

"I visit now and then," he said, and winked at the little girl, who grinned even wider.

Joe left and drove the quarter mile to the festival grounds and pulled the truck into a field that had been transformed into a parking lot. Tour buses lined the back of the lot, along with motor homes and trucks with horse-trailers attached. The rest of the lot was filled with cars and trucks.

Joe parked at the outer reaches of the lot, walked a ways back to the entrance, paid his money and entered the fair grounds. Booths of Native American arts and crafts stood in long rows. Signs advertised buckskin pants and vests, moccasins, traditional dresses, belt buckles, bone chokers, porcupine quill work, and a few war bonnets.

People milled around the booths. Tourists. School kids on vacation. A large group of Asians with cameras hanging around their necks stuck together like a school of fish as they darted through the crowd from booth to booth. Cars continued to pour into the parking lot, stirring a fine sprinkling of dust into the air, and Joe breathed in the dry whiff of dirt mingled with the tantalizing aromas of festival food.

Behind the vendors, a whole teepee village had sprung up where native families camped, sprawled in lawn chairs, and cooked on portable gas grills while music wafted from a smattering of boom boxes.

As the heat of the day started to fade, the sun sinking in welcome relief behind dark clouds on the horizon, Joe bought a dinner of buffalo stew and fry bread and settled on the rodeo bleachers. He watched as a sultry Native American girl no more than eighteen basked in the attention of two young men, which dredged up the image of Shawna kissing another man, then of Claire sitting in her kitchen as he explored her tender skin for shards of glass after the rattler incident. Two women he would never see again.

The drums started up outside of the rodeo arena. Joe finished eating and left the bleachers, mingling with the crowd as they headed into a gigantic tent.

He barely made it inside when a beautiful young woman rode into the tent on horseback. A diagonal ribbon across her beaded costume proclaimed her Miss Shoshone Bannock. She dismounted and stepped up to a microphone, tried to speak a few words, only to create a high-pitched tone that made children squeal and adults cover their ears. A hefty Native man rushed to the sound equipment by the stage, fiddled with some dials, then gave a thumps-up to the queen, who shyly tried her speech once again, words reverberating in the early evening air. She welcomed the crowd, said a few words about the history of the celebration, originally called a *social powwow*. She invited dancers and drum groups to get ready, the dance contest was about to begin.

Contestants lined up, most dressed in traditional costumes. Painted faces peered from beneath elaborate feather headdresses. Leather costumes with intricate beadwork evoked an era gone by. In the crowd, moccasins stood by cowboy boots, leather leggings by blue jeans. Lining the edge of the dance floor, Native drummers pounded out a rhythm, and the dancers began to dip and swirl. As time passed, the dancers worked themselves into glistening sheens of sweat. Some grabbed torches, illuminating shining faces in a flickering orange light.

A few young men standing in front of Joe passed a flask back and forth, taking pulls, joking and laughing and growing louder. *What is it about drinking that makes people loud*? Just then a Native American man sporting a deputy badge walked up behind the boys. He had a football coach's belly, pushing out the wrinkles out of his shirt and wore his salt and pepper hair cut short. His weathered skin had seen its share of sun. When the flask passed again, he plucked it mid-air. The young men turned in unison to protest but spotted his frowning face and thought better of it.

"You boys go find a better way to enjoy the festivities, you hear?" The man said, and the boys skulked away.

"I swear these kids are drinking younger every year," he mumbled, and glanced at Joe. "Well, I'll be damned."

"Tuff," Joe replied.

The two men bear hugged.

"What the hell," Tuff Kellerman said.

"Just rolled into town," Joe said. "I planned on making my way to your place soon."

"Mom will be delighted. Hell, I'm delighted. Thought we wouldn't see you this summer."

"And I thought you weren't going to do this gig again." Joe tapped the badge pinned to Tuff's shirt.

"Ah, hell. They talked me into helping out with crowd control again. Every year I say it's my last, and every year I cave like milk toast. You come on out tonight and stay with us."

"How about tomorrow night? You're busy this weekend, and I don't want to bother Esther. She's probably already in bed and sound asleep by now."

"You got that right."

A ripple pulsed through the crowd; a couple of men scuffled together in fun or in anger.

"Here we go," Tuff pushed the flask into Joe's hands. "Take this, will you? We'll look for you tomorrow then." He took off and plowed through the crowd.

Joe pushed the flask into his back pocket and made his way through the crowd, half dreading and half looking forward to visiting his cousin the next day.

***

After the powwow, Joe found his way to his car and back out onto the highway. He drove, headlights slicing through the dark, searching for a place to spend the night. He pulled onto a side road and drove a piece. He pulled over in a wide spot next to a grove of trees around midnight, and tried to stretch out in the cab, which was a good sight narrower than he was long. He curled on his side and drifted off, Native drums echoing in his dreams.

At first light, there came a rapping on the window. Joe opened his eyes to see a frowning farmer glaring at him. Joe sat up, waved his hand in reassurance, started the truck, and headed down the road, pulled back on the highway, and drove until he found a rest stop. He stuck his head under the spigot in the bathroom sink, using the hand soap to wash his face and hair, and wetted paper towels to take a sponge bath.

Relatively clean, he felt pretty good for a moment, but when he pointed the truck back to Pocatello, all the harsh emotions he had been trying to ignore came crashing down on him.

The Rocky Mountains loomed behind Pocatello, a sight he usually found captivating. Today he barely noticed. He drove toward something with a familiar feel to it—the university.

He pulled into a campus parking lot, killed the engine, and stared morosely at the buildings, the sidewalks, the acres of grass dotted with trees. A smattering of backpacked students wandered about. The campus wasn't packed, typical for summer quarter.

The overwhelming urge to be part of a campus again swept through him, followed by self-pity. He hadn't done anything wrong, yet here he sat in a university parking lot, longing to be a part of a world that had chewed him up and spat him out.

The flask Tuff had taken from the kids lay on the passenger seat floor. He stared at it, then leaned over and picked it up, unscrewed the lid and breathed in. To his surprise, it didn't smell bad—vaguely caramel-like mixed with wood. He screwed the top back on and threw it on the seat. He glanced at the flask again. Why did anyone drink? He hated how it made his mother behave. Or like those kids the night before. Loud.

Claire drank. Did she drink because the family business was flowing through her fingers like blood from a nicked artery? The night of the rattlesnake, it wasn't only the broken glass and whiskey bottle that gave her away. The way she had stared at him boldly with no restraint. That's what liquor did, right? Dissolved your inhibitions. He had nearly drowned in the blueness of those eyes until he remembered, with guilt, that he had just come from Shawna's bed.

Shawna drank wine, but never seemed inebriated, at least in the short time they'd been together. Maybe she was too ambitious to let drink get in the way. When he'd seen her kiss another man his ego had suffered a severe puncture wound. She'd drawn blood.

Classes must have gotten out because students poured out of a nearby brick building. Joe leaned his head back and took a deep breath. He, who had never failed at anything in his life, had fallen flat on his face. On impulse, he picked up the flask, unscrewed the lid and took a swig. He shuddered, then took another drink and coughed. Liquor drippled down his chin and onto his shirt. Two young women had been walking toward the parking lot, but when they spotted Joe, flask in hand with booze dripping from his face, they glanced at one another nervously, and quickened their pace.

"Bad idea," Joe mumbled, opened the car door a few inches and poured out the rest of the liquid, whiskey he guessed, onto the pavement and tossed the flask back onto the floor.

About ten minutes later, campus security arrived—two guys in blue shirts and holstered guns. One of them knocked on Joe's window.

"Hey, buddy."

Joe rolled the window down.

One of the guys ducked his head near the window and sniffed. "Smells like a brewery. You been drinking?"

"I believe you mean distillery," Joe said, "and I had a couple swallows before I dumped it out." He pointed to the wet pavement by the truck door.

"Or took a piss." The other guy said, then walked away at a good clip.

"Why would you dump out a perfectly good bottle of..."

"A flask," Joe corrected. "I'm guessing it was whiskey."

"Guessing, are you? Well then, why would you throw away a perfectly good *flask* of whiskey?"

"Didn't much care for it," Joe said.

Ten minutes later, the sheriff arrived, and it wasn't temporary-duty deputy Tuff Kellerman.

Chapter 34

Poe Riddle commenced his crusade at the employment office in South Wenatchee, where men huddled in groups outside, waiting for orchard jobs. Cars with California license plates lined the curb, a few with Oklahoma and Arkansas plates. Pickers moving north. Many had already hired on at orchards picking peaches and apricots. But the big crop in this valley was apples.

Poe sauntered over to some guys standing near a beater van.

"Welcome," he smiled. "Y'all speak English?"

The men frowned.

"Lots of work here," Poe went on. "You boys worked here before?"

"Yakima, not Wenatchee."

Poe's smile faded. "Got news for y'all."

Poe nonchalantly pulled out a hunting knife from a sheath attached to his belt. Though bulky and dangerous to carry around, the long stainless-steel blade was too impressive to resist. Poe examined his fingernail with concern, then used the sharp tip of the blade to pick imaginary fragments from beneath the nail. He pressed the tip to his own flesh until a bright red drop of blood appeared.

"Ow!" He stared at the knife in mock surprise, holding it in front of his face and flipping it back and forth, blade glinting in the sun. "It's so sharp," he said, as if to himself. Then, as if remembering there were others present, he focused on them. The men glanced at one another, shifting uncomfortably.

"I reckon you best steer clear of the Courtney Orchard in East Wenatchee. Guy was murdered there last year." Poe leaned closer and whispered loudly. "Mexican Mafia says stay away. *Comprende?*"

One guy rattled off something to the others. They nodded.

He replaced the knife into its sheath, sucked his bleeding finger, stared at each man, one at a time. "Y'all tell the others, hear?"

He moved onto the next group of men. After he finished there, he headed to a couple of taverns, and continued his campaign.

If Carlos Barbosa wouldn't tell him what really happened to Billy, he'd make sure Carlos and the boss lady would feel a little of the same pain he and Billy's family were feeling. He knew they were hiding something—had known since the day Billy got dug up. He'd make them tell or make them suffer.

***

A week after Poe's warnings, Juan found Carlos near the spray barn first thing in the morning. Juan was dressed in clean, going-to-town clothes instead of his usual work clothes.

"Something going on today, Juan?" Carlos asked when he took in Juan's appearance.

Juan fidgeted, trying not to look the older man in the eye. "I must quit today," he said, high-pitched voice cracking.

"You sick?"

Juan shook his head.

"Okay, whatever it is, go take care of it. We'll see you tomorrow."

"You don't understand," Juan said, shifting from one foot to the other. "I'm quitting for good. I want to get paid and get going."

Carlos frowned. "What are you taking about?"

Juan shook his head. "I have to quit."

"Why?" Carlos couldn't believe his ears. "I need you, Juan. It's almost harvest. You're my right-hand man."

Juan, restless, glanced over his shoulder, worked the muscles in his jaw, finally looked at Carlos. "The word's out. Anyone working here's going to get hurt."

"What are you talking about?" Carlos took Juan by the shoulders, looked him in the eye.

"Poe," Juan whispered. "He's hooked up with the Quincy gang. He's put the word out. The Mexican Mafia wants revenge for Billy's murder. They'll hurt anybody who works here. I have to leave, Carlos. Send me my check, okay? You have my address."

Juan broke free from Carlos's grip and hurried away.

Chapter 35

"Morning, Stu."

"Morning, Tuff. How'd it go?"

"The usual. Once a year is plenty for me. Do me a favor. Don't call me next year." He tossed the badge onto the sheriff's desk.

"Say, Tuff. Take a look at this guy we picked up yesterday. He says he knows you." The sheriff keyed open a door and walked down a hallway to a couple of holding cells. "You seen him around here before?"

Tuff peered into the cell. Joe sat on the bunk, then, seeing Tuff, stood.

"What the hell?" Tuff turned to the sheriff.

"Found him sitting in his truck, drunk, in the university parking lot. Scared a couple of little college gals who say a drunk Indian, no offense Tuff, looked at them in a bad way. Nobody saw him drive in. Must have sat there for a while. The truck was cold. I'm trying to figure out what to do with him. Probably drunk and disorderly. You know him from the reservation or something?"

"I wasn't drunk," Joe said, staring intently at Tuff.

"Of course, you weren't drunk," Tuff said. "You don't drink."

"You *do* know him." The sheriff sounded surprised.

"Yeah, he's my cousin."

"Well, I'll be damned. Sorry, Tuff, but he had a boozy flask with him and he smelled like a brewery."

"Distillery," Joe mumbled.

"Whatever." The sheriff glared at Joe. "He stunk of whiskey, so we brought him in."

"I asked him to give me a breathalyzer," Joe said. "But he refused."

"Why'd you have the whiskey?" Tuff walked over to the cell.

"It was the flask you handed me at the festival," Joe said. "The one you took from the kids."

"Oh, shit," Tuff said.

"I took a drink on a whim. Thought about seeing what drunk felt like, but I couldn't stomach the stuff. I spilled it on my shirt and dumped the rest on the ground. That's when campus security arrived."

Tuff considered Joe for a moment, then to the sheriff, "Can I take him off your hands? No charges?"

"Why the hell not. It'll save me the paperwork." The sheriff fetched his keys and unlocked the door. "His truck's impounded at Pocatello Towing. Nice GMC. It'll take some bucks to get it out of hock. Thanks, Tuff." He looked at Joe. "Come on, before I change my mind and charge you with something."

Joe followed Tuff out the building, squinting in the sunlight. Tuff's old, faded blue Chevy pickup was parked at the curb with a blue-eyed border collie wagging its tail like a windmill in the back.

Joe scratched the dog behind an ear. "How you doin' Charley?"

They climbed in the Chevy. Tuff pumped the gas pedal, worked the choke, turned over the ignition and convinced the old truck to start one more time. He glanced at Joe. "What'd you want to get drunk for?"

"Why do people get drunk, Tuff?"

"All sorts of reasons," Tuff said. "Women mostly."

They hesitated, then grinned at each other.

"Maybe some of that," Joe agreed. "And a few other problems."

Tuff studied Joe for a minute, then put the truck in gear, and headed to the impound garage.

Joe slid out of the truck. "Thanks."

"See you at the house," Tuff said. "Mom knows you're staying.

***

Joe headed east, turning onto a dirt road a good ten miles out of town, a road he'd traveled countless times over the years to Tuff's house. The yard was filled with a tangle of flowers—bachelor buttons, poppies, and lilies. Three elm trees with thick trunks shaded the house and yard. Joe breathed in the sweet, clean air as he noticed Esther's vegetable garden with corn stalks, tomatoes, potatoes, raspberry and blackberry bushes.

To the east of the old but immaculate white house stood two lumbering wood barns, and beyond them fenced pastures stretched out of sight, cattle in one, horses in another, and beyond them a field with long rows of cut alfalfa drying in the sun.

On the porch of the house sat a tiny Native woman snapping beans into a bowl.

Joe climbed the steps to the porch. "Esther."

The woman smiled up at him, wrinkles radiating from kind eyes. She carefully laid the beans and bowl to the side and stood.

"There's my boy," she grinned a picket-fence smile and gave him a hug. "You're late!" she admonished. "It's August and you usually get here in June."

"Didn't think I was going to make it at all this year."

"Wouldn't have been the same without you. Your room's all made up. There's iced tea in the fridge. I better keep working on these beans so we can have dinner."

Tuff stepped out of the house. "You ready to work?"

"Sure."

"Go freshen up, and whenever you're ready, I'll be in the barn," Tuff said. "I'm on my second cutting and it's been drying for a couple of weeks. I need to get it bailed and put away."

In his bedroom, Joe found the cowboy hat he always wore, put it on and caught himself in the dresser mirror. The summer version of Joe Running stared back at him, all cowboyed up.

The afternoon was hot and the work exhausting. Just what Joe needed. He rode on the trailer behind the baler, hooking ninety-pound bales as they slid out a chute, and stacked them. When the trailer was loaded, they drove to the barn and restacked the bales.

When the dinner bell sounded it was a welcome relief. Tuff pulled the tractor into the barn, and they walked side-by-side to the house.

Esther stood on the porch. "You each have time for a quick shower before dinner."

Joe stood beneath the spray, scrubbed off the dirt and sweat, and worried about what he would tell Esther and Tuff about why he ended up here, now.

***

The hot afternoon cooled to evening, and they ate outside in the backyard under the shade of one of the ancient elm trees. The air smelled of grass and hay and the heady aroma of Esther's flowers. Tuff barbecued T-bones and Esther set out the green beans, salad, and a bowl of small red potatoes. "All from the garden," she bragged. "Except the T-bone's from the pasture."

Neither Tuff nor Esther questioned Joe during dinner, but as they finished up, Joe steeled himself, dreading disappointing the people he loved the most.

"I should tell you why I'm here," he said at last.

Tuff and Esther watched him expectantly.

"You know I was working on a Clovis Dig in Wenatchee, Washington," he began.

"Yup," Tuff said.

"Well," Joe said wryly. "It didn't go so well." He went on to tell them all the details, from Claire hiring Spencer Grant to the discovery of a body, ending with the artifacts found in his apartment in Pullman and how he chose to handle their unexplainable appearance, ending with getting fired from the project. "I may not have a job at WSU anymore either," he finished, unable to look Tuff or Esther in the eye.

The three sat silent, listening to the robins and the killdeer chattering as darkness settled in.

At last, Tuff spoke. "You were framed."

"Yeah," Joe said quietly.

"Why?"

"To get rid of me, I suppose."

"Grant, the city guy?" Tuff quizzed.

"Seems unlikely."

"Who else, then?"

Joe sighed. "I wondered about the Colvilles, since I wouldn't agree to spy on the dig for them. But they're the ones who bailed me out. It doesn't make sense. But Grant, the Philadelphia guy, he's too big and important to stoop to anything so low."

Tuff guffawed. "Some people get too big for their britches, son."

"In any case, I can't prove anything, so I'm off the project. Maybe fired from the university."

Esther reached out and patted his hand with her own bony and veined hand. "You have a place here, Joe. Always have, always will. You could work on the ranch or teach high school. They're desperate for teachers."

Joe gave a half smile. "Thanks, Esther."

"Now I know why you tried drinking." Tuff leaned back, took a toothpick from his shirt pocket, and poked around in his teeth. "That kind of bullshit would drive any man to drink."

And somehow this sparse conversation seemed to lighten the burden on Joe's heart.

***

Joe worked with Tuff each day, followed by showers and dinner, and attempts at sleep. The first week of ranch work awoke long forgotten muscles. Sometime during the second week the exhaustion eased up, and by the end of the third week he began to feel as fit as he had playing college ball. The physical labor defined his muscles. He worked shirtless in the heat, the sun warming his skin to a darker shade.

When the work didn't exhaust him to sleep, he lay in bed fighting off haunting thoughts. The dig. His graduate students and what they must think of him now. Claire. Shawna and Sam. Sometime in the dark of night, each night, he managed to push the thoughts to the back of his mind, and pretend life was simple.

This life wasn't so bad, working with people he loved and who loved him, at a job with clear outcomes, with no politics or egos to get in the way.

But an ache in his gut always lingered in the background, a constant reminder of the injustice that had befallen him.

Chapter 36

Poe switched off the headlights as he turned the old Subaru onto the dirt road that ran behind the orchard, killed the engine, and let the car coast to a silent stop. He grabbed a newspaper and a gas can out of the back and headed toward Carlos's house. Overhead, the stars disappeared behind the thick canopy of branches and leaves as he dropped his supplies on the back porch and tried the door. Locked. He crept along the side of the house until he spotted an open window.

***

Carlos lay in bed and stared at the ceiling. Although the sound of the window screen being removed was no more than a whisper, he heard it. He'd been waiting, knowing this day would come.

Soundlessly, he rolled out of bed to the floor. With excruciating care, he eased open the bottom drawer of the nightstand and pulled out a loaded revolver, a Colt Python. It trembled in his hand.

He listened as a floorboard in the living room squeaked. He waited and tried to control the labored noise of his breathing. He peeked over the bed and spotted a crouched silhouette in the doorway. Carlos raised the pistol.

A hushed voice spoke with an unmistakable southern twang. "Gonna kill me, Carlos? Like you killed Billy?"

"I didn't kill Billy, and I don't want to kill you."

"Let's swap stories," Poe said. "Me first. I'm pissed off at you and the boss lady. Billy died under your watch."

Poe was pissed at Claire? Carlos hadn't considered that before. "Was it you who tried to scare Claire?" Carlos asked. "The coyote head? The rattler? Was that you?"

Poe laughed. "You're slow, old man. Yeah, it was me. It's me keeping all the workers away from here. I'm a powerful man, Carlos. Don't you know? Powerful enough to make you pay for what happened to Billy."

Poe stopped talking and the only sound was the two men breathing hard.

"Your turn," Poe said, "tell me what happened to Billy."

Sweat beaded on Carlos's forehead. The hand holding the pistol felt slick. He longed to wipe it on the bedspread but dared not move.

"Billy started selling drugs," Carlos panted. "He showed up here one night, high out of his mind and sick with drugs, looking like he'd been hit by a truck, all bruised and battered. He was out of his head, and he attacked some boys. They fought him, defending themselves, and things got out of hand. Things went too far."

"Went too far? Being' the boys killed Billy?" Poe's voice took on a hard edge.

"Billy ended up dead. I'm sorry."

"Sorry? Some boys killed Billy and you did nothing about it?" The silhouette swayed.

"What good would it have done? Ruined the lives of three boys? To be honest, Billy looked half dead already."

"Those boys are free," Poe's voice grew louder, "and Billy's dead."

"They're just kids. Stupid kids," Carlos argued. "Billy sold them drugs. Maybe those boys should have gotten arrested, but I made a choice, to hide it all, and I've had to live with it. I guess I'm paying for it now."

"Oh, Carlos," Poe drawled. "You ain't begun to pay."

Poe's silhouette disappeared. Carlos half stood and Poe slammed into him. The pistol fired into the ceiling as Poe knocked Carlos onto his back, pinned the hand holding the revolver to the floor with one knee and put his full weight on his other knee on Carlos's chest, as heavy and suffocating as a heart filled with grief.

"For Billy," Poe panted.

Carlos could smell Poe's sour breath and the pungent odor of sweat. Poe lashed out and Carlos's cheek felt on fire.

Poe paused, knife poised over Carlos's neck. "Scared to die? Billy mighta been scared to die." His voice broke.

Poe stood abruptly and walked away, back to the kitchen and outside. Oxygen flooded back into Carlos's lungs.

***

Poe grabbed the gas can and lugged it into Carlos's kitchen. He poured gasoline onto the linoleum floor where it puddled beneath the birch table. He crumpled up the newspaper, lit it and dropped it. The gas ignited. Flames raced across the floor and licked the legs of the table. The linoleum began to bubble and stink. Poe was filled with harsh waves of grief at the thought of Billy facing death alone. They'd always been there for each other, but the one time it really counted, Poe had let Billy down. He'd make up for that now.

Poe retreated outside. As he headed toward his car he glanced back at the house. A flicker of light appeared in the window, as if Carlos had a cozy fire in the fireplace. Oh, how he longed to watch the place burn to the ground but couldn't risk sticking around. He turned and broke into a stumbling trot, tears running down his face for Billy.

***

The sharp report of a gunshot in the distance woke Claire from a shallow sleep. She lay there for a long time, trying to figure out if the sound came from a dream; listening for a repeated sound that would prove she'd really heard it. She finally gave up, threw the bed covers back and wandered to the window. An amber glow flickered above the orchard near Carlos's house. A bolt of fear shot through her. She threw on jeans and a t-shirt, stopped long enough to call 911 and bark out the word *fire* and her address, and ran downstairs and outside, sprinting down the dirt road to Carlos's house.

Flames licked up through the roof and out the window from the kitchen end of the house.

"Carlos!" Claire screamed. She ran to his bedroom window and peered inside. Smoke was beginning to waft into the room, and she spotted a dark lump on the floor near the end of the bed. She pulled the screen off. Thank God the window was cracked open—she raised it and hoisted herself up and through.

She rushed to his side and dropped to her knees. The air was clear near the floor. "Carlos! Are you all right?"

Carlos grunted and reached out.

She grabbed his hand. "Can you stand?" He felt like dead weight, but she managed to pull him to his feet. "We have to go out the window, now!"

He leaned heavily on her as they stumbled to the window and he poked his head and shoulders outside, bent at the waist. This was no time for a gentle exit, so she gave him a hard shove and he was through. The smoke, thicker now, followed him out the window, and so did Claire.

He had crawled far enough away that she didn't land on him when she fell to the ground. She grabbed him under the arm and half carried half dragged him away from the house, until they both dropped in the grass. They lay on their backs, breathing hard as the distant wail of sirens grew louder.

Claire looked over at him. The fire cast a flickering glow, illuminating his face. "You're bleeding!" She rummaged in her jeans pocket, found a tissue, and pressed it to his face. "What happened?"

He flinched and met her eyes. "Revenge," he breathed.

***

Carlos sat at Claire's kitchen table. The firetrucks still pulsated light in the orchard, but Carlos's house had been saved. His cheek was bandaged, but he had refused to be taken to the hospital. "I'm fine," he had said as he gruffly waved the paramedic away.

Claire placed a glass of ice water and a cup of tea in front of him. He gulped the water, winced with the effort, and avoided Claire's eyes.

Claire sat across from him, a cup of tea untouched before her. "The firemen said someone set your house on fire," she said. "Arson. Who would do such a thing? The same people who broke into my house? Who hates us so much, Carlos?"

"The fire is only part of the picture," he said slowly. "Juan quit."

"Juan quit? What do you mean?"

"He told me today that he had to quit, told me to send him his last paycheck."

"But why? He's been with us for years. He has a family. What's this all about?"

"He won't be the only one to quit. I've been trying to get a crew together, without much luck."

"I don't understand anything you're saying. What does this have to do with the fire? We'll have a crew. We always have a crew."

He had dreaded this moment. It was time to tell Claire the rest of the story. "It has to do with Poe."

"Poe? Carlos, you're not making any sense."

Carlos gazed around the kitchen, trying to take comfort from the old, familiar feel of it. He wished Claire's dad were still alive. Maybe none of this would ever have happened. "It's about Billy. I know more about Billy than I told the sheriff."

"Oh shit, no." She leaned forward. "What? What do you know?"

***

After torching Carlos's house, Poe ran to his old Subaru, which was full of gas and ready for the two-thousand-plus mile drive to Arkadelphia. The more miles he could put between himself and all these Yankee two-by-fours—the most common pieces of wood known to man—the better. Poe figured he could make it in four days, easy. Maybe three. He drove all the way to Montana that first night, catching a few winks at a rest stop off I-90, only after the road started going blurry on him.

The next day, he relived every moment of his revenge as he drove, first on Claire, with the coyote head and the rattlesnake—what an inspiration they had been—then the skirmish with Carlos. He'd wanted to kill the man, stab him through the heart, but his mama didn't raise no fool.

By the third day on the road, he could think of nothing but Billy, and he spent the day wobbling between tears and rage. He reminisced on growing up together, two skinny, scraggly cousins who got themselves in all kinds of scrapes. But they always had each other's backs, until the time it mattered. Poe still couldn't quite believe that Billy had drifted away from him. Lived a secret life—the only time in all their years he'd hidden something from Poe. It hurt.

By the time he reached the plains of Kansas, he was a horse headed to the barn, so close to home that he could barely stop to take a piss.

The afternoon he drove into the outskirts of Arkadelphia, the old Subaru squeaking and moaning with the effort, he rolled the window down and inhaled the smell of the river and trees, the dizzying tang of home. And when he fell into his mama's arms, snot and tears gushing out all at once, he swore on the Confederate flag that he would never, ever leave Arkansas again.

The day he had to face Brenda was the worst day of all. He told her what little he knew, and cried with her. But he didn't really know how it happened, how sweet Billy had gotten mixed up with dangerous men, and how Poe hadn't suspected anything. He wished he understood the whole story of how Billy drifted away.

Chapter 37

Things had gone well for Billy, at first. Pedro taught him the ropes. Once a week, ten at night, the phone rang in Billy's apartment. A voice on the phone gave instructions for a pick-up spot—always a different intersection on rural roads around the perimeters of Quincy or Waterville, farm towns with miles and miles of dirt roads with alphabet and number names. *Meet at the intersection of Q Road NW and 7 Road NW. Meet at the corner of Road R NW and Rd 11 NW.* He drove to the designated intersection at midnight, stopped, and slid out of the car, smooth as water moccasin slipping into the river on a hot, summer's day. He opened the trunk. After a while a car skimmed up the dirt road at high speed, stopped, a guy threw packages of marijuana, crack and meth into Billy's trunk, and Billy handed the guy a paper bag full of the money he had made from the last drop. Somewhere, somehow, an accountant kept track of everything.

At first, he sold marijuana to some of the guys he knew around orchards. Teenagers, mostly. He sometimes ducked out of work in the afternoon and drove around East Wenatchee. He stumbled upon a few apartment buildings where folks hung out during the day. White guys with greasy hair; skinny women who had teeth missing. Luck was on Billy's side. Their supplier had vanished, so when he worked up the nerve to walk up to them, all sweaty and shaky, they had been cautiously receptive, and soon they became his gold mine. Crack and meth users. The skinny gals ogled this cute little cracker when their men weren't looking. They loved his southern drawl. Not only did they buy, they told Billy other places where people needed a dealer.

After a few months, he had enough money to buy a well-used BMW, and still send money home to his ma and Brenda. Hiding his activities from Poe was becoming a problem, so he rented his own apartment just down the hall from the room they shared. Every now and then, he dipped into his supplies and indulged in a little meth and dreamt of Brenda's smooth skin. One hit and Billy felt on top of the world, high as a kite, yet ambitious and energetic and wishing he could screw Brenda for hours on end. He couldn't wait for the day when he returned to her, a rich man.

He was afraid of the fat man, so every time he skimmed a bit of meth or crack, he charged extra to cover the loss. The buyers bitched about these occasional surges in price, but he told them it cost more because the shit was special. Better shit. They paid more.

One day Billy came up with a great idea. Not only would he charge more, but he would give his customers a little less of their drug-of-choice and pocket the difference. Soon, he was getting high almost every day *and* hiding cash under his mattress and inside the back seat of his BMW, where he had carefully slit the seat cushion to hold his stash. To play it safe, he also dug a hole in the ground behind the apartment and dropped in plastic bags of money and drugs, pushed dirt over it and crowned it with a chipped terra cotta pot of dead flowers.

As the months ticked by, business thrived. He felt increasingly jittery, true, but a little more meth kept his head on straight. He maintained. Yeah, he maintained very well.

He kept careful track of product and payment because he knew somewhere, somehow, an accountant kept track of everything.

But he must have messed up.

One night in late October after the last apples came off the trees, the gringos went nuts buying meth, and he capped off the best two months ever. He sold so much it made his head spin, and he skimmed money and meth carefully, oh so carefully. One night after the best season of his short but prosperous drug-dealing life, it all came crashing down.

***

Midnight at the designated drop spot, an intersection near Quincy, the driver pulled up, took the sack of money Billy held out, but instead of putting the usual package in Billy's trunk, the guy said to follow him. El Gordo wanted to talk.

Sweating bullets by the time he pulled the BMW up to a trailer at the end of a long, lonely dirt road, Billy wished he had smoked meth before setting out for the rendezvous.

He climbed out of his car on shaky legs. The night air held a cold bite. One of the refrigerator guys patted him down and shoved him into the trailer, where the air was thick with cigarette smoke.

The huge hombre sat on the couch, sweating despite the cold, autumn night.

"Remember, little man, trust..." The fat man began in broken English, and Billy's ears began to ring so loudly he could barely hear the rest of what the fat man said. "My people say you up to something. A little funny at first. Now, every week. Explain why the numbers are wrong. Always wrong."

El Gordo knew! Fuck, fuck, fuck! The shit was about to come down fast and hard.

"I can't imagine..." Billy scrambled through his brain to come up with a plausible explanation. *Shit.* He should have had a better plan, just in case this day ever came. Now here it was, and his mind was blank. "I followed all the directions. I was very careful. Perhaps your people are mistaken? Or maybe not trustworthy?"

El Gordo's expression darkened. He let loose with a tirade of words—half Spanish, half English—voice simmering with rage.

What Billy finally got out of the rant was the guy who reported the irregularities was married to El Gordo's sister. Billy had just accused El Gordo's brother-in-law of cheating him, and the big man was really pissed now.

El Gordo stopped talking, panting like a bull, and gave a nod to one of the refrigerator guys, who grabbed Billy's hand and yanked the ruby ring off his finger and shoved it in Billy's mouth.

"Eat it," El Gordo commanded.

Tears sprang to his eyes as Billy tried to work up some spit, but his mouth had gone bone dry. He swallowed and swallowed until finally the cursed ring went down in a strangling lump.

The thugs pushed him outside, threw him on the ground and began to kick him. The punches and kicks rained down until he blacked out. When he woke up, someone had shoved him behind the wheel of his BMW and told him to drive. Somehow, he managed to put the car in gear, turn around, and grope down the long dirt road. He spat some hard pieces into his hand. He clicked on the interior light, squinting at the brightness, and saw two bloody teeth in the palm of his hand. He dropped them in his shirt pocket, clicked off the light, and began to cry. It wasn't until he pulled in front of his own apartment that he saw every seat in the car had been pulled out, except the driver's seat, which had been slashed. He fell out of the car to the ground. It took him a good five minutes to stand, and he lurched inside. His place was ransacked.

He staggered outside, kneeled down in front of a planter of dead flowers, pushed it aside and dug in the dirt. Billy began to chuckle. They hadn't found his stash. He took the packages inside.

Every part of him ached. With shaking hands, he lit the pipe and inhaled. The meth eased the pain of his scalp where they had pulled his hair, soothed the bruised, no, broken ribs, eased the nausea from the kicks to his gut where a gold and ruby ring lay in a hard knot. He had nothing now, except the meth.

He emptied the plastic bags of cash onto the table and counted out a thousand dollars. That was good, but another thousand would be better. He'd make a couple of sales then head home—home, to Brenda.

He took a few more hits, and when he started to feel human again, he grabbed the bags of drugs, got back into the BMW and drove toward the apartments where the meth heads lived. He made it about halfway when the car sputtered to a stop. He rolled to the curb and looked at the fuel gauge. Empty. *Shit.* He stuffed the drugs in his shirt and set out on foot. The gringo apartments were too far, but he knew some Mexican kids who lived near the Courtney Ranch who might be in the market for drugs.

Chapter 38

Claire dreaded what Carlos had to say about Billy, but she had to hear it. "Go on," she prodded.

"Billy was a good kid at first, but he must have gotten mixed up with some bad guys. The second year he worked for us, he must have been selling drugs." Carlos looked grim.

"Why didn't you tell me?"

"I wasn't sure. He wasn't doing anything obvious, and he showed up to work every day. Then one night, in the middle of night, someone came pounding on my door. Three boys, barely twenty-years-old, were in a panic—local boys who lived near here and had worked for us off and on since they were sixteen. Good kids going to school and getting good grades. They were going to college—all of them—the first in their families. They said they were in trouble. They'd done something bad and needed help. They begged me to come with them. I went. They led me to Billy." Carlos rubbed his hands over his face.

"Billy wasn't breathing by the time I saw him. The boys told me they sometimes bought marijuana from him, but they knew Billy also sold crack cocaine and something called meth. The boys said Billy had approached them when they were walking up Grant Road near here. They said Billy looked like hell, all beat up with a black and swollen eye and a split lip. He shrugged it off when they asked him if he was okay, and offered them marijuana. They all came into the orchard together to make the deal. Billy was acting weird, all fidgety and wide-eyed and hard to understand. Billy pulled out some baggies of marijuana and shoved it into one boy's hands. Billy said he needed the money. The kid gave him ten bucks. Billy said he needed a thousand dollars. The kid tried to give the marijuana back, but Billy kept shoving it all back into the kid's hands. The two of them began to kind of wrestle.

"One of the other boys tried to pull Billy off, and the third kid spotted a shovel leaning up against a tree. We had just dug up that part of the orchard for the new irrigation lines, so somebody must've forgot to put it away. The kid grabbed it and took a swing. It hit Billy on the back of the head. They said Billy made a little sound, like a whimper, then went limp and dropped to the ground.

"They stood around Billy, terrified. In a dead panic they ran to my house and asked me to help them. They didn't mean to kill him."

Claire felt numb. Billy had been killed, and Carlos had known about it.

"I was tired, and there I was in the middle of the night with three scared boys. By the time they led me to Billy, he wasn't breathing. It was the worst night of my life. I knew if I called the sheriff, the boys would go to jail. And for what? Some drug selling son-of-a-bitch. They're good boys. They said they bought marijuana from Billy, nothing more, and I can promise you they haven't used drugs since that night. Like I said, we had just put in new irrigation lines, so the dirt had already been dug up. The digging was easy, and we dug a deep hole. I got a trash bag from the shed, and we stuffed him in the bag."

Carlos's voice cracked and he rubbed his eyes until he could talk again. "We dropped him into the hole and covered him up. Not long after that, it snowed, thank God, and no one noticed until..."

"The dig," Claire finished.

"Yeah. After they dug him up, and the sheriff didn't seem to care much, and I hoped, maybe it would be over. Then came Poe, Billy's cousin." Carlos fell silent.

Claire's emotions jumbled together. Disbelief. Horror. Sympathy for Carlos, having to carry this burden. "Oh, Carlos," she said at last. "What are we going to do?

"Poe's out for revenge. Juan said Poe's spreading the word that the Mexican Mafia says that no one should work for Courtney Ranch. Work here, and you'll regret it. No one will work for us now."

It took a minute for the words to make sense. "We have the best apple crop in years, and no one will work for us?"

"Yeah."

The oxygen evaporated from Claire's lungs. After a long while, she could breathe again. "It doesn't matter. What matters is that Poe tried to kill you."

"He could have killed me. He blames me, he blames you, for Billy's death. The coyote head, the snake..."

"Oh my God! Poe?"

"I didn't know until tonight. I'm sorry. It's my fault."

The something important occurred to her. "What you all did was wrong, burying Billy like that."

Carlos hung his head.

"But Carlos," she waited until his eyes raised to meet hers, "the boys didn't kill Billy."

Carlos looked skeptical. "What do you mean?"

"I read the entire autopsy report. The detective gave it to me and talked to me about it. It mentioned a laceration to the back of Billy's head," Claire leaned forward, "as incidental. It said the probable cause of death was internal bleeding. Billy's ribs were broken, and his internal organs were most likely damaged, causing a slow bleed, it said. Not only that, but the detective called me a few days ago. The ring they found in Billy's stomach matched a ring worn by gang members—a Mexican drug gang that operates out of Quincy. He said they were leaving the case open but figured something had gone wrong between Billy and gang."

"Juan said something about the Quincy gang." Carlos sounded stricken.

Claire leaned forward and looked Carlos in the eye. "The crime committed was you and the boys burying a man who died of internal injuries sustained before he met up with the boys. If you'd have called the police that night, no one would have gone to jail, at least for very long. But you buried him, and hid it, and that's a crime, but the boys didn't kill Billy. He was already dead."

Chapter 39

A few days later, after the fire trucks were long gone and cleanup had begun on Carlos's house, a woman showed up on Claire's doorstep late in the afternoon. As Claire walked toward the house from the orchard at the end of the workday she spotted a tall, dark-haired woman wearing a sleeveless sundress knocking on the front door of the house.

"Can I help you?" Claire asked.

The woman turned and smiled. "Claire Courtney?"

"In the flesh."

"I'm Shawna Ross, a friend of Joe Running. I'm looking for him."

Claire stood at the bottom of the steps. "Can't help you there."

"I need to talk to him. And I was hoping he would show me around the Clovis Cache."

"He left and didn't tell anyone where he was going."

Shawna looked disappointed and walked down the steps. "Would you mind showing me the dig? Maybe we can talk about Joe."

"Yeah, I don't do that. Good luck." Claire started up the stairs, but the woman stopped her.

"I know it's a lot to ask. Joe and I are friends, and when I found out he was working here, I intended to come visit. But I never made it until now. I've read about this whole incredible artifact find, and I was hoping Joe would give me a tour."

Claire stared, unmoved.

"I've come a long way," Shawna said, "for Joe. Now that he's not here, it would really mean a lot to me. To see what he was working on."

Claire hesitated. For some reason, this woman was hard to say no to. "All right. This way."

They walked without speaking to the dig site. When they arrived, Spencer Grant was kneeling by one of the pits. No one else was around.

"Oh good, you're here," Claire said. "We have a visitor who wants a tour."

"You must be Spencer Grant." Shawna walked up to him and held out her hand. "I've read about you. It's a pleasure to meet you."

Spencer took her hand. "You are...?"

"A friend of Joe's. Shawna Ross. I've been wanting to come visit, but my schedule's been crazy. How lucky you're here." She looked past Spencer to the pit. "Oh my God," she whispered, kneeling down. "Hearing about them is one thing. Seeing them is something else entirely. These are astounding."

"They're an awe-inspiring sight, aren't they?" Spencer agreed, looking suspicious. "How do you know Joe?"

Shawna stood. "We studied Native American cuisine together, once. I'd read that he was working on this archaeological dig and I meant to come and say hi. To reconnect."

"He's off the project," Spencer said. "He's gone."

"I guess I'm a day late," she sighed, then perked up. "Listen, I've just come from the grocery store. I couldn't resist a bottle of sauvignon blanc, chilled, that would be lovely to share. I would be so grateful to hear your expert explanation of what you've found here. And Claire, I'd like to thank you for bringing me out here to the dig, when you didn't have to. It would be my little way of saying thank you. What do you say?"

Claire wasn't particularly interested in hearing any more about the dig, but something about Shawna made her curious. The woman had a charisma that was hard to dismiss. "We could sit on the veranda," she heard herself say.

Shawna seemed elated. "That would be wonderful."

Spencer still looked skeptical, but shrugged. "I wouldn't mind a glass of wine."

Fifteen minutes later they were settled on the veranda, wine bottle uncorked, glasses full.

"This is the perfect wine for this ungodly hot time of year," Shawna said. "Cool and light." She raised her glass. "To our mutual friend, Joe, and this wonderful archaeological discovery."

Spencer frowned, and glanced at Claire, then all three clinked glasses.

"I appreciate your time, and I'm here to listen," Shawna said. "So please, tell me what you've found, your theories on the time period, anything at all." She sat forward like an eager anthropology student, and Spencer had never been able to resist a lecture in front of an attentive audience. Especially when the audience was an attractive woman.

Chapter 40

"What are we going to do if we can't get pickers?" Claire asked Carlos in the next morning as she shoved a prop under a branch.

Although they were in dire straits to get the fruit picked, Carlos seemed calm. The news that the boys hadn't killed Billy seemed to have lifted the heavy burden of guilt from him. "We work, like we always work. We pick if we have to. We'll do it all."

"That should only take us eight months or so."

"Sarcasm does not become you," Carlos replied.

It struck Claire as funny, a phrase coming from Carlos so unlike him, and she burst out laughing.

Carlos laughed, too.

"You two seem in good spirits." Spencer said, walking toward them through the trees.

Carlos's levity dissolved. "I gotta go," he said, and climbed on the tractor and drove off.

Claire, still smiling, kept working. "Morning, Spencer."

"Good morning, Claire. I know you're busy and everything's been crazy, the fire and all. How about dinner out tonight? I think we could both use a break."

Claire's first instinct was to turn him down, but in truth, she had actually enjoyed their little wine party with Shawna, and a dinner out would mean she'd get fed without having to cook. "All right," she said.

"Pick you up at six? I know you're early to bed, early to rise, so I don't want to keep you out too late."

"I turn into a pumpkin at nine."

She took him to a local steak house called the Windmill. They both ordered ribeyes with salad and a bottle of wine, this time a cabernet sauvignon.

"That woman's visit," Spencer said after their wine was poured, "Shawna Ross. What do you suppose she really wanted?"

"She said she was looking for Joe."

"She's Native American. I kept waiting for the politics, but they never came. She's an excellent listener, but I don't trust her."

"Are you a suspicious man, Spencer?"

"Under these circumstances, yes."

"She's certainly striking, and there's something about her that made it hard to say no. I'm not in the habit of entertaining strangers, especially this time of year with all the work I have to do."

"You're starting harvest soon."

Claire coughed out a bitter laugh. "We should be. The apples are nearly ready, but we're having trouble rounding up a crew this year."

"Why?"

"It's a long story, and it won't help my digestion."

"Well then," he raised his glass to her. "We won't discuss it."

They took their time enjoying their meal, but stuck to one bottle of wine and skipped dessert. True to his word, Spencer delivered Claire to her doorstep well before nine. He walked her up the steps, took her hand and raised it to his lips, then leaned in and kissed her on the mouth.

Claire felt the heat rise to her face.

He touched his forehead to hers.

Tongue-tied, Claire stammered, "Thank you."

He laughed softly and pulled back. "You know what I love about you? No woman in Philadelphia would thank a man for a kiss. You're a delight."

He kissed her again, squeezed her hand and walked down the steps to his car, waving out the window as he drove away.

Love about her? Had he really said that?

She lay in bed that night, thinking over the events of the last weeks. Joe's arrest had been the worst, until Poe showed up and set Carlos's house on fire. And the whole revelation about Billy's death, and Carlos's part in it.

Then there was Spencer getting friendlier by the day. He was definitely sending her signals that their relationship could be more than business. Way more.

She had a hard time sleeping.

The next morning over her first cup of coffee, she picked up the phone and called WSU and asked for Bradley Randall.

"This is Claire Courtney," she said when Bradley answered.

"Ms. Courtney." He sounded tentative. "I extend Washington State University's deepest regrets for the unfortunate events..."

"Forget it," she interrupted. "Do you know where Joe is now?"

"No idea."

"No address? No phone number?"

"No," Bradley said. "Personnel is waiting for him to call so they can forward his checks."

"Bradley." She didn't know why she should bother to ask but couldn't help herself. "Do you think Joe stole the artifacts?"

"No, Ms. Courtney. I *know* he didn't. I don't think Joe would steal his way out of a blindfold."

"Do me a favor then. When Joe does get a hold of you, give me a call."

"I can't divulge confidential information."

"Don't you think you owe him? Owe me?"

After a short silence, he said, "I'll see what I can do."

***

A couple days later, Shawna Ross showed up on Claire's doorstep again late in the afternoon.

"Hello again," Shawna said, and handed Claire a small paper bag.

"What's this?" Claire reached out hesitantly, took the bag, and pulled out a wine glass. She held it up, bemused.

"Your glass made it home with me the other night," Shawna said nonchalantly.

"That's odd."

"Not odd. Intentional. I'm Shawna Ross, Claire. Sam Moses is my grandfather. He's the Tribal Councilman of the Colville Confederated Tribes."

Claire felt a dawning sensation. Spencer had been right to be suspicious of this woman. Shawna was here for more than a wine glass. "Do we need to talk?" Claire asked, already knowing the answer. She held the door and Shawna stepped inside.

***

Bradley Randall called her back a few days later. Joe had contacted the university and gave them a post office box in Pocatello, Idaho. "I shouldn't be telling you this," he said.

"Thank you," she said, writing down the information. "Thank you very much, Bradley."

After hanging up, she stared at the paper, an insane idea forming in her mind. A crazy idea without any merit whatsoever.

Chapter 41

Bleary-eyed and bone tired, Claire drove into Pocatello. She had left home twelve hours before and driven straight through, stopping only for calls of nature and a quick lunch in Boise. Full of doubt, she had nearly turned back a dozen times. What the hell was she doing? She didn't know.

The first thing she needed to do was get a motel room then find the post office. She had no photograph of Joe to show people, so she had only herself to rely on to spot him.

She drove around until she found the Pocatello post office, then found a Thunderbird Motel less than two miles away. Claire showered, changed clothes, and went for a stroll to stretch after the long drive. Except for the dinner in Olympia, she hadn't been out of Wenatchee for years. How exhilarating to walk unknown streets, to be a stranger in a new town. She found a diner and asked for a table in a back corner, where she savored the best meatloaf and mashed potatoes she'd had in years.

First thing the next morning, she found a bench close to the post office and spent hours sitting, watching, waiting. The postal boxes were accessible twenty-four hours a day, and Joe could show up at any time of day or night, or not at all. Maybe he knew the day his paycheck would arrive and would come for it on only on that day. What other mail would he be expecting? Maybe she'd have to sit on the bench for a month before she spotted him, and she didn't have the time. She should never have left the orchard at all, with harvest coming on and no help to speak of.

On day two, a tall, dark-haired man appeared heading toward the post office, and Claire's heart gave a jump. She would go inside after him. No. She would wait until he came out, then talk to him. Or maybe she should stay undercover and follow him.

It wasn't Joe.

After her breathing slowed to normal, she realized if he did show up, she should have her truck nearby. On day three she drove to the post office and parked, moving the truck every few hours to avoid a parking ticket.

Just after noon, she settled onto the bench after a trip back to the glorious meatloaf café, this time for a pastrami sandwich on rye. I'll give myself two more days, she mused as she devoured the sandwich. This had been a stupid idea to think she could find him, and crazy to have driven more than six hundred miles on a wild goose chase.

But at three o'clock, Joe showed up at the post office. She almost missed him. The cowboy hat threw her. Cowboy boots, yes, he usually wore those, but she'd never seen him in a cowboy hat.

He left the post office and climbed into his truck. Claire took off at a sprint to her own truck and tried to pull out as one slow car after another chewed up precious time. By the time she made it onto the street, he had vanished. *Damnation.* She had lost him. She kept driving. The street turned into a road leading out of town and she just kept going. A few miles out, beyond a couple of pickups and a hay truck, she spotted Joe's white GMC. She took a deep breath, loosened her grip on the steering wheel, and tried to calm herself down. She had him now.

They drove about ten miles north of Pocatello, then Joe took a left onto a dirt road. Claire slowed. It looked like a long, private driveway. Out here, in the middle of rural Idaho, she would stand out like a sore thumb. No sneaking up on anybody out here.

She took a left onto the same road and stopped. What now? She sat for five minutes. Ten. She wasn't going to be able to do a drive by, so she may as well face the music. She took a deep breath and shifted the truck into gear.

***

A mile down the road, she came upon a white house surrounded with flowers. Two trucks were parked out front, and one was Joe's. She slowed to a crawl and rolled down her window. The air smelled of dust and freshly cut alfalfa.

To the east of the house was a large barn and several fenced-in pastures, one with bales of hay drying under the intense, afternoon sun. Joe and another man, both wearing cowboy hats and a leather mitt each, were in the pasture closest to the house throwing a ball. A dog ran back and forth with each throw, tail wagging, barking whenever the ball smacked into a glove. Throw, smack, bark. Throw, smack, bark.

The hell, she thought. *Joe's playing catch.* She got out and walked over to the fence, leaning on the top rail. Joe glanced over at her, paused, then threw another ball. The other man, older and broader than Joe, kept the ball, and both men walked her way.

Self-conscious, she stood a step back from the fence, stuck her hands in her pockets, and squirmed.

"Claire?" Joe looked surprised.

"In the flesh."

The blue-eyed mutt squeezed under the fence and wiggled over to her and stuck his nose on her jeans.

The other man looked from Joe to Claire and back again. "Gonna introduce me, Joe?"

"This is Tuff Kellerman," Joe said at last.

Tuff reached a hand over the fence.

She took his hand. "Claire Courtney."

"Pleased to meet you. That there's Charley. He's a friendly cuss and wouldn't hurt a fly."

Joe's hair looked longer than she remembered. Black and glossy, he wore it pulled back in a braid almost as long as hers. His shoulders seemed bigger than she remembered. He didn't look like a professor. He looked like a cowboy, with some baseball player thrown in for good measure. She felt dwarfed by him and out of place, standing on this foreign, Idaho soil.

"What are you doing here? How'd you find me?" He stared at her as if she were some unexpected and harmful insect.

"I, uh, called Bradley and he gave me your forwarding address. I waited 'till you showed up at the post office and, uh, followed you." It seemed utterly ridiculous to have followed him, to be standing here trying to explain her presence.

"What do you want?" His voice had a funny tone she couldn't quite figure out.

Tuff cleared his throat. "So, you two know each other. Good. For a minute I thought you were a census taker or tax collector. It sounds like a serious conversation might be about to happen, but I, for one, am parched. How 'bout we go see if Esther's made any lemonade or iced tea? Dinner's nearly ready, I'm guessing. After we all get acquainted, you two can sit down in the shade and talk."

Claire breathed again. "Thank you. That sounds great!"

Tuff walked down to a gate, but Joe put one leg on the lower rail of the fence and vaulted over. He turned to Claire with his back toward Tuff, and leaned down, holding her eyes with his. "I've told them everything," he said quietly but firmly.

"I wouldn't have expected anything less."

"But we don't need to talk about it in front of them." He stood back to full height, pulled the mitt off his hand, and walked toward the house.

Esther Kellerman stood on the porch, smiling and looking as curious as a cat. "Welcome, dear."

"Hello. What a beautiful place you have. I'm Claire Courtney."

"Thank you. We enjoy it. I'm Esther Kellerman, Tuff's mom. Come on in while I finish getting dinner ready. You're joining us, of course."

"I don't mean to impose."

Esther glanced at Joe. "Don't be silly. You're more than welcome."

"May I help?" Claire offered.

"No, dear. You relax."

***

A warm breeze trickled in through the open windows and doors. Around the dinner table they passed heaping dishes of food—red potatoes, salad, steak, corn on the cob.

"Esther grows all these vegetables," Joe said, handing Claire the plate of corn.

"I saw the garden when I drove up." Claire took an ear of corn and passed the plate to Esther.

"Do you garden?" Esther asked, eyes twinkling.

"I'm a grower," Claire said. "Apples and cherries. No time for a vegetable garden, I'm afraid."

Tuff said nothing, but his eyes flicked back and forth between Joe and Claire as he ate.

Claire tried to mind her manners, but the food defeated best intentions, and she ate ravenously.

"Are you staying long?" Esther smiled.

Claire's eyes jumped to Joe. "Not long."

"And where is home, dear?"

"Washington. East Wenatchee, Washington."

"Lived there long?" Esther asked.

"All my life. My grandparents bought the land I live on. My dad planted the orchards, built the house. It's all I've ever known. These potatoes are wonderful."

"I see," Esther said and looked knowingly at Tuff, then at Joe. "The place where Joe was working."

"Mother." Tuff gave Esther a hard look.

"How about this place?" Claire asked between bites. "Been here long?"

"Tuff bought this place about forty years ago, when he got married. Isn't that about right, Tuff?"

"Yup."

"I moved in about thirty years ago," Esther hesitated, "when Tuff's marriage went south. Tuff takes care of the cattle, horses, and fields while I do the gardening and the house. He also helps out with the Tribe's buffalo."

"Really?"

"Over four hundred head roam the bottoms on the reservation," Tuff said. "It's a good business investment for the Tribe, good job for me. I help look after them all year. Feed them in the winter. Herd 'em from their summer pasture to the winter land, and back again."

"What a sight it must be," Claire said. "I'd love to watch."

"It's an event," he said.

After dinner, they took their coffee outside to the porch. Two swallowtail butterflies played on a warm breeze, danced along the porch, and disappeared into the garden.

"What's the secret to your garden, Mrs. Kellerman?"

"Call me Esther, honey. Partly, it's fertilizers and planting at the right time, plenty of water. Mostly, though, it's because I ask for a good crop, I accept gifts graciously, and I pass a portion of my harvest along to others."

"Oh?"

"First, I ask the Creator for exactly what I want," Esther explained. "Good growing weather. Rain to help out with irrigation. Plentiful corn. Sweet, juicy tomatoes. Usually, I get what I ask for, unless the Creator decides otherwise, for reasons I'm not privy to. A poor crop can be a gift, though it usually doesn't seem like it at the time. No matter what, I give thanks. It's more fun to give gifts to grateful people, isn't it?" Esther smiled, cheeks wrinkling. "Lastly, I share some of my crop with others. Sharing your bounty is powerful. It works with fruit trees, too," Esther peered at Claire. "You ought to try it."

"Mom," Tuff scolded her.

"Aren't you about to start harvest?" Joe asked.

"I'm having trouble getting a crew together. The pickers are sort of on strike."

"What's the problem?" Joe asked.

"It's a long story," Claire said slowly. "But it has to do with what your graduate students found in the new pit. In the garbage bag."

Joe coughed and stood. "It's getting late. You'll be wanting to get back to town."

"Thank you for a wonderful dinner," Claire stood and took Esther's callused hands in her own.

"Will we see you tomorrow?"

Claire glanced at Joe. "Yes, I'll come back tomorrow."

With a hand lightly on Claire's back Joe gently guided her off the porch and walked her to her truck.

"They're lovely people," Claire said.

"You don't know the half of it."

Claire gazed upward. The sun was heading towards the horizon and a few wispy clouds took on a pale pink shade. "Look at the sky. It looks bigger than at home. The sky must be closer to the earth here in Idaho."

Joe looked bemused. "You don't quite seem yourself. You're, I don't know, relaxed."

She gave a small smile. "Maybe it's being away from home. My troubles seem far away. I guess I forgot, for a minute, the two hundred acres of apples ready to pick. Did I mention I have no crew? This will finish me off, financially."

"Why no crew?"

"It's complex."

"I'm sorry," Joe said. "Truly sorry."

"Thanks. It's almost a relief. The thing I've dreaded for years is coming to pass."

"Claire," Joe stopped by her truck. "Why are you here?"

If she didn't know better, she would say his voice betrayed some unidentifiable emotion. She gazed up at him, wondering how she could ever convince him to come back. "I'm beat," she said. "If you don't mind, let's talk about it tomorrow."

She climbed in the pickup, rolled down the window. "Wonder what Esther will be making for dinner." And drove away.

***

Joe watched her leave, then walked back to the house, where Tuff and Esther still sat on the porch.

"It's not what you think," Joe said.

"It's never what you think, my boy," Esther said. "That's what makes life so interesting."

Chapter 42

Claire forced herself to wait until afternoon to drive back to the Kellerman ranch. She wanted to go first thing in the morning but knew they all had work to do and she didn't want to interfere. And she still didn't know what she was going to say to Joe, which made it easy to drag her feet.

She pulled into the long driveway as Tuff and Joe walked in from the alfalfa pasture, looking dirty and hot, with the dog, Charley, at their heels. Charley spotted her, his tail whipped back and forth, and he made a beeline to her. She crouched down, like a baseball catcher, and waited for the impact. Charley didn't bowl her over but slowed when he reached her, wiggled his rear, nosing her and licking her face. She laughed and scratched behind his ears with both hands.

She looked up as Joe and Tuff towered over her.

"Let me take a quick shower, then I'll be back," Joe said.

"Come on in," Tuff said, "and we'll get a glass of iced tea."

She gave Esther a hug when she walked inside.

"Welcome back, baby girl," Esther grinned, and set about getting glasses of tea for all of them.

The shower hissed from the back of the house while she chatted with Esther about flowers, and soon Joe joined them with wet hair loose around his shoulders and the aroma of *clean* about him. Tuff disappeared to shower, and Joe gulped his tea.

"Why don't you two go for a walk," Esther suggested. "You've driven a long way to talk with Joe, so I'm guessing you're wanting to get to it. Off with you two. Take your time. Dinner's not for a couple hours."

They walked along the perimeter of the first pasture, and on to the next, where five horses grazed. Joe leaned on the fence, putting one foot on the lower rail, and Claire followed suit.

"They're beautiful."

Two of the horses stood nose to nose.

"The two brown horses looking like they're about to kiss are Morgans," Joe said. "The brown with a white spotted rump and face is an Appaloosa, and the little blonds are Norwegian Fjords, the gentlest creature you'll ever set eyes on. Tuff has a thing for horses."

"I love them," Claire whispered.

"Want to ride?"

"Now?" Claire looked up at Joe. "I've only ridden a few times, but it's been a long time."

"Then we'll put you on one of the Norwegian Fjords. If you fall off, you won't have far to go."

Joe saddled them up and handed off the Fjord to Claire. Claire took the leather lead and gazed into the moist, brown eyes of the horse. "What's its name?"

"*Her* name is Yellow Cloud. Need a hand up?"

Claire put her left foot in the stirrup and threw the other leg over the saddle. "I'm good," she said, pretty proud of herself.

Joe mounted his horse, and the other Morgan nickered and trotted to the fence. "Don't you worry." Joe pulled his horse around so the two Morgans could touch noses one more time. "I'll bring him back to you soon."

Joe took off at a comfortable walk down a dirt, two-track road and Claire joined him, feeling like a kid again. Soon the road sided a stream, with grass and shrubs growing alongside. Away from the stream, scorched earth and sagebrush took over. They rode for a long way, side by side, without conversation.

She glanced sidelong at Joe now and then. He sat a horse as if he'd been doing it his whole life. Every now and then he'd reach down and absently stroke his horse's neck.

After a few miles, they came upon a wide grassy spot near the water where couple of Hawthorne trees cast shade.

"How about we give the horses a rest," Joe suggested.

They dismounted and led their horses to the stream and let them drink. Then Joe tied each horse loosely to low hanging branches.

They sat on the green grass and listened to the murmur of the stream.

Joe turned to her. "Why are you here, Claire?"

"Shawna Ross came by a couple of times."

Joe tensed, eyes guarded. "Came to see you? Why?"

"She was looking for you." Claire studied Joe full on. She had almost forgotten his ebony eyes, high cheekbones, straight nose, full lips. His body had filled out since she saw him last. Her eyes drifted to his muscled forearms.

She stood, brushed loose grass from her jeans, walked over to the Norwegian Fjord and laid her hand on the mare's back, her head on the horse's warm neck. "I like it here," she said gently. "You picked a good place to escape to. But that's not why I'm here. I didn't come here to escape my life." She hesitated. "I didn't even come here to fall in love."

Joe's expression changed; his eyes softened. He unfolded himself from the ground and moved to her. Claire's heart thudded with the boldness of her words. Joe gently took her into his arms and kissed her. They clung to one another for a long while.

Reluctantly, she stepped out of his embrace and faced him. "I'm here because you're the underdog. The losing team. Circumstances have not gone in your favor, and I'm a sucker for underdogs. Not only that, but I came here to find you, Joe Running, because I need your help."

***

Claire floated through Idaho and Oregon as if she had helium in her engine instead of gasoline. Every time she tried to sort out her emotions, her mind wandered back to the feel of Joe's body, his strong arms wrapped around her, the scent of him, the tenderness, his lips on hers. She grinned as she drove, then scolded her face back into a seriousness. She wasn't sixteen, for crying out loud.

She broke the long drive up into two days, staying overnight in Kennewick after crossing into Washington. She arrived home before noon, only to find the street along her property lined with cars and trucks. Her elation evaporated. *What now?*

She turned into her driveway, pulled in front of the garage, grateful to get out of the truck and stretch. She started walking toward the house when she spotted Chester, the stoic Colville guard of the dig, in the first row of apple trees on the far side of the clearing. A harness and canvas picking bag hung from his broad shoulders as he reached overhead, plucking golden delicious apples from the tree. She stopped in her tracks. In nearby trees, some on ladders, some on the ground, men and women she didn't recognize picked her apples. They were all Native Americans.

She walked slowly toward them. "Chester?"

Chester glanced down. "Claire," he said.

She wasn't sure she'd ever heard him speak. She moved past him like a sleepwalker.

Out of a nearby tree, a familiar voice called her name. "Hey, Claire!"

She turned. Gabby stood on the ground. Scott perched halfway up a ladder. They both waved at her, grinning.

Weren't they supposed to be back in school? "What's going on here?"

It seemed obvious, what was going on, as she walked through her orchard. People she had never met before, mostly Native Americans, were picking her fruit. Some of them waved. Others smiled.

Claire didn't trust her voice at first. The lump in her throat was too large. But she gave it a try. "Hello. Thank you," she said as she walked up and down the rows. "Thank you so much." She wandered back toward the house as if in a dream. When she reached Chester again, he was on the ground, gently rolling a full bag of apples into a bin. "Thank you, Chester."

He gave a nod.

The dull roar of a tractor grew louder. Carlos pulled up, hauling a load of bins. He climbed off the tractor. "Almost too late for the goldens," he said. "But I think we might make it. Then we'll head straight to Galas and Fujis."

"How did you do it?"

"I didn't do anything. They just showed up. All I did was show them what to do."

Claire tried to get a grip on her emotions. "If the goldens are too ripe, they can be sold for juice," she said.

"You learned that from me," Carlos teased.

"I believe I did," she said, and hugged her old friend.

Chapter 43

When the knock sounded on her front door, Claire took a deep breath, suddenly nervous. Could she pull this off? She reminded herself that she wasn't alone. Reinforcements were on the way. She opened the door. "Spencer. Come in."

Spencer closed the door behind him and took Claire in his arms. He kissed her. She gave herself over to the kiss. Studied it. Analyzed it.

When it was over, she felt nothing. No racing heart. No chills up her spine. Just a blank space inside. She took his hand and led him to the living room. On an end table was a bottle of champagne nestled in an ice bucket, alongside two flutes.

"What have we here?" Spencer grinned. "May I?"

"Please."

He eased the cork from the bottle and filled the flutes. "What's the occasion?" he asked, handing her a flute. "A successful and unusual harvest? When I saw all those Colvilles show up, I braced myself for another protest. I couldn't believe it when they put on harnesses and started picking fruit. Your man Carlos had them organized and working in no time."

"My friend, Carlos." Claire corrected.

"Yes, of course. It's nice to have you back, Claire. I missed you."

They touched flutes and drank the champagne.

When their glasses were nearly empty, the crunch of tires on gravel announced the arrival of another car. She wasn't sure if she should laugh or cry from utter relief. *Finally,* she thought.

A few minutes later, Joe walked into the living room with Bradley Randall on his heels.

Claire practically tingled with excitement. Now what? Should she be brazen? Or play her cards close to her chest. A scenario played out in her mind.

She walks up to Joe, reaches up and places a hand on the back of his warm neck, and pulls him down into a kiss. Nothing long and messy. Just enough. When the kiss is finished, she takes Joe by the hand and turns to Spencer, who is staring, predictably, open-mouthed. Claire feels giddy as she watches a mix of emotions play over Spencer's face. Dismay, followed by anger, which segues into eye-narrowing suspicion, and finally, hurt – Spencer looking wounded. "It's shocking when someone you trust betrays you, is it not, Spencer?" Claire says cruelly.

But she doesn't have it in her to be cruel. Spencer *did* look shocked, kiss or no kiss, and his expression turned suspicious. "Can I get you something?" she said to the newcomers. "Coffee?"

"Nothing for me," Bradley said, glancing at Spencer and looking uncomfortable.

Another knock sounded on the door.

"I'll get it." Joe disappeared for a moment, reappearing with Frank-with-the-sideburns, whose expression mirrored Spencer's.

"Thanks for coming." Claire said. "Please, everybody, make yourself at home."

Joe and Bradley sat on the couch. Frank walked to Spencer's side of the room and they each sat in an easy chair.

"What's this all about?" Spencer sat ramrod straight, what might pass as a pleasant expression on his face.

Claire moved in front of the fireplace and set her glass on the mantle where the coyote head once hung. This was not her forte. She'd tried to talk Shawna into managing this little gathering, with no success. She gathered her courage as she looked around the room.

"As we all know," she began, "three artifacts were found in Joe's apartment in Pullman. In the freezer. A freezer in a refrigerator that had somehow tripped the circuit, rotting the contents and bringing it to the attention of the landlady and anyone else who walked within fifty feet of the apartment. When Joe discovered the artifacts, he was shocked. He knew nothing about how they got there. He went directly to Bradley," Claire indicated Bradley with a nod, "his department chair at WSU. Bradley suggested they say Joe had brought the artifacts to the lab to study, to avoid any possible trouble."

"Well, I just thought..." Bradley began, then clamped his mouth closed.

"Joe refused, because that wasn't the truth." Claire hadn't made a speech this long since college speech class, and it wasn't any easier now than it had been then. She took a deep breath and forged ahead.

"Instead, Joe returned here and reported to Spencer that three artifacts had appeared in his freezer in his apartment in Pullman. Spencer called the sheriff, who arrested Joe – in front of a crowd of people, I might add."

"We were there, Claire," Spencer spoke up in an irritated tone. "What's the point of all this?"

"I'm headed down that road, Spencer." Claire threw him a look. "I refused to press charges. However, Spencer insisted Joe be dismissed from the project, and encouraged Bradley to fire Joe from WSU. They placed Joe on administrative leave."

Claire paused, let the silence in the room stretch out, all eyes on her. "Before Joe left, he gave permission for a security team to search his apartment. The team, detectives from the Colville Confederated Tribe, searched the place thoroughly." Claire pulled a folded paper from her back pocket, unfolded it and read aloud. "The search included the assessment of shoe prints, glove prints, tool impressions and fingerprints. "Claire lowered the paper. "Most of the fingerprints were Joe's. But one fingerprint, found on the handle of the toilet, belonged to another individual. The FBI cooperated with Colville Confederated Tribal police, and their database found a match." Her nerves kicked in, and her hands shook a little as she held the paper. "The fingerprint belonged to Franklin Vanderhoff, whose prints were on file due to a reckless driving conviction at age eighteen."

All eyes turned to Frank. He jumped to his feet, features twisted in anger. "You're not pinning this on me."

No one said a word.

Frank frantically searched the room like a caged animal, then turned and pointed a finger at Spencer. "He made me! He paid me five hundred dollars to do it. I'm innocent."

Spencer stared at Frank. "I have no idea what you're talking about."

"Liar..." Frank's face turned red.

"It's all right, Frank," Claire said softly. "We understand. We're on your side. There's no law enforcement here. Tell us what happened."

Frank whipped around to her. "Dr. Grant gave me the artifacts and the address of Dr. Running's apartment. He gave me five hundred dollars and told me what to do. He said we needed to get rid of him. He said Joe was a real troublemaker because he used to be in charge, and now he wasn't. He said Running might go postal."

"Tell us what you did in Pullman," Claire urged.

"I found his place, and used a bump key to get in. Lock was a piece of shit, anyway." He looked absurdly proud of himself, given the circumstances. "I stuck the artifacts in the freezer, then stuck a piece of wire into the outlet to trip the breaker. Child's play. But it's not my fault. He's my boss." Frank pointed at Spencer again. "He made me do it. He *ordered* me to do it."

All eyes turned to Spencer, who took a deep breath, sighed, gave a thin smile, and gazed coolly up at Claire. "What now?"

"I'll be damned," muttered Bradley.

"I think there might be a solution." Joe stood and moved to Claire's side. "We have a proposal."

Spencer stared at Joe, then back to Claire. "I'm all ears."

Chapter 44

Sam Moses asked Joe to pick him up at his office, then directed him to a place on Lake Chelan called Wapato Point, a large boot of land jutting out into the water. Sam had Joe drive to the farthest point, the end of the road, where green meadow bordered sandy beach. As Joe stepped out of the truck a strong gust caught the door. Joe held on and closed it, then loped around to the passenger side, afraid Sam might get knocked off his feet. Sam waved him off, climbed down from the truck, closed the door firmly, and strode across the grass, leaning into the wind, until he reached the beach.

"This water," Sam swept his arm out to the lake, chest puffed out, "is the purest, clearest water you'll find on the planet."

They stood shoulder to shoulder and watched the churning lake, stoked into whitecaps by the blustery weather. The wind and water sounded to Joe like the roar of a home game stadium after the crack of a bat and a home run. A good sound.

"You were wronged, son. That man nearly ruined your life. A few press releases saying it was all a mistake doesn't begin to make up for what he put you through."

"Thanks to your help, he didn't get away with it. If your security guys hadn't come to my apartment, we'd have never known who planted the artifacts. I'll never be able to thank you enough."

"It was Shawna who insisted on the search." Sam glanced up at Joe. "I hoped you and Shawna might become more than friends. I thought I saw a spark there."

Oh, there had been a spark all right. "She's one of the most intelligent, capable women I've ever met. But she has another..." the word *boyfriend* sounded too juvenile, "... another friend."

"James." Sam sighed again. "You're the better man, if you ask me. But nobody's asking."

They stared out at the lake again. "I brought you here for business, Joe."

"Okay."

"We have an opening for an archaeologist." Sam pulled a paper out of his back pocket and handed it to Joe.

"The Tribe has a history and archaeology program. We maintain a collection of artifacts and treasures of our People. We work with the feds and the state on cultural issues, among other duties. This brochure explains everything. The salary range and benefits are on the back."

Joe skimmed the front, then flipped it over. The salary was appreciably more than he made at WSU.

The offer blindsided Joe. After his arrest, he figured he was finished. He had come to grips with it in Idaho—figured he could spend the rest of his life bucking hay and working on a ranch. Maybe teaching high school. Now this.

But return to a reservation? Taking the job in Pullman had been as close to a reservation as he had wanted to get. He hadn't once considered going back to the Spokane Rez. Maybe he had deliberately escaped the reservation all those years ago when he left for Reardan High School, and then again when he struck out for the U of Michigan, hoping to never return. What had he been escaping? The poverty of the rez? The tribal culture? Or simply his own family?

"What do you say?" The old man raised hopeful eyes to Joe.

"Thank you, Sam, for all you've done for me."

Sam waved away his words.

"Now this," Joe held up the brochure, which flapped in the wind.

"You've earned your own way."

"I have nothing but respect for you. I need some time to think it over."

"Of course. Take all the time you need. And remember, Shawna might get tired of the James's of the world. But you? Never."

They stayed a while longer. Talked sports some, then casinos. Sam shared his dream of someday building a spectacular hotel and casino right here on the shores of Lake Chelan. People would come from all over the world. How fabulous would that be?

The next day, Bradley Randall called.

***

Bradley was hunkered behind his mammoth desk when Joe walked in. Bradley jumped up and grabbed Joe in an uncharacteristic bear hug. "Welcome back, my boy, welcome back."

Bradley pushed him back to arms-length, beaming like a proud father. "Vindicated! You've been vindicated! I never trusted Spencer Grant, the arrogant bastard. Sit, sit." Bradley returned to his chair and sat facing Joe. "We missed you around here."

Joe took all the beaming and pampering in stride. This was a side of Bradley he hadn't seen before. "Thanks, Bradley."

Part of the deal they had made with Spencer that night in Claire's living room was that Spencer and his museum publicly exonerate Joe. Press conferences, news releases, and public announcements offered apologies, explaining that the whole mess was a college prank gone horribly awry.

"Martin Smith himself came to my office last week and we had a long talk," Bradley said of the university president. "Spencer Grant met with him and explained how embarrassed he and his museum were, and they deeply regretted the pain and suffering the prank had caused. Spencer said he knew nothing until the young man confessed, full of remorse and guilt. I'd sue his ass if I were you."

It sounded like Spencer was holding up his end of the bargain.

"Your teaching position is waiting for you!" Bradley delivered the news like a big, fat Christmas present. "You'll be put on a tenure-track associate professorship, free to pursue field work in a rotating schedule with the other faculty. And the time you spent on administrative leave will in no way affect your salary." He sat forward and held Joe's gaze. "We want you back, Joe."

Joe took a deep breath. This felt damned good. Good to be sitting in Bradley's office. Good to be wanted again. He could picture himself living in Pullman again. The academic feel of the campus as young people trudged up the steep hills to their next class, greeting him as they passed by. Teaching and working with students. Attending department meetings and the occasional weekend cocktail party. Watching the leaves of the gigantic elm trees fade to yellow in late October, followed by the cold bite of the wind and snow in the winter. He could envision it all. Still.

"I need some time," Joe said.

Bradley's smile faltered a bit. "Of course! Take all the time you need."

Joe stood, as did Bradley, and they shook hands across the desk. "Thanks, Bradley."

Later that week, Joe received another phone call.

Chapter 45

Joe pulled the GMC up to Claire's house, as he had done countless times before, only this time the dig site was locked up tight and the orchard silent. As he climbed the stairs to the house, he rehearsed in his mind what he would say, but all thoughts flew out of his head when she opened the door.

"Care to take a walk?" he asked.

"God, yes. We need to talk." She closed the door and fell in beside him.

They sauntered into the orchard, hidden from the world within the sanctuary of trees.

"The Colvilles offered me five hundred thousand dollars for my place! Can you believe it?" Claire blurted out, peering up at Joe. "I was shocked, as you can imagine. Sam Moses said they wanted their people's tools and bones and belongings. He said to him and his people, the artifacts are full of life. He said he knew I'd lived here for a long time, but this place belonged to his people from the beginning of time." Her words came out in a rush. "Shawna showed up a few days later with a real estate listing for an orchard north of Manson. It's a young, organic orchard. It might not turn a profit for a couple years, but it's priced to sell, and with the money for this place, I could make it a few years. Shawna says organic is the way of the future."

"That's quite an offer," Joe said. "It would be a big change."

"Yeah." She quieted down. "I've lived my whole life here. The idea of up and leaving, well, it's hard to imagine."

He loved the way she smelled. The way she talked. The way she treasured her life here, even as difficult as it had been.

"I thought about it, long and hard," Claire continued as they walked. "I told them the deal depended on Carlos keeping his house and the twenty acres of cherries. He and Carmen needed a place to live, and Carlos and I made an agreement a long time ago for him to buy that place. I didn't think they'd agree, but Sam countered, dropping the offer forty thousand dollars, which seems a fair price for the house and the acreage."

"Are you going to take it?"

"I think I should."

"Well then, congratulations," he said.

Claire exhaled a half-laugh. "Yeah, we'll see."

They strolled. There was a cool promise of autumn in the air. The steady sound of sprinklers hissed rhythmically in the distance, dampening the aroma of leaves that were growing weary of clinging to branches.

"I have some news myself," Joe said after a long while.

"Let's hear it."

He told her about Sam Moses inviting him to join the Colvilles, and Bradley offering his old job back to WSU. And, that he had received a third offer—an offer that involved baseball.

"Baseball?" Claire laughed. "What?"

He explained.

The third phone call he had received came from The University of Oregon in Eugene. They had suffered a budget crisis in '81, and axed the baseball program from the athletic budget, changing it to club-sports status. The team still played a regular season against other college teams including WSU, but the games counted only as exhibition games. The U of O baseball coach knew Joe's Michigan coach, and he'd read about Joe in the newspapers, about the whole missing artifact fiasco, and later, the apology, and Joe's exoneration.

The coach had called and said he needed an assistant coach, but one who could teach, and the anthropology department had an opening. Joe could teach fall and winter quarters, and coach in the spring and summer.

What he didn't tell Claire was that after the phone call he had hung up, stunned. He needed time to think. He drove to Wellpinit, stopped in to see his mom, who he found sleeping off a doozy of a hangover. He left her trailer on foot, and walked for miles and miles that day, losing himself amongst the ponderosa pines that breathed oxygen into the rez. He listened hard for some kind of guidance; he searched deep inside himself for direction. In the late afternoon, the old ponderosas began to murmur. A wind crept through the forest, eventually swelling into a tempest. Joe gazed upward. The trees, some a hundred feet tall, thrashed back and forth like ancient people raising their hands skyward in a worshipping trance. The birds fell silent as the forest rumbled. Pine needles began to pelt Joe. A branch snapped off with a loud crack, brushing Joe in its plunge to the ground. The welcoming forest had turned hostile. The wind roared and, together with the trees, pushed Joe out of the forest.

He figured he had his answer.

The only thing that almost stopped him was the fact that moving to Oregon meant moving farther away from Claire. If everything wasn't so new between them, he might have talked it over with her, or even turned down the offer. In the end, he made the call on his own.

"I accepted the job."

They stopped, deep in the shadows of the orchard and turned to face one another.

Claire looked thoughtful, but not horrified. "This leaves us in a fine pickle, doesn't it?" she said lightly.

"It does," Joe agreed. He gathered her into his arms and kissed her.

"I could get used to that," Claire said, a little breathless, when they parted.

He pulled Claire close and savored the feel of her. A fine pickle, indeed.

Chapter 46

"Not only did they have manners, they thought them worth preserving. They treated the opening of a door for a lady or the hand-scripted regret the way an archaeologist treats a fragment of pottery—with all the loving care that we normally reserve for things that matter."
Amor Towles, "Rules of Civility"

***

Two Years Later, May 1990

The sky was so blue it almost hurt Claire's eyes. Azure. Sapphire. Cornflower blue.

She stood in the midst of her orchard, in the Fuji tract, gazing up through the white and pink blossoms at the intoxicating sky, inhaling the sweet blossom scent.

The organic orchard was still new to her, but she was excited to learn. The Alar Scare in '89, a public panic over a chemical used in apple orchards, reduced traditional orchards into pariahs. The apple market tanked. Except organic. Organic apples were like gold bullion now, and Claire had fifty acres of pure gold.

When Claire met with Sam and Shawna to sign the papers, she had nearly backed out. It was too damned hard to leave her home and all she had known. But reason overcame fear, and she signed.

After her signature was on the page, she felt somehow lighter. She knew it had been the right thing to do.

After the paper signing, when Sam stepped out of the office, Claire had asked Shawna how she had known it really had been Frank alone who broke into Joe's apartment, and not Spencer, too.

"Fingerprints," Shawna had said.

"Frank had a police record," Claire said. "Don't you have to have some prior conviction to get fingerprinted? I can't believe Spencer would have fingerprints on file."

"Oh, he doesn't," Shawna said. "We checked. But he did leave some very nice prints on the wine glass at your house."

"The wine glass? The one you returned to me later?"

"One and the same."

"You did that on purpose?"

"I did. There were no prints that matched Spencer's at Joe's place. Either he wasn't there, or he did a very good job cleaning up after himself."

Claire was impressed. Shawna had thought of everything.

After the public apologies, Spencer and his crew pulled up and out of the dig, then Spencer vanished. Claire stayed away from the dig on the day he departed. She later heard from Bradley that The University of Pennsylvania Museum of Archaeology had sent a letter of apology to WSU and said that Spencer was no longer on staff. That was a shock. Perhaps they had known about Spencer's predilection for selling artifacts under the table. Who knows? Claire figured he would eventually rise like the phoenix from the ashes, somewhere, somehow. He wasn't the type of man to succumb to failure. She hoped she'd never see him again.

A month after that fateful gathering and Spencer's subsequent disappearance, Carlos and Carmen married. The wedding had taken place at St. Joseph's Church, followed by a fiesta at Carlos's house—the happy couple's new home. The men roasted a goat, a Mariachi band played, and everyone danced until the wee hours.

Carlos had taken Claire aside late in the festivities. "Sam asked me to stay on and manage the orchard," Carlos said. "I said, yes. But it won't be the same without you."

Her chest caved in at his words, but she managed to congratulate him. No, nothing would ever be the same again.

***

Claire heard a truck approaching, and she practically tingled with excitement. She headed toward the driveway, arriving in time to see Joe emerge from the pickup, all legs and cowboy boots and long, black braided hair. She drank in the sight.

He spotted her and waved, walked to her, leaned down and planted a quick kiss on her lips. He hesitated, then went in for a long, lingering kiss.

"Hi there," she said when they parted.

"Hi, yourself."

"Missed you."

"Then you'll be doubly glad to see me. I brought dinner."

"What?" she asked, giddy.

Joe returned to the truck and pulled a small cooler out of the back. "Barbecue from Stormy Mountain Brewery."

"My favorite." Claire eyed the cooler with hunger-lust.

"By the way," Joe said as they strolled toward the house. "Scott called this morning. He and Gabby are flying to Italy next week to work at Pompeii."

"They got the grant?"

"They got the grant."

"How perfect for those two. I'm so happy for them. And you?" Claire asked tentatively. "When do you leave?"

"Early tomorrow. I'm lucky I could get away at all."

"I should be able to finish spraying by Wednesday. Sulphur." She wrinkled her nose. "This organic farming is one stinky business, let me tell you. I'll drive down Thursday to watch your last few games."

Joe threw his free arm over Claire's shoulder and she leaned in, savoring the solid warmth of him. "This long-distance romance is putting some miles on my truck," she said.

He kissed the top of her head. "I would stay, if you asked," he offered earnestly.

"I would never ask you to do that." She hesitated. She knew what she *should* say. If he's willing to stay for her, she should be willing to move to Oregon, for him. But damnation, that's a tough commitment to make. "I could lease out the orchard and move..." She began half-heartedly.

"It's okay, Claire." Joe laughed—a kind, accepting laugh.

Relief swept through her.

They ambled toward her new house, a white, two-story farm style with a wrap-around porch and tangles of wild roses twining through the railings. A shrill shriek sounded from above, and they stopped and craned their necks.

In the sky above them two raucous red-tailed hawks circled counter to one another until they appeared about to collide. They tilted away at the last second, wingtips brushing. After a few passes, one of the hawks changed course to follow closely behind the other. As Claire and Joe watched, the hawks rose higher and higher, spiraling in tandem on invisible currents. Then abruptly, first one, then the other tucked its wings and plummeted toward the earth. At the last possible moment, they spread their wings and shot skyward with breathtaking velocity.

Together, they soared.

AFTERWORD

This novel was inspired by a true archaeological find—the Richey-Roberts Clovis Cache which was discovered in East Wenatchee, Washington in 1987. The excavation yielded some of the largest stone Clovis points known to science. The cache also held decorated mammoth bones and other tools and implements dating to roughly 11,000 radiocarbon years before present, or about 13,000 calendar years ago. The site was originally excavated by anthropologists from Washington State University, and later a second excavation was led by an archaeologist from the Buffalo Museum of Science, New York. There was controversy over the dig, including protests by local Native American Tribes.

In July 1992, the Washington State Historical Society purchased digging rights to the site from the owners, with the agreement that the site would not be excavated again for 15 years—until 2007. The State Historical Museum director told the Seattle Post-Intelligencer, "The points have been in the ground thousands of years. A few more years won't hurt. The passions seem to require a cooling period so a different generation of people can deal with it, and I wish them better luck." (July 8, 1992)

The orchard owners donated all of the artifacts that had been removed from the site to the Society. Prior to this time these artifacts had been at the Buffalo Museum of Science.

The dig site was covered with concrete slabs and the area was once more planted with apple trees.

***

A note on food, then an interesting discovery of Clovis Culture ancestry:

The dinner of indigenous food Shawna prepared for Joe was inspired recipes created by Sean Sherman and his company, The Sioux Chef. Sean and his company are revitalizing Native American cuisine and reclaiming an important culinary culture long buried, much like the artifacts in Claire's orchard.

I was fortunate enough to tour the East Wenatchee Clovis Site (also called the Richey-Roberts Clovis Site) in 1988. I found it fascinating and collected all the newspaper articles and journal articles about the find, in those pre-internet days. I wrote the first draft of the book in the late 1990's. At the time, the theory was that the ancient Clovis people had no connection to the present-day Native Americans. The Native Americans disagreed.

I returned to the manuscript in 2018. During those interim years, progress in science—in particular DNA testing—had grown significantly. As I researched Clovis sites in North America, I came across a site in Montana called the Anzick Clovis burial site.

In May 1968, Sarah L. Anzick was two-years old when the ancient remains of a male infant were discovered at the base of a bluff on her family's ranch near Wilsall, Montana. The artifacts were found by construction workers whom Sarah's father had permitted to excavate fill from their land for a local school building project. The workers returned with their wives the evening after unearthing the find, loaded up artifacts, and took them home where they washed them, rinsing away much of the red ochre that coated the artifacts. Sarah's dad, a veterinarian, learned a few days later about the find and contacted local archaeologists. The subsequent exploration discovered the infant had been carefully buried with more than 100 stone and bone tools, all stacked neatly in a meter-square vault on top of the skeletal remains, which were just a few skull fragments, some ribs and a clavicle. The remains were determined to be 12,600 years old. The Anzick infant is one of just a handful of ancient skeletons to have been found in North America and the only known Clovis burial site.

Here's the part I found more fascinating. Sarah Anzick went on to become a molecular biologist at the National Institutes of Health (NIH). At the time of this writing, she works in the genomics unit at NIH's Rocky Mountain Laboratories in Hamilton, Montana, where she brings genetics to bear on the study of allergies, immunology, and infectious diseases.

Sarah was on a research team that read the genetic sequence of the Anzick Clovis baby. They determined the most obvious conclusion from the genetic study is the Clovis people who lived on the Anzick site in Montana were genetically very much like Native Americans throughout the Western Hemisphere.

I found it intriguing that the discovery of Clovis artifacts on her family's ranch led Sarah into a career where her research discovered common ancestry between the Clovis people and Native Americans, a fact that was hotly disputed during the time of the Richey-Roberts Clovis dig, which inspired this novel.

ACKNOWLEDGEMENTS

Thanks to my publisher Dave Lane (aka Lane Diamond), a talented author, editor, and businessman.

I give thanks and appreciation to my editor Robb Grindstaff. Your expertise and guidance made all the difference.

Dale Pease is the gifted graphic artist who designs the covers for my novels. Thank you, Dale.

I so appreciate my early readers who gave me feedback, suggestions, and steered me in the right direction: Tracy Fitzwater, Lloyd Smith, and Cathie West. I value your opinions and advice. Thank you for always taking the time to make the book better.

I appreciate the assistance from members of the archaeology department of the Colville Confederated Tribe for taking the time read an early draft and suggesting changes to help make the cultural details accurate.

Thanks to Chelan County Coroner Wayne Harris for checking out the autopsy details.

Thanks to the Icicle Creek Center for the Arts and their film *The Winter's Tale Dragon Spexman*. In the film, oral Historian Randy Lewis brought to life the Native legend surrounding the Clovis Cache, while geologist Nick Zentner explained the geology of the Wenatchee Valley and the Clovis cache.

Although this story is a work of fiction, it was inspired by the discovery of a Clovis Cache in East Wenatchee, Washington in May 1987, and subsequent archaeological dig.

ABOUT THE AUTHOR

Teri spent her early childhood years in Redondo Beach, California, before her family traded the beaches of the Pacific Coast for the apple orchards of Wenatchee, Washington. Her career has taken her from librarian, to corporate writer, and communications officer before becoming a novelist. Her writing has won literary awards for both fiction and nonfiction. She's a member of the Pacific Northwest Writers Association and Write on the River. Teri and her husband live on beautiful Lake Chelan in central Washington State.

For more, please visit Teri Fink online at:
Website: www.TeriFink.com
Goodreads: Teri Fink
Facebook: @TerriAnnFink
Twitter: @TeriFink

MORE FROM TERI FINK

INVISIBLE BY DAY

Beautiful young Kate has three men in her life—the aristocrat who wants to bed her, the suitor who wants to marry her, and the man who must save her.

- **WINNER:** Pinnacle Book Achievement Award - Best Fiction
- **FINALIST:** Beverly Hills Book Awards - Historical Fiction
- **FINALIST:** The Kindle Book Review Awards - Literary Fiction

Born into the Scottish working class, Kate McLaren is a servant. When Lord Des McGregor, a member of the wealthy elite, woos her, she falls in love. Her life in tatters, she escapes and marries James Casey, a young man from her village. They live in London, where James' career thrives, they start a family, and Kate struggles to find her place in society.

Lord Mark St. John, owner of the shipping company where James clerks, becomes the couple's benefactor. Mark divides his time between London and his country estate, Stonebeck Hall, where his traditionalist mother, independent sister, and shy wife reside.

When Kate crosses paths with Des again, he becomes obsessed with her.

Then the Great War comes along and changes everything. As Kate struggles to make a new life for herself with James away at war, she suffers a grief too great to bear—a dark night of the soul—and stumbles upon a secret that threatens her very existence.

MORE FROM EVOLVED PUBLISHING

We offer great books across multiple genres, featuring high-quality editing (which we believe is second-to-none) and fantastic covers.

As a hybrid small press, your support as loyal readers is so important to us, and we have strived, with tireless dedication and sheer determination, to deliver on the promise of our motto:

QUALITY IS PRIORITY #1!

Please check out all of our great books,
which you can find at this link:

www.EvolvedPub.com/Catalog/

Thank you!

CPSIA information can be obtained
at www.ICGtesting.com
Printed in the USA
LVHW010302100222
710694LV00013B/1815

9 781622 530861